# MOLLY
## Companion

*Also by Maura Stanton*

**Snow on Snow**

# MOLLY Companion

by
## Maura Stanton

**THE BOBBS-MERRILL COMPANY, INC.**
Indianapolis/New York

Published by The Bobbs-Merrill Company, Inc.
Indianapolis    New York

Designed by Gail Herzog Conwell
Manufactured in the United States of America

First printing

---

Library of Congress Cataloging in Publication Data

Stanton, Maura.
    Molly Companion.

    1. Paraguayan War, 1865-1870—Fiction. I. Title.
PZ4.S7923Mo [PS3569.T3337] 813'.5'4 77-5257
ISBN 0-672-52353-1

*For my mother and father*

*I would like to thank*
*the National Endowment for the Arts*
*for its support in writing this novel.*

# MOLLY
# Companion

# One

That first night in Paraguay, I ate soup made from parrot meat. The split beaks had been tossed in for color, like clamshells in some chowders. When I finished and set the tin dish down on a stone, one of the soldiers grabbed for it and began sucking at the pieces of beak. Another soldier pulled some sugar lumps from his pocket and offered me one. He seemed surprised when I refused. I had thought that all three soldiers were wearing boots, but now in the firelight I noticed that their feet were bare and covered with thick, reddish slabs of mud. Their after-dinner pastime seemed to be whittling away at this mud with knives, gradually freeing their toes, which they then wiggled pleasurably for several minutes. At one time, they told me, there was a village that manufactured sandals made out of clay and rope, but during the war people had discovered how much more comfortable it was simply to allow the mud to accumulate naturally.

"Tell me about the war," I said.

"Lopez will tell you about the war," they grunted, as they had been grunting all day. The harsh rum they had passed around in a gourd hadn't loosened their tongues any, but my own head was spinning. I lay back on the ground. One of the soldiers began to strum a charango made out of the shell of an armadillo, while another sang about a monkey who once fell in love with a woman (although my knowledge of Guaraní, which I had studied diligently for the past two months in Buenos Aires, was still not perfect). In one of the verses the monkey gives the woman a silver comb to stroke its fur, but around that point I fell into a daze, looking up at the strange southern constellations, remembering the ship I had sailed on from New York, jostled at the rail by a group of naturalists from Massachusetts as we watched the mysterious smoke cloud over the Virginia coast. Much later in Brazil we had learned it was the battle of Petersburg. Everyone had shivered then, thinking how close we had been to war as we floated down the calm Atlantic.

Now I was in the middle of a war. In the distance a gun fired, and I buried my head in my arms. Washington, where I had gone searching for news of my husband, who had deserted from the Union army, had been full of soldiers and hospitals, but there had been such a grim efficiency about everything that the war lost its reality. I shivered, realizing the stars were gone. I must have fallen asleep without knowing it, for my face was covered with a cold dew, and I could hear faint snores from the soldiers around me.

The next morning we continued through the *carri-*

*zal* toward Nduré, where the soldiers said the main Paraguayan army was encamped since the retreat from Paso la Patria two days ago. We kept to a narrow path between a lagoon on the one hand and deep, impenetrable jungle on the other. Occasionally the jungle would give way to a field of grass six to nine feet high, the strands intertwined so tightly as to be impassable except for a few small brown *chilin-chilin* birds nesting there. The path itself, usually under water, was so muddy that after a while it became difficult for me to lift my boots as the red mud caked quickly in the steaming heat. I had my skirt tied around my waist with a strong vine, and shimmering insects settled on my pantaloons and stung through the cotton until my legs grew numb. The soldiers seemed not to notice the insects at all. Every so often, as a joke, one of them would kick another into the lagoon, then shriek and laugh as he clambered out wet and stuck with leeches.

Around noon the dull booming of the guns from the Brazilian fleet began in the distance. The soldiers stopped, their faces sharp, looking at one another. After that we hurried, although the high sun was thickening the air almost to the consistency of the mud, and it was painful to breathe. Then we emerged onto a high, open plain, dotted at wide intervals with palms, which we crossed hurriedly to the South Estero. At the bottom of the bank an enormous barefoot soldier in white drawers and a scarlet shirt was waiting beside a *pelota,* a stiff, dried hide turned up like a dish. He did not seem very happy about taking me across the narrow passage through the reeds, and muttered something about gunpowder.

3

"Lopez is waiting for her," one of the soldiers who had accompanied me from the outpost said sharply. The big soldier shrugged and dragged the pelota to the edge of the water.

I got in carefully. "How do I steer it?"

"You don't. He pulls it across."

The soldier looped the pelota's rope around his neck and plunged into the water of the Estero. The hide floated delicately, but I had to maintain such careful balance that I was almost afraid to move my tongue. The three soldiers from the outpost waved and clambered back up the bank, where I could see their bobbing heads through the brush. The water was about chest deep. The reeds, which had been mashed down to allow for this narrow passage, rose about six feet tall on either side of us. The water was so clear in places that I could see the twisted strands of the reeds that had been trampled to cover the mud below, and even the occasional flash of a fish. Small birds somewhat resembling sparrows screamed up at the whistling splash of the soldier's arm. Yesterday, across a stream, the soldiers had pointed out some pale yellow birds hopping along a basking crocodile, eating its parasites, and I looked around nervously when a similar bird suddenly looped overhead. Twice the pelota tilted and left me breathless. I was glad to see the dense yellow-green mass of the Yatai palm forest looming ahead. The light grew dim and green like the inside of a cathedral. We ducked under some low fronds. The air smelled faintly of garlic, for the fruit on the trees was ripe. After he dragged me ashore, the soldier of the pelota picked me a handful of this fruit, which looked like dates.

"Lopez is at Nduré," he said, pointing down a path

4

that led into the underwater atmosphere of the forest. I thanked him and hurried forward, for I was anxious to be alone a little bit and consider my impressions of the Paraguayan army. I did not know how I was going to send a dispatch, but I thought I might get some help from Washburn, the American minister at Asunción. When I got a little way into the forest, I sat down against the rough trunk of a palm and ate some of the fruit, which also tasted like garlic. As the sun grew warmer, gnats rose up from the marshy places in the forest to shimmer around my head, and I got up, brushing red ants off my face. A large, pinkish parrot squawked over, and I started to run, for the soldiers yesterday had told me about a certain species of parrot that could pluck out a human's eye. They had pantomimed the process with much hilarity. They had also told me, I remembered as I tripped on a bit of soft, marshy ground I hadn't seen because of the deep shadows, about a snake with the head of a dog that lived in the marshes. At that moment I heard a dog barking in the distance.

I came upon the clearing at Nduré quite suddenly, and the sun blinded me. Something leapt against me, and I squinted down to see a skinny, almost hairless orange dog licking at my hands, which were sticky from the Yatai fruit. Near me in the clearing, which widened out toward the silvery waters of the North Estero, hundreds of women were encamped, and it was the murmur of their voices that I had mistaken for wild bees for the last few minutes.

A few of the women looked up as I approached, but they quickly turned back to the big soup pots they were tending over open fires or to the soldiers' uniforms they were sewing. It was strange to see so many arms lifting and falling with the thread at once. It was like looking at a field of hobbled birds. Most of them wore blouses embroidered in black silk, with red sashes around their waists and several layers of mended petticoats. A few still wore bright-colored shawls, but most had thrown them off because of the heat. All were barefoot, although a few of the younger women had silver bracelets around their ankles. There were women whose mouths had almost disappeared in their potato-colored faces, young women with waxy red lips, fat women with black hair stubbled along their arms, women with swollen feet, women suckling babies, and women so ancient that their faces seemed matted with spider webs. One woman absently looped her black hair into curls around her fingers, over and over, then clawed it straight again. A girl with blackened teeth halfheartedly chased some naked children around a fire with a stick. Other women, rags tied around their hair, stirred the pots. Long jets of rancid steam rose in the air. The ground gleamed with the litter of orange peels and half-eaten Yatai fruit, with bones and chicken feathers. The murmur of their voices rose and fell, sometimes steady as bees, but more often, especially as I walked among them, stuttering into a sound like a general sigh, although when I caught a snatch of conversation it usually concerned merely goats or bean shoots or somebody's boiling stew. Yet there was something dim about their faces, as if each had been ground in by a pestle.

I heard a shout and caught sight of a scrawny officer in a red jacket with a torn blue collar. A few of the women turned and stared dully as he came riding over. His face streamed with sweat, and there was a dead mosquito smashed against his cheek.

"Are you the American lady?" he shouted breathlessly. "The one they telegraphed about at the outpost?"

"Yes."

"Then I have orders to tell you, if you write anything without the permission of Lopez, he'll cut off your hands." He bowed stiffly from his saddle. "I'm Lieutenant Leopoldo Camilo Cela." He pointed behind him to a man who was approaching slowly on a skinny, saddleless horse, his legs stuck out stiffly at the sides, an oilcloth cap tied on his head with a piece of string. "That's Doctor McPherson. English. McPherson!" The officer stuck his thumb at me. "Over here!" He lowered his voice. "He'll show you around the camp. By the way, Lopez has invited you to the ball."

As McPherson approached, Lieutenant Cela saluted, wheeled his fly-encrusted horse, and galloped off with such a loud crack of his whip that McPherson almost tumbled into the red mud as he dismounted, puffing. The exertion must have affected his chest, for he almost doubled over, coughing. "Damn weather," he muttered at last. "So goddamn damp." He wheezed, catching his breath. "My wife is consumptive, you see. We thought it would do her good, coming to a warm climate, but she's worse, thin as a twig. And now I've got this damn cough. . . ."

"Where is your wife?"

"Asunción. In a house where the sheets are always damp. I shouldn't be here." He looked around at the field of women. "Neither should they."

"Camp-followers?"

"Oh, a few. Mostly they're women rounded up from nearby villages. Literally *no* Paraguayan will be left behind for the enemy, Lopez claims." He turned away, choking into his sleeve. When he caught his breath again, he was pale. "Martha—that's my wife—has been badgering Lopez with letters, trying to get me back to Asunción, at least, if not England. No luck. Meanwhile, she's getting weaker, and I'm not there. Excuse me." He tried to raise his cap, then realized it was tied with string. "Sorry. I'm Ralph McPherson. I take it you're Mrs. Companion. That pup Leopoldo spotted you and took off at such a gallop, I wasn't sure what was happening. So you're the Reuters correspondent Lopez has been cackling about."

"Cackling?"

"He claims you'll justify his ways to the world."

"I thought he was going to cut my hands off."

"If you write anything he doesn't like, he means." McPherson finally unknotted the string and took his cap off. He was bald, with the mark of a severe sunburn over his smooth skull. He extended his hand. "A pleasure, Mrs. Companion. But I must warn you, if you think you're another Jessie Meriton White—Lopez is no Garibaldi."

"That young officer said there was a ball tonight." I shook my head. "Was he joking?"

"Lopez is always having balls." McPherson pointed to a rise in the distance where a group of soldiers scrambled around an awning of palm leaves. "For morale. It works, too. These soldiers are fanatically loyal. Or else scared of their shadows. Who knows?" McPherson added with a sigh, "If you'd like to rest, Mrs. Companion, there's a little lean-to where we're keeping the medical supplies. Not that we've got

8

much. Lopez insisted on trying to cure the cattle with most of it."

McPherson led his horse and we walked slowly through the camp. Most of the soldiers napped in the open, their faces hidden from the sun under ponchos or blankets. Some of the women were going about collecting the tin plates smeared with the remains of stew and licking the gravy greedily from their fingers. "He brought a lot of cattle over from Corrientes in a retreat, and they ate *mio-mio*." McPherson scratched his neck. "That's a poisonous herb which the Paraguayan cattle have the good sense to avoid. They died by the thousands. The smell was terrible."

I looked at the women. "They act as if they're starving."

McPherson glanced over. "They aren't allowed any rations, only scraps or what the soldiers give them. Lopez would shoot them if they took even a bite of that stew first." He pointed to a couple of palm trees where several dozen men lay on grey blankets. "That's the hospital, for today at least. Lopez is out reconnoitering positions on the North Estero for the new camp."

Some of the men in the impromptu hospital leaned on their elbows and stared at us with the huge, shining eyes of the feverish as we walked by. One thin boy with a dirty bandage over his ear lifted a tin cup of water to his lips with shaking hands, spilled it, then bent down to suck at the grass. An old woman hobbled among them with a basin, washing their faces or fetching more water. At the edge of the shade another doctor was binding up an old man's shoulder.

"They were caught in the shelling. They'll all live, though. No one was killed in the retreat."

"Why did Lopez abandon Paso la Patria? I'd heard those trenches were impregnable."

McPherson looked at me closely. "Don't question Lopez," he said in a low voice. "Of course he could have held that fort forever. Everyone knows that. But for God's sake don't *say* it. Even to me. Here's the lean-to." He pointed to an old man dozing just outside. "That's my herb gatherer, Monkey-Snout. I'll be back. I want to see what's going on around here."

It was nice to sit down in the shade. The lean-to had a dry, astringent medicine smell mixed in with the smell of the fresh palm-leaf roof. When the doctor was gone I propped my head against a crate. The old man, Monkey-Snout, out of politeness, had stood up at the sound of our footsteps and bowed. Now he sat in the sun just outside the lean-to, his hands clasped in front of him. I wondered why he was called Monkey-Snout, for although he was wrinkled and dried from old age, the bones of his face were sharp and well formed.

"You gather herbs?" I asked.

He nodded, grinning, and moved a little closer. He had no teeth. "For the doctor."

"Why are you called Monkey-Snout?"

"Because I used to hunt monkeys for the army." He gestured up at the sky with one aged, bluish hand. "They needed the tails for their helmets and jackets. They said, 'You give us the tails, keep the snouts'; then, 'Hey, Monkey-Snout, bring us some tails.'"

"Did you always hunt monkeys?"

"Before that I was a fish vendor." He screwed up

10

his face so that it resembled gnarled tree bark. "It was better."

"Why did you stop, then?"

"Because I sold a fish to the servant of El Defuncto." He lowered his voice to a whisper. "Francia, our dictator before Carlos Lopez, the father of Francisco Solano Lopez. The fish was infected. El Defuncto ate the fish and vomited. I heard that the soldiers were coming, so I hid in the Chaco, eating monkeys. Later on, that's when I began to sell the tails, after everything was forgotten."

"Had you always been a fish vendor?"

He smiled. Without teeth, his mouth was a dark hole. "Oh no, I was a musician."

"What did you play?"

"The harp. But see—" He held out his right hand, and I saw for the first time that two of his fingers were only stumps. "El Defuncto did not like musicians who wandered from village to village begging for money, because we might be spies. So he cut off our fingers. They pinned fingers to a tree outside every village, as a warning." He reached in one of his pockets and brought out two small yellowed sticks. "Luckily, I stole mine back. Otherwise, what a sad ghost I'd be later. I'd have to find the bones after I was dead." He replaced the bones in another pocket. I looked closely at his faded grey shirt and trousers. Small pockets had been sewn all over his clothes, three on each leg from the knee to the waist, two on each sleeve, six down the front of his shirt. Each bulged with some little object and was fastened with a wooden button.

"*Then* you became a fish vendor?"

"Why, not right away. I was a bullfighter, but I couldn't goad the bulls to fight." He swept his hands in an arc over his head. "I flung my cape, I whipped them with burrs . . . they wouldn't fight. I had to slit their throats, and no one had fun. It's an art, they say, getting a bull to fight."

"But I thought bulls were ferocious."

"Not oxen."

"You fought oxen?"

"They were bigger than bulls. The bulls could kill you, too."

"How did you go from being a bullfighter to being a fish vendor?"

"I married a fish vendor. A widow. She had a regular stall and her sons owned boats."

"What did she do when you had to hide from the soldiers?"

"She was dead then. Her sons wouldn't let me beat them, and ran off. I used to go down to the docks and buy directly from the fishermen, all the scum fish, for I hadn't much money then. I knew the trick of shining up the scales when a fish was bad, and getting rid of the smell. How did I know the fish was meant for El Defuncto himself? I thought the cook would eat it."

"Where did you learn about herbs?"

"From the Indians—the Maca. When I was eating monkeys in the Chaco, I was bitten by a snake. The Maca found me and cared for me. They taught me special things, for I was bitten in their sacred grove, and they thought I would haunt them if I died."

"What sort of herbs can you find?"

He moved a little closer into the shade, but he seemed to think it impolite to move totally out of the sun. Sometimes his face did not seem like a human face but something carved out of old mahogany for a stair newel post. "Good herbs. To cure bellyache, or fight snake's poison. Also, I find spider webs."

"You mean, to staunch wounds? I've heard of that."

He shook his head. "For the lace makers. They use spider webs for their patterns. I bring them perfect spider webs from the woods . . . without breaking them."

"Isn't that difficult?"

He picked an ant from his sleeve and set it delicately back in the dust. "Impossible, some say. Would you like a spider web? No, you would rather have the lace." He squinted at me. "I'll give you some lace. The first lace maker found her lover's dead body covered with spider webs, and imitated the webs for a shroud." He closed his eyes. His lids were strangely flat and unwrinkled, as if coins were set in the sockets. I thought he was meditating what to say next, but in a little while his mouth opened and he snored.

From where I sat, I could watch the swirling movements of the temporary camp over his shoulder. A company of mud-splattered soldiers poured into the clearing from the palm forest, breaking formation with wild, ecstatic leaps as they caught sight of the stew pots. One tripped, lost his leather hat, and a wad of paper money fluttered across the mud. A bullock cart of old men wearing tall black hats plodded past. One of them had a knife and made slashing gestures in the air, at the same time screaming, "Cut off their ears!" A girl with long braids was chaining a mule between the traces of a green cart and cursing a soldier who dozed against the wheel. Two women with reddish mud caked like stockings up to their thighs, where their skirts were tied, dragged a crate of chickens behind them on a litter. Other women led cows loaded with sacks of grain among the big artillery pieces scattered haphazardly between hide tents. The soldiers working on the awning of palm leaves had almost finished. It was difficult to imagine a ball in the midst of such a confused retreat. Yet stranger things had been written of Mariscal Francisco Solano Lopez, dictator of Paraguay, in the Buenos Aires papers. I had pored over them diligently during the two months I had waited for a boatman who could be bribed to take me up the Paraná River.

Now at last behind Paraguayan lines, in the hands of the monster—for so the Brazilians and the Argentinians called Lopez—I felt a surge of elation. I was here! I was not in Boston, looking at the pale-colored pieces of a map, while my aunt gasped in horror at my plan to locate my husband somewhere within Paraguay's imprecise boundaries. I was not still contemplating my decision, shivering as I lay in bed under a bright quilt in her best bedroom.

In a few minutes Doctor McPherson squatted down beside me, wiping his hands on his trousers. "Lopez will see you after the ball tonight, his aide says. We're invited to supper afterwards. It may be the only decent meal you get here, unless he takes a fancy to you." He pointed to the left, where I saw a dozen men struggling with a red-and-white-striped tent. "It'll be a feast. Lopez still has huge stores, in spite of the blockade." He sighed. "You know about Madame Lynch, of course."

"Yes."

"Before the war, the wife of the French ambassador made the mistake of snubbing her. She and her husband are now in prison—if they aren't dead by now, that is."

"The ambassador? But isn't that cause for war?"

"For war?" He laughed. "Paraguay's completely cut off now; you know that. The only country Lopez tries to appease anymore is the United States. Unfortunately, I'm British."

"Lopez won't let you go, then?" I frowned. "Sometimes Paraguayan newspapers got through the lines to Buenos Aires, or some personal letters—"

"I've heard about those *personal* letters!"

"Also consular dispatches, which indicated that the foreigners in Paraguay *refused* to leave. They wouldn't desert Lopez. They offered both their money and their lives."

"Do people believe that down there? Really believe that?"

"No one knows what to believe. But it's convenient for a neutral country to believe it, I suppose."

"You're the first correspondent Lopez has allowed through the lines, Mrs. Companion." McPherson shook his head. "Try to get back! Your only dispatches will consist of lies, signed by you."

My hands felt cold and I buried them in my skirt. "It's that bad?"

"Oh, no." McPherson rolled a cigarette. "Much worse." He glanced meaningfully at the old man, who whistled a little as he snored. His chin had fallen on his chest, but he still sat cross-legged and erect.

"You don't trust anyone, do you?"

McPherson coughed. "Another day, and you won't trust *me*. It's not pure maliciousness people fear around here—it's what their friends might say about them under torture. Enough said. I've got to check on some new measles cases." He sighed and adjusted his damp lilac cravat. "Over a thousand men died of measles last month. Sometimes I have nightmares about all those corpses covered with rashes and red bumps. Weird flowers. Like those parasites you see strangling the palms."

He gave a listless shrug and disappeared around the back of the lean-to. The doctor's description of his nightmare had caused my hands to tingle. I remembered the bright red patches I had seen on the sea coming down the coast of Brazil—sea flowers, I thought. But when the sailors dipped up a portion in a bucket, they had proved to be a brood of rapidly moving little crabs. The naturalists on board immediately began sticking them into jars of alcohol.

The damp breeze was making me rather chilly, as it was getting close to nightfall, so I put on my shawl and decided to walk around the camp. The preparations for the ball were almost completed. Under the thatch awning a military band was tuning up and waxing its instruments. The men had small harps propped on chairs, or guitars, and a few swung tambourines or beat on triangles. The music, coming at irregular moments in loud, unmelodic spasms, was disturbing. Though the men wore black shirts embroidered in brilliant square patterns of red, green and yellow, they seemed more unhappy than the other soldiers sprawled on the ground picking their toes or playing dice in small groups. They did not smile—not, it seemed, because the business at hand was a serious one for professional musicians, but because they were in the grip of some internal sadness that had drained them like a fever. They paid no attention to me as I walked by; they looked dully past me at the air or remained intent over their instruments. One man began to sing about Lake Ypacarai in a mournful, furry voice. The soldiers who were at work beating down the weeds into an acceptable dance floor hopped about much more cheerfully, whistling and joking and pushing one another into the dust. The sad-eyed musicians did not glance their way.

At the edge of the clearing a crowd of soldiers and a few anxious-looking women had gathered in a loose semicircle around a marshy space. Because of the sudden deepening of the shadows, it was a moment before I saw the man tied to a palm tree with leather thongs around his waist. His curly head was shiny with sweat and he was shaking visibly, not with fear but with an apparently uncontrollable ague. Only the thongs kept him upright. He attempted to lift a thin black hand to ward off one of the swarms of flies that rose up from the marshy ground, but it was too much effort, and he let the hand fall. When the flies were bad he kept his eyes closed, allowing them to settle in clusters over his lids and mouth, but at other times he seemed to be trying to locate someone in the crowd and would move his head slowly from side to side, the whites of his eyes gleaming.

"What is it?" I asked a woman with a stern, set face and a basket balanced on her head. She had pulled a cigar out of her blouse and was lighting it.

"Smallpox."

I stared at the sick man. "Why have they tied him up like that?"

She shook her head, but in a moment it was obvious, for a group of soldiers had come forward with rifles. One of them tied a big palm leaf around the sick man's eyes, and he grew still, although his lips twisted in a silent mutter. The other soldiers roughly shoved the crowd back and knelt in formation with their rifles aimed at the man's heart.

The sudden ringing in my ears was caused by the violence of my own pulse. I don't think I even heard the shots, although I watched the sick man's head fall forward as a stain spread out from his belly. Someone clutched my arm, and I turned to see a civilian in a stained calico shirt and knitted waistcoat staring at me. He was trembling.

"How could you watch it?"

"It was so sudden—"

"Do you want to throw up? I did." The man, an American, guided me around the puddle of his own vomit, and now I remembered dimly that as I watched the execution someone had been retching at the edge of my peripheral vision; I had smelled the sourness. I turned my head. The soldiers were untying the body.

"What did he do?"

"He had smallpox." The man leaned on me for support, although he made an outward effort to appear to be supporting me. "He was a Brazilian, a deserter. Some poor slave. Lopez claims he was sent on a mission to infect the Paraguayan army with smallpox."

"Do you believe that?"

The man's mustache seemed to catch in his teeth as

he spoke, and it was hard to understand him. "I don't know. I'll believe . . . "

"What?"

"I said, I'll believe anything. Just tell me what you want me to believe."

Tallow dips had been lit around the edge of the dance floor, and the man's starched collar shone as he bent his head toward me. "I'm Porter Bliss. You're Mrs. Companion, of course. We've all been waiting for you, ever since the telegram from the outpost." He swallowed hard. "You know, Mrs. Companion, I do everything to avoid these executions. When I hear them announced, I stop up my ears with my fingers. I go out of my way to walk around the orders nailed to trees; I refuse to listen to rumors. But I always find myself *there*. Watching. Imagining it's *me!*"

"But why was the man shot? It was obvious he would die within hours anyway."

"Who knows?" Porter Bliss winced. His stubby white eyelashes were in stark contrast to the sore red color of his face. "All I know is that anyone can be bayoneted for anything—that's the usual method around here, you know. Saves ammunition."

"Why did you come here?"

Bliss cleared his throat, embarrassed. "I was a fool. I knew a few merchantmen who wouldn't mind turning pirate under the Paraguayan flag—it was done in our civil war, you know. But Lopez wouldn't hear of it. Now he won't let me go." He shuddered. "I'm afraid he thinks I'm a spy, although he's made me his historian. But at least there's only myself—poor McPherson, always talking about his wife. You were crazy to come here, Mrs. Companion."

19

I said carefully, "I'm looking for my husband."

"Here? I know all the Americans—there's no one named Companion."

"Calvin may have another name. He's a big man. His left earlobe is torn in a rather noticeable way."

Bliss's hand jerked along my arm. He breathed sharply, then said hurriedly, "He's not here. Perhaps he's dead. A lot of people are dead. A fellow named Kruger was blown up last week."

"Are you sure?" Bliss was looking fixedly away from me. The gathering darkness obscured the expression on his face somewhat, but I had the impression that a very specific nervousness had replaced his more general fear of a few moments earlier. "People don't forget Calvin."

"If they've seen him. I've never seen him. Although he might be in Asunción—no, he's probably dead."

"That's comforting."

He finally looked at me. "I can't tell if you said that bitterly or not."

"I don't know."

"Sh! . . . " He pressed my arm. "It's General Bruguez."

A fat man covered with braid and medals approached, wrinkling his greasy forehead. His eyes were lost in the puffy expanse of his face, and pinkish moles dotted his chin and flat earlobes. I thought he was going to pass without a word, but his left leg, which should have glided him forward, stamped in the dust, attempting a bow that could never be fully completed because of his swollen stomach.

"So you are our American correspondent?" He

grabbed for my hand with his own, which was the consistency of soft soap. "Welcome to Paraguay."

I made some inarticulate murmur.

"Were you a friend of Mr. Abraham Lincoln?"

I shook my head. Bliss, who had his arm in mine, trembled slightly and pressed against me to steady himself.

The General clicked his tongue. He had several gold teeth; the rest were black, or perhaps even missing, for it was hard to tell in the uncertain gleam of the tallow dips. "A tragedy. Mr. Lincoln was a great hero of mine. Is it true he went barefoot to your Congress? And gave his cows to the poor? I admire that."

I was about to mutter something agreeable when a young soldier with huge ears and an endless high forehead came running up. He held out an official-looking piece of parchment and broke in breathlessly: "From the Marshal, General Bruguez. A sergeant from the 9th Battalion has just brought nine heads in a sack! He killed nine Allied sentries single-handedly and has their heads in a sack. You can hardly lift it!"

Bruguez let go of my hand and stared at the boy, turning over the parchment. "And what am I to do?"

"They've piled the heads outside staff headquarters, General. You're to promote the sergeant, the Marshal says."

Bruguez looked carefully at the parchment, holding it upside down. "Of course, you fool!" He glared angrily at the young soldier. "Get out of here!"

While the soldier hurried away, almost tripping, Bruguez smoothed a wrinkle over his belly. His uniform jacket was glossy with grease. "Good night,

Señora. I hope I will see you at the ball." He twisted his head in the direction of Bliss and pursed his lips to say something, then thought better of it. I smiled, my mouth dry, and Bliss hurried me away.

"Who is he?"

"Our Minos." Bliss was actually panting a little. "He signs his big 'X' on all the orders for executions—at Lopez's direction, of course, but nevertheless . . . I think I'm going to have to go see them."

"What?"

"The heads." He looked at me.

"No, I'm not going." I pulled away from him. He was beginning to hurt my arm.

"You think I'm a fool, don't you?"

"Not exactly a fool—"

"It's not death, you see. . . . " He rubbed his fingers through his hair until it stood out in wild peaks. "It's this not *knowing!*"

"Does Lopez hate you for some reason?"

"He doesn't need a reason. He doesn't trust me; I told you, he suspects I was sent here as a spy—from God knows who!"

The musicians were beginning to play in earnest now, and groups of soldiers gathered around the dance floor. At one end of it several high-backed leather chairs had been set out next to a punch bowl on a spindly table. An old woman was filling the bowl with champagne and fresh orange juice that she squeezed on the spot after tearing a hole in each orange with her teeth. The rapidly growing crowd parted suddenly and a group of women with high, glittering combs in their dark hair flooded into the dusty circle, red dust rising like scarves around their bare

feet. They wore brilliant dresses of lace and satin, cut
low to display strings of gaudy beads. Soon they were
dancing with the officers, while just outside the roofed
area the common soldiers, with loud whoops, stamped
their feet. Dust rose in a lacy screen that burned my
eyes.

"Those are the Golden Combs," Bliss whispered.
"Lopez's official prostitutes." Suddenly he whirled as
if he had been hit by a rock. "My God! McPherson,
for Christ's sake!"

"I only tapped you on the shoulder." McPherson
laughed harshly. "Get hold of yourself, Porter."

"You crept up; you're always . . . " He blew air
over his lips, making a blubbering sound. "My nerves
are shot."

"Look at the stars." McPherson pulled me a little
out of the glow of lamplight. "I can't get used to the
sky here. I keep looking for the Great Bear."

"It's disorienting."

"That's the Centaur up there—that group. That's all
I remember from school." He put his hand around his
throat as if pressing in a cough. "It's like somebody
messed up the whole sky. Rather frightening."

"If the sky's all you find frightening, Doctor—" Bliss
shrugged elaborately. "You've been invited to supper,
I suppose. *I* haven't."

We all turned to watch the dancing, which grew
more frenzied. The women's skirts swirled out like
pinwheels, and the great jewels in their ears gleamed
and tossed in the light. I noticed several cauldrons
that must have contained rum or beer, for soldiers
surrounded them with tin cups. The Golden Combs
danced only with the officers, it seemed, and con-

tinuously, for as one man tired, his partner was passed to another. There were washes of shadow under the women's eyes.

"Pancha Garmendia"—Bliss pointed to a woman I hadn't noticed before because of the whirling patterns of the other dancers—"the only woman in Paraguay who ever refused Lopez."

She was dancing alone, very slowly, and because her dark hair was dressed as elaborately as the other women's and her old-fashioned gold comb was perhaps higher and more bejeweled than the others, I did not at first see the fetters on her bare feet, hooked together by a chain that dragged in the dust. They must have been heavy, for her ankles were caked with dried blood and she could do little more than turn around and around in crooked circles.

# Two

Doctor McPherson found us a divan in an inconspicuous corner of the tent where we could watch the milling officers around the punch bowl without being stabbed by the huge silver spurs on their boots. An oil lamp with a red glass chimney on a polished table at my elbow threw ruddy shadows over McPherson's pale face and over my hands, which had begun to burn and itch. I turned up the edge of my sleeve and saw the bumps running up my arm. It was the rash again. I was never without it for long. It had appeared for the first time a few weeks before my wedding. I had been put to bed, rubbed with stinging lotions; forced to drink thick black oily potions; to take baths and roll in the snow in my nightgown; sleep one night on silk sheets, the next on the hard wooden floor. The doctors had spread grey sticky clay over my body which had dried, causing unspeakable pain when they chipped it off and pulled the hair on my arms. They had smeared me with assorted oils: some black, some translucent, some thick as honey. On the recommendation of a neighboring midwife, they had even tried honey, and I woke up one night to find myself swarming with ants. They had opened the windows to blizzards some nights, and closed them other nights in order to burn various smelly leaves that sent me choking for air. Finally, when they were going to smear me with glue and ashes, I said, Enough! I had a vague hope that the wedding would be called off, but my fiancé, my cousin Calvin, had insisted I pull the white dress over my polluted flesh and meet him at the altar, even though his hand shook when he took my arm.

The rash bloomed and faded from my body at intervals. I tried diets, sometimes drinking only milk or refusing vegetables for weeks at a time, but nothing I did affected its erratic course, unless I thought about it, or looked at it, and let my horror of it get the better of me; then it got worse. Luckily it never touched my face; only the backs of my hands showed it publicly. No one here would suspect how it flowered under my clothes. Forcing myself to focus on something other than my body, I took the glass of punch offered me from a tray and drained it.

"Are you all right?" The doctor looked at me curiously.

"Oh, yes." I set the glass down on the table beside me. "It's rather warm in here."

"Beastly." McPherson cleared his throat. "Are you a widow, Mrs. Companion?"

"No," I said. "As I was telling Mr. Bliss, I think my husband may be here. In Paraguay."

"Here?" The doctor licked off a speck of saliva that had foamed on his lip. "How's that?"

"He came here. I had a letter."

"He's expecting you, then?"

"No. You see . . . " Glimpsing my hands, I quickly turned them palms up in my lap. "It's hard to explain. He doesn't know I'm here."

"Companion." The doctor squinted. "I know most of the English-speaking foreigners here. The name doesn't . . . Companion."

"He's a big man with a chewed ear."

McPherson rolled back his upper lip. He looked away from me, shaking his head vigorously. "No, no. He's not here."

"Doctor, are you sure?"

"Positive." McPherson clenched and unclenched his fist. "Absolutely."

"You looked startled for a moment, as if you'd recognized my description, like Mr. Bliss. Is something wrong?"

McPherson coughed harshly into his palm, then wiped his mouth quickly with a handkerchief that was stained pink when he took it away. "This isn't the place. . . . Mrs. Companion, please, don't tell anyone, *anyone*, about your husband until I've had a chance to explain. That fool Bliss—why didn't he tell me . . . " He coughed. His throat sounded full of scrap metal. "Will you promise me that?" His voice dropped to a whisper as he glanced quickly at a nearby group of drunken officers. "I can't explain here."

"All right."

I looked around the tent, recognizing only General Bruguez, who was shoving his way to a table where plates of food were being laid out for a cold supper. One officer with a triangular face and small, pointed beard stared at me, and as our eyes accidentally met, he nodded.

"Who's that?" I asked McPherson, pretending to look elsewhere. "The man near the purple chair."

"Diaz, one of Lopez's favorites."

The officer must have sensed that I had inquired about him, for he suddenly loomed over the doctor, grinning a little. His teeth were yellowish but straight. "May I join you?" he asked, at the same time kicking out his foot behind him, hooking a chair leg, and dragging it forward.

"Mrs. Molly Companion," the doctor muttered, swatting at a fly that had landed on his mustache. "Lieutenant Colonel Jose Eduvigis Diaz."

Diaz, sitting directly opposite me on a chair so that our knees touched, grinned again. His dark eyes slanted slightly because of his high cheekbones, and shone glossily, as if he were either slightly feverish or slightly drunk. His skin was sallow. I felt uncomfortable because he kept looking at me with obvious warmth. Doctor McPherson, beside me, stiffened, the planes of his face rigid, although his upper lip quivered.

"Molly Companion." Diaz repeated my name slowly. "Molly. I don't know that name. English. You speak Spanish well, they say."

"My grandmother was from Barcelona. She taught me."

"Ah." He clicked his tongue. "I've never been to Europe."

"Neither have I."

"No? You've never seen the bears in the Tower of London?" His yellowish teeth flashed. He looked at the doctor. "You, Doctor, are English?"

"Of course. But I've never heard of any bears in the Tower of London."

"No? Trained bears that play the accordion?"

"I've never heard of such nonsense."

Diaz frowned, sucking in his cheeks. "No bears? Have you been to the Tower, Doctor?"

"Actually not." The doctor cleared his throat, making a trumpeting sound. "I've never been much in London. I'm a Liverpool man."

Diaz leaned forward. "You've met the queen?"

"Certainly not. You don't *meet* the queen." The doctor grabbed at a can of oysters that was being passed around and stuffed cne emphatically into his mouth.

"I think," Diaz said, glancing behind him, "that Major Godoy wants to speak to you, Doctor. He's just outside. I think it's important—medical supplies."

"What?" The doctor jumped. "Why didn't you say so before? Outside, you say?" He stood up, spilling the can of oysters on the Oriental carpet. He looked down agitatedly at the slimy grey shapes. "Oh, Christ!"

"Hurry, Doctor." Diaz stood up, giving him a little pat. "Don't worry about it." He kicked the oysters under the divan with his boot, then rubbed the oil off his sole onto the carpet. "Go on; he's waiting."

After the doctor disappeared in the crowd, Diaz sat down beside me. Again he was grinning. "Major Godoy will be very surprised." He looked at me carefully to see how I had reacted. I didn't say anything. Diaz tapped his boot nervously and pulled a hair out of his beard, growing suddenly embarrassed. Rapidly he began to point

out the other officers in the room, the names spilling
over his tongue: Lieutentant Colonel Benitez, Major
Gill, Captain Cabral, Lieutenant Quinteros, Lieutenant
Urdapilleta, Colonel Alen. I couldn't follow the darting
movements of his hand and had no clear idea which
name fitted which face. The uniforms of the officers
were varied and fantastic. Some wore short blue jackets
trimmed with gold; others wore long frock coats crossed
by a sash and jingling with medals. They were passing
plates of white asparagus, artichokes, cheese, little liver
sausages in gold papers, smoked salmon and tongue,
hand to hand; and when a little grey earthenware jar of
*foie gras* came our way, Diaz, after glancing around at
the backs conveniently turned to our corner, pocketed
it with a wink. Then I noticed a stir in the crowd of officers, a hesitation in conversation—not exactly a pause,
but a momentary drop and a quick, forced start. Lopez
stood in the entrance between two red, white and blue
Paraguayan flags.

He surprised me by his shortness. Although I had
glimpsed him earlier at the ball, it had been at a distance, and I had been unable to form any true impression. I would not call him fat, in the manner of Bruguez,
who had great gobbles of fat hanging under his chin,
but, rather, stout; his skin seemed to ooze a little, like
aspic, under his tight clothes. He wore a gold uniform
trimmed in silver, with a scarlet fur-lined poncho tossed
over his shoulders. He looked like a man with amnesia
who had constructed a suit of clothes for himself after
studying the portraits of ruffled dukes and statesmen in
some dim ancestral gallery, for there were strange little
flourishes to his costume—bits of lace here or embroi-
dery there, gold facings at a cuff, or some velvet but-

tons—that could not be attributed to any one style or period.

"There's been a miracle," he said solemnly, pulling off one of his white leather gloves. His hands struck me as especially small. Even though the tent was noisy, everyone seemed to hear him; I wondered if they had all learned to read his lips out of the corners of their eyes. A softly plump man in a black cassock had followed Lopez into the tent. Lopez now turned to him. "Who would deny it's a miracle?"

A whisper like the hiss of wind over grass rose and fell in the tent. I could hear the flies buzzing over the punch bowl.

"No one, Marshal. Of course it's a miracle." Diaz, beside me, jumped up, holding his glass high. "A toast to the miracle!" He lowered his glass to his lips, then paused, stroking his beard. "But tell us about this miracle, Marshal. We've heard nothing."

"Tell them, Bishop." Lopez kicked his companion's leg with his patent-leather boot.

"But, Marshal . . . !" The Bishop sighed, pulling at a strand of his thinning white hair. "All miracles must of course be verified by the papal authorities. However, in this instance, the proof is so clear—" He folded his hands over his belly. "It reminds me of the story of Lazarus, or even . . . but I hesitate . . . "

"Or even?" Lopez prodded.

"The man literally rose from the dead. Or was it a trance? It's difficult to determine if it was a real resurrection or merely a trance."

"A resurrection," Lopez added coldly.

"Yes, probably. He was shot in that little battle on the sandbank two weeks ago, through the heart, and buried

at Paso la Patria. . . . Why, one of my own priests re-
members performing the service! There were maggots
on the man!"

"And he's alive now?" General Bruguez leaned forward, almost dumping a plate of sliced veal off his lap.
He licked a bit of grease from his finger.

"Not only alive, but healthy. They say there's a small
scar in the shape of a single teardrop over his heart. He
was found sleeping peacefully in his own bed in Asunción."

"You're sure he wasn't just a deserter?" someone
muttered.

"He was *dead!*" Lopez screamed. A purple sheen
spread over his cheeks. Even the fiercest general in the
tent seemed to be holding his breath, and the youngest
officers took hurried gulps of their punch.

"To the miracle!" Diaz cried loudly, raising his glass.
Everyone in the tent did likewise. "Tell me more about
this, Palacious."

"There were some curious details involved in the
affair." The Bishop pulled a dirty letter from his pocket
and glanced at it. "For example, the man's room in
Asunción, which hadn't been slept in for months,
smelled of incense. That's how his mother discovered
him. And he's dumb."

"Dumb?"

"His tongue's missing. God replaced his heart with his
tongue." The Bishop lowered his head. "God's will be
done."

"So he himself can tell us nothing about the miracle,"
added Lopez. "But the facts verify it. And when they
bring the man from Asunción, you"—he pointed toward
the table where Doctor McPherson, whom I hadn't

noticed returning, was standing quietly, with an olive
between his fingers—"will prove it, Doctor."

"Me? How can I prove it?"

"Surgery. You'll cut him open and find the tongue."

"Good God—!" McPherson turned scarlet, his words
cut off in a fit of coughing.

"And in your sermon to the men this Sunday, Bishop
Palacious," Lopez went on, "you'll tell them: If they die
fighting for Lopez, like that—what's his name?"

The Bishop consulted the letter. "Diego Limpio."

"Like Diego Limpio, they'll be resurrected in Asunción. They'll fight like devils—"

"And die like angels," the Bishop finished piously.

A spattering of applause followed this remark. Diaz
sat down and abstractedly pinched his little beard between his fingers. Lopez strutted from group to group,
talking more quietly, occasionally grabbing some breast
of goose or a sausage off the plates of delicacies. The
Bishop, in an overly loud voice that was surely meant to
carry to Lopez's ear, explained several other local miracles to General Bruguez, who now balanced two plates
on his knees and managed to nod and chomp at the same
time. The Virgin had appeared to two starving boys
from a remote village, giving them a roast lamb. A velvet
box had turned up with an intact breast in it, obviously
St. Agatha's, and then more mysteriously disappeared.
The urine of a dying woman had turned into a golden
fleece. Saint Francisco Solano had been seen flying over
a woods, his cape spread like wings, crying out that all
sinners would be damned; and that night two of the
three men who saw him died in their sleep, with looks of
horror frozen on their faces. The third man had applied
for admission to the priesthood. And a pious old dame

had discovered flowers growing out of the tumor that had disfigured her face since birth. The Bishop demonstrated the shape of the tumor by puffing his cheek with air and squinting. General Bruguez belched, and a little froth of masticated food appeared on his lips, which he licked off with his tongue. A few bottles of champagne had been brought out for a special toast to the Marshal. Bruguez managed to get a whole one for himself and kept it stuck securely between his knees.

Diaz poured me a glass of champagne. I felt lightheaded. He kept his shiny dark eyes constantly on me. Finally he leaned closer. "Why are you here, Mrs. Companion?"

"To see your war."

He grinned, then broke into such a deep laugh that several heads turned our way. "Oh, no, Mrs. Companion."

"That *is* why," I said stiffly, remembering the real tremble in Doctor McPherson's voice as he asked me not to mention Calvin. "I like adventure."

"A woman like me." His thick lashes flashed down over his eyes as he picked up my hand. "Why is it so red?"

I pulled my hand away and stuck both hands under my armpits as if I were cold. "I don't know."

"How many crocodiles have you killed, Mrs. Companion—since you love adventure?"

"None."

"You never went crocodile hunting as a child?"

"They don't have crocodiles where I grew up."

He looked genuinely surprised, sucking his cheeks in with a whistle. "None? How strange."

Diaz then began to tell me sad stories about his child-

34

hood: how he had broken his leg trying to kill a crocodile, how his favorite little sister had disappeared into
the jungle while calling her dog, and how his old mother
had gone mad and cursed him on her deathbed, thinking
he was a robber. He interrupted himself only for
another toast to the honor and glory and health of
Mariscal General Francisco Solano Lopez, President
and savior of Paraguay. Then a space in the center of
the room was cleared for a game of dice, and soon a
group of officers were down on their knees with little
piles of gold coins, cut into quarters, before them. Diaz
stopped talking to watch them. It was a game in which
luck was strictly hierarchical; the pile of gold in front of
Bruguez, who did not kneel but merely stooped a little
from his divan, grew fastest, for he had a trick of scoop-
ing up his throw before anyone called it, or accusing the
other officers of nearsightedness. One of the officers
peeled off some paper money from a big roll, but he was
hooted away. Just when Bruguez had won most of the
gold and was toeing it with his boot, making it ring and
jingle, Lopez, who had been talking to some officers not
far from me about maneuvers and trenches, glanced my
way. Up until now he had, rather carefully I thought,
avoided me.

"Well, Mrs. Companion, would you like to join the
game? Are you going to let General Bruguez win everything?"

General Bruguez quietly moved his boot away from
the pile of gold.

"No, I don't have any money to lose."

"But if you win?"

"General Bruguez is too lucky."

Lopez, in a quick movement, tossed a coin in my di-

rection which Diaz caught in his cuff. He plucked it out
and gave it to me.

"Give the lady the dice," Lopez said.

Someone handed me the dice, a fine ivory pair. I
threw them out haphazardly from where I was sitting.

"A five! Now, General Bruguez—" Lopez nodded.
"Highest roll wins."

Bruguez threw. His dice came up two sixes.

"A three!" Lopez cried. "Mrs. Companion, you've
beaten the General. You've won everything."

The gold was heaped in my lap by one of the younger
officers. General Bruguez, although trying to smile, was
clenching his fists. Out of the corner of my eye I saw him
cover a forgotten piece of coin with his boot. Diaz con-
gratulated me and got up, offering his place to Lopez,
who sat down with a swirl of his scarlet poncho.

"I was just your agent. The gold is yours, Marshal."

"Nonsense. It was your luck. You threw the dice." He
glanced over at the Bishop. "Enough gold to buy your
way into heaven, eh? But think of it as your salary."

"My salary?"

"I'm appointing you as the chief field correspondent
for my newspaper, *El Semanario*. They say you speak
Spanish and passable Guaraní."

I stared at him. The bits of broken gold jingled against
each other in my lap. "Is it possible for me to also send
dispatches back to the United States?"

"Nothing can get through the lines at present. Later,
perhaps."

"But don't American gunboats occasionally come
upriver with the diplomatic packet for Mr. Washburn?"

"Mr. Washburn is on leave."

"On leave?"

"He went to New York." Lopez bit heavily on his lower lip. I could see the indentations left by his teeth, which were almost black. "He promised to get me some guns. Also to intercede for me, to persuade the Senate to declare war on the Allies—but I don't trust him." Abruptly he stood up. "Elisa's coming. Let me introduce you to the most beautiful woman in Paraguay."

A blond woman in a pink hoop skirt looped with flounces had paused at the entrance to the tent. Officers who had passed out on the divans were hastily shaken awake by their companions and prodded to their feet. I stood up also, my fists full of gold, nervous about the protocol involved, for if I were too polite, it might be taken as a worse insult than if I weren't polite enough. Madame Lynch had a small green parrot perched on her shoulder. Her hair was coiled with ropes of pearl. She crossed the tent briskly, swinging her arms, ignoring the officers who were bowing to the waist around her like toy dolls.

"My headache's better, Francisco, so I thought I would come meet Mrs. Companion." She looked at me frankly, and I was surprised at the friendliness of her smile. "Hello. I'm so glad to meet another English-speaking woman at last." She sank down on the divan and gestured me to join her. "Now go away, Francisco. I want a little time alone with Mrs. Companion."

Lopez kissed her hand with a loud suck. "My sister has written again about her trousseau. Did you see the letter?"

"Yes, yes." Elisa Lynch clicked open a purple fan. "Such a bother. Doesn't she realize there's a war?"

"Not Inocencia. She wants to be married in the Cathedral. She wants me to be there." He sighed. "She

37

wants to keep her fiancé in Asunción for another week, but I think we need him here."

"Oh, let her. It'll be weeks before the new camp is in order. What can he do until the supplies are ready?"

Lopez shrugged, then glanced at me. "I've followed your suggestion, Elisa. I've appointed Mrs. Companion my field correspondent."

"Ah, good!" Elisa Lynch smiled at me. "Now go talk to Diaz, Francisco. Leave us alone."

"What is the parrot's name?" I asked shyly, my voice catching in my throat. Her prettiness made me suddenly conscious of the streaks of red mud across my plain calico dress and the oily strands of unwashed hair escaping my chignon.

"This is Napoleon." She stuck her finger near the parrot's beak. "Say something, Napoleon." The parrot squawked, his wet eyes darting everywhere, but I could not make out any words. "Come on, Napoleon. Speak! Speak!" She touched his tailfeathers. "Speak, Napoleon!"

"Empress! Empress!" the parrot squawked in the midst of some unintelligible sounds. It dipped down, rubbing its beak along her cheek. "Empress!"

"I taught him that." She kept her chin tilted high to hide the thickening flesh below it; nevertheless, she was beautiful, with clear, colorless eyes under pale lashes, and a smooth complexion. "I hope we'll be friends, Mrs. Companion—Molly. May I call you Molly? I so need a friend." Biting her lip, she flung her hand outward at the drunken officers. "You understand."

Suddenly a few of the men in the tent leapt to their feet, shouting, "Resquin! Resquin!" A swarthy, thin man of about forty in a mud-caked uniform had staggered in, breathless. Soot streaked his high cheekbones; he brought the sharp odor of woodsmoke into the hot air.

"Well, General?" Lopez shouted. "It's done?"

"We've burned Paso la Patria behind us, as you ordered, Marshal. And the Allies are taking possession of the village."

"You can hear the church bells ringing!" someone shouted. "And the sky!"

Everyone shoved outside. Stuffing the gold bits into my pocket, where they felt sharp and uncomfortable, I followed Elisa Lynch. The cool, humid air sponged my tired eyes. Over the feathery tips of the palms the sky glowed faintly red; occasionally, when the wind veered, bells clanged faintly in the distance. Lopez threw his gloves up with a wild yelp.

"Don't look down, Mrs. Companion." Diaz, suddenly beside me again, grabbed my arm fiercely.

"What—?"

Of course I looked down. I had almost stepped into the pile of human heads flung into the slime. They appeared like soldiers who had fought on quicksand and had now sunk up to their necks, their mouths open in soundless wrath.

In my dream I had been floating along on the bank of a centaur which had rapid silver hoofs and Lieutenant Colonel Diaz's face. As we rode along, through some northern forest of pine and oak, he kept turning his head to look mournfully at me, biting his thin, sorrowfully twisted lips. I was afraid he would plunge us over a cliff into a river of crocodiles, and kept pointing ahead, trying to get him to look where he was going. Then a fly brushed my cheek and I woke up; lately I had been sleeping in so many strange places that I always visualized where I was before opening my eyes so as not to feel a giddy sense of dislocation. I knew I was now in Diaz's tent. He had insisted that I sleep here, claiming that he himself preferred the open air. He had given me a sheepskin and had left me a candle that had been extinguished by a moth.

I opened my eyes. The same triangular face I had been dreaming of grinned down at me. Diaz sat cross-legged beside me, his shirt off. An ant traveled through the dark hair on his chest. He scratched his flat belly leisurely. "So you're waking up at last, Mrs. Companion."

I sat up. My clothes, which I hadn't changed for days, stuck to me unpleasantly in the thick, humid air. Nevertheless, it was chilly, and I grabbed for the shawl I had tossed over my valise. "Good morning."

"Some *chipa?*" He handed me the piece of flat orange bread that rested on his knee. Although my mouth was dry, I discovered that I was amazingly hungry, and devoured it quickly.

"Molly Companion." My name sounded funny as he rolled it over his tongue. "Molly." He took a puff of his cigarette. "Where is your husband, Molly Companion?"

Luckily I was chewing the chipa, and very naturally took a moment to swallow. "He's dead, I think," I finally said. "He joined the Union army during our civil war and never returned."

He nodded. "You will marry again, perhaps?"

"I have no idea," I said stiffly. Then, suddenly annoyed with the melodrama of Doctor McPherson and Porter Bliss, I added, "Perhaps he isn't dead."

Diaz's eyebrows flashed together. He looked at me searchingly. Today his eyes were not glossy but a strange, thoughtful amber brown, much lighter in color than they had appeared last night. "Do you have reason to think that?"

"No."

"Did you love him very much?"

I turned my head away. "I don't wish to discuss it, Colonel. I'm sorry."

I heard him swallow hard. When I glanced at him, he had flushed slightly and would not meet my eyes. "Forgive me, Señora," he said in a formal tone, "but I, Jose Eduvigis Diaz, have never been married. It is a subject of great curiosity for me."

For a long moment neither of us spoke. I licked the crumbs from my fingers while Diaz ground out his cigarette. Finally he said, "We're moving headquarters to Paso Pucu. It won't be so damp."

"Where is Paso Pucu?"

"Over the North Estero, beyond the marsh. About three miles from the main fort at Humaitá." He drew big loops in the air with his fingers. "The enceinte will be enormous, but there are only a few positions to hold. Most of that area is impassable—marsh, jungle, quicksand; no army could get through except at a few points. Oh, we'll need to dig a lot of trenches, of course." He shrugged. "But the Brazilians are so slow moving, we'll have plenty of time."

We were startled by a shout. "Ghost!" I thought I heard, then, "Holy Ghost!"

Men ran by outside, babbling. Diaz leapt up, and I hurried through the tent flap after him. The air was misty, as if a thin cloud had settled over the camp, but the sun occasionally broke through. We hurried down, past long rows of tents where naked officers peered out at the commotion. A horde of soldiers, some still pulling on their trousers, had gathered in the open space before Lopez's striped tent, leaving a little circle around Lopez and his staff. Elisa Lynch stood next to Lopez in a blue wrapper. Above the tips of the palms about half a mile away a red balloon floated, ascending gradually as it moved closer to camp. A little basket with the figures of two tiny men in it dangled underneath. People were alternately shading their eyes from the sun, which streaked through at intervals, and crossing themselves. I was standing beside Bishop Palacious, who danced nervously about in his fine linen cassock, fingering the crucifix around his neck and muttering to himself.

"Is it Satan?" a tall, gaunt-faced officer asked him eagerly. He shook his head, crossing himself rapidly.

The balloon disappeared into the mist. "Mother of God!" The Bishop went down on his knees, and those around, observing, did likewise. A man with long, tangled black hair fired his gun into the air. Two chickens roosting on a crate squawked wildly into the crowd, flapping their dingy wings. "It's invisible!" The Bishop pointed up where the balloon had been. "Marshal, it's invisible!" he shouted. "This is sorcery!"

Lopez, who had been observing the balloon through a pair of field glasses, turned around, grinding his teeth. "Look at the ropes, idiot!" He flung the glasses at Palacious, who almost toppled over, catching them. The cloud passed from the balloon. It was not any closer. A pair of field glasses circulating among the officers came my way, and I too could see the ropes now, stretching down into the trees. The Bishop scrambled up, searching the sky. "It was just a cloud, just a cloud," he assured the men around him.

"Another balloon was found in the woods, near Sauce," Lopez said to Elisa Lynch, who had moved to where she was now standing beside me, her gold opera glasses trained on the now stationary balloon. "Some soldiers shot it down. It was filled with poison."

"Poison?" I said it at the same time as Elisa Lynch, and for a moment we looked at each other. She dropped her lids.

"Horrible poison. Enough to kill the whole army. Captain Amarilla examined it, along with a priest and Doctor McPherson. Eh, Doctor McPherson?"

Doctor McPherson stood a few paces behind Lopez. He nodded gloomily. Bags of loose skin, like change purses, hung under his eyes as if he hadn't slept. When he caught sight of me, he began to move obliquely in my direction as if he were simply stretching his legs. Officers began dispersing the crowd. Elisa Lynch smiled gently at me over her shoulder as Lopez put his arm around her waist, pulling her toward the tent. Diaz had disappeared. While I waited for Doctor McPherson to catch up with me, I stood next to a horse that had swarming blue flies like flower clusters over its open sores.

"It was filled with hydrogen," the doctor muttered under his breath. "You see what he does?" Taking my arm, he added loudly so that everyone could overhear, "Come with me to the hospital, Mrs. Companion. I need you to make an inventory of my supplies."

We circled the edge of the camp where tents were being pulled down and oxcarts loaded, staying under the yellowish light of the palms. Hammocks on which soldiers had spent the night stretched from trunk to trunk. Occasionally McPherson stopped to cough,

harshly and painfully. I suspected that was why he
hadn't slept. "How did you come to Paraguay, Doctor?"

"Lopez has an agent in England, an old sea captain.
He pours you claret and tells you about mango groves
and breadfruit." He choked and spat. "He told me I'd
have a villa with orange trees, and a position as govern-
ment doctor—there were new hospitals in Paraguay, he
claimed, and no disease to speak of. People died of old
age. Old age!" The doctor's voice rose. We had reached
the lean-to where Monkey Snout dozed in the sun, and I
was almost afraid he was going to go over and kick the
old man. "I made a few bob in Liverpool—my wife was
ill; I couldn't do anything in London. We were starving.
Paraguay? Why not?" He laughed. "Old Captain
Nicholson gets half an ounce of gold for every fool he
ships over here, I found out later."

He led me to the back of the lean-to, out of earshot of
Monkey-Snout. Porter Bliss sprawled against the wall, a
quill in one hand, a piece of parchment on his knee, and
a clay pot of ink beside him.

"Mr. Porter Bliss," McPherson said dryly. "Recently
appointed historian to his royal pigface, Lopez."

"Shut up, idiot!" Bliss craned quickly around the edge
of the lean-to, watching Monkey-Snout, who gave a
fierce snore where he lay wrapped in his poncho, and
rolled over. "What are you trying to do, get us all
killed?"

"Ha! It's safer to speak treason in this country than to
hear it."

"What is this all about?" I asked sharply. "What do
you know about Calvin?"

"Calvin Ferris," Bliss hissed. "That's his name now.
We didn't know he had a wife, of course."

"Well?"

"He's engaged to be married to Lopez's sister."

I gasped. "To be married!"

"Oh, that doesn't matter," Bliss said nastily. "But it's to Lopez's sister."

"Lopez would kill him if he found out." McPherson sat down, sighing. "So you see why we stopped you."

"Or," Bliss grinned, "he'd kill you, making Calvin a widower. Why break Inocencia's heart for your sake?"

"I'm confused." I knelt down in the dust beside the two men. "Does he love her?"

Bliss laughed, leaning so close to me I could see the red pits across his nose. "Now that's a woman's question. You don't know your husband very well, do you?"

I stiffened. "I know him."

"You see, Mrs. Companion, it's our only chance—your husband is our only chance to escape. He's gotten closer to Lopez than any other foreigner."

"What does he intend to do?"

"Help us escape. All of us."

"How?"

"We don't know yet—steal a boat, perhaps. It's not going to be easy." McPherson brushed a beetle off his trouser leg. "Things have gotten much worse since Washburn, the American minister, left—not that he'll be much help when he returns. Lopez hates him. But he's still hoping the United States will intervene, so he's careful."

Bliss snorted. "He has one of his Jesuit scribes forge a British passport if he wants to execute an American. Not that it matters. Who would ever know?"

McPherson untied his cap and began to brush the dust and seeds off the short brim. "As long as you perform some useful function for the war effort, you'll be all right—unless he suspects a plot. He's always suspecting plots."

"Which is why your husband is dead, Mrs. Companion—dead, dead." Bliss squeezed my arm. "Or we're all dead."

I shrugged. "All right."

"I don't think she fully understands her position." Bliss looked at McPherson, shaking his head. He turned to me. "How long did you plan to stay here?"

"I had no plan—it depended—no, depends—on Calvin. But not long, I hoped."

"Unless Calvin's plan works, you'll be here until the end of the war, Mrs. Companion. Which will never end, I'm now convinced. Or until you're dead."

# Three

At the staff meeting last night, I remembered, just when my eyes ached from looking at the maps and my ears sang from the babble of orders and instructions going on around me, that Lopez had shocked me awake by catching a green moth. He had pinned its wings to a map on the wall of his new office, right over the position of the Argentine vanguard. "That's Mitre!" he had cried, to the jubilant shouts of his officers. The moth had wiggled its frail body helplessly. Later, someone must have smashed it with his thumb, for I found only a trickle of pale juice and a fragment of wing on the map. I closed my eyes, trying to recall the black strokes that marked the water of the North Estero, the balloon-shaped island of Yataity Cora drawn in the middle; the Portero Sauce, a clearing in the middle of thick jungle with a hidden road of fine ink drawn carefully toward it; the palm forest, a thick series of broken lines; and the zigzags standing for Paso Pucu, Lopez's headquarters. At the bottom of the map—Was it south or west?—the Paraná River swept in front of Paso la Patria, now thoroughly in Allied hands, and at a right angle from it rose the narrower band of the river Paraguay which the Allied fleet had not yet dared enter. Last night those maps had seemed indelibly burned on my memory; now, in the little clearing where my horse had stopped uneasily at the nearby rumble of guns and artillery, I realized I was lost.

The air, thickened by an invisible smoke from the howitzers pounding ahead, made my eyes sting. I could see nothing through the underbrush of thorns and creepers, but occasional wild yells, louder even than the steady, uninterrupted sound of the musketry, laid back the ears on my horse. I went cautiously down the path on the other side of the clearing, hacking at the trailing parasites and vines with a long knife. The birds seemed to be raging at the guns, for they continually beat up from the brush, screaming; small Karayá monkeys, ordinarily rarely seen, swung and chattered maniacally over my head, spinning the petals of some red flowers like confetti over my face. I could see the smoke now, sifting in tatters around the wet trunks of the smaller trees. I was approaching the actual fighting, and I shivered, remembering Porter Bliss's ironic laugh about how King David had sent Bathsheba's husband, Uriah, into battle with the hope that he would be killed. "But it wasn't his idea to make me field correspondent," I had insisted. "It was Madame Lynch." Bliss had merely looked at me over his rum and lemonade, which he drank all day in a squalid hut while working on his his-

tory of Paraguay. I had my own hut in the new camp at
Paso Pucu, where I wrote exaggerated stories about
Lopez, the "Cincinnatus of America," which were then
sent to Asunción and printed on thick white-brown
paper. It had quickly become apparent that I would
never be allowed to send a dispatch through the lines,
unless Lopez wrote it; in effect, I was a prisoner. At
night I slept badly in a hammock, under a cloud of pre-
cious mosquito netting that Diaz, promoted to general
on a whim of Lopez's, had procured for me. Occasionally Elisa Lynch spoke of Calvin to Lopez, and I had the
impression that he had returned from Asunción to work
on some project, but I never saw him.

The ground grew marshy. A centipede fell from a leaf
onto my hand and I knocked it into a pool of water,
where it floated upside down. As I rode deeper into the
marsh, I noticed that some of the trees were white with
mold halfway up their trunks, or covered with green
moss. Others were nubby with strange mushrooms I had
never seen before. At the same time, smoke eclipsed the
air itself; I had the impression that noon had lapsed
magically into twilight, although when I looked up
through the haze, I could see the round disc of the sun
beyond the palm fronds.

The noise of the firing grew terrifically loud. A bullet
spangled through the vines at my left as I emerged,
startled, from the jungle onto a low, wet plain facing a
stream, where a trench had been dug. A mass of
soldiers, naked to the waist, their white trousers caked
with mud, were firing furiously across the stream at a
mound of freshly turned earth; red flames spurted over
the top of the mound, which was all but obscured by

dark smoke. A howitzer barked over the heads of the soldiers, and great spurts of dirt flew up on the other side.

I had to pass this space, I supposed, to get to the main army—or at least to the center, commanded by Diaz, which was my objective. A few hours after the fighting started, Lopez had descended on me with an important message that he claimed only I could be trusted to carry. I thought of the message Uriah had carried to Joab, but I did not think General Diaz would deliberately endanger my life. I suspected he was in love with me. However, I had to reach him. I kept as far back at the edge of the trees as I could. Luckily the enemy had no artillery here. No one noticed me. I felt weightless, invisible even to the bullets that seemed to occasionally sear close, although in reality I was well out of range. I passed a dead soldier who had crawled toward the underbrush to die. Flies in great fistfuls covered his eyes. He still had the iron corkscrew, used for cleaning cannons, in one hand. I kicked my horse sharply, and he flew forward, almost knocking me off. The path I had been on for an hour twisted a little farther through the marsh, then suddenly ascended a steep hill, where I had to lead the horse. By now I had adjusted to the noise, so that even though it must have been much louder than before, it buzzed and stung my ears at a more tolerable level, and I no longer felt sharp jolts through my skull. From the top of the hill I saw the same stream again, although here it was much wider where it entered a laguna. Thousands of men were massed on both sides of it; the rust-colored water was so thick with bodies that they seemed to form a bridge on which the living fought.

A new battalion moved up on the Paraguayan side. They stood out from the other men, who were half naked or splattered with mud, for their white trousers shone ghostlike through the smoke. Suddenly they ran wildly toward the water. For a moment the lines on the other side fell back at their fire, but as the new battalion reached the stream, the first ranks floundered, waist-deep, trying to shove the floating bodies out of their way. But the mass of men behind them were an unstoppable force. They began to crowd and trample one another. In a few moments the whole battalion was beating this way and that in the stream, turning on itself like a huge, eyeless sheep. All the while the Allies kept up continual fire. It was hard to tell the dead from the living who had stumbled and were trying to scramble back up the low bank before being shot in the back.

The enemy, on the other side of the stream, moved back and forth in vague blurs, emerging out of the smoke at times as precise little islands of blue. Great mouthfuls of smoke shot from the howitzers and were answered by the artillery of the Paraguayans.

I rode around behind the artillery wagons, looking for Diaz or one of his aides, but the smoke disfigured everyone I saw. A line of wounded hobbled toward a grove of Paraiso trees. One tall man with a bloody gash down the side of his head carried his own ear in his fingers before him, calling in a high, querulous voice, "Thread? Got any thread? A little piece of thread?"

"He's got a hat full of thread under his arm!" an old man with a dangling arm shouted up at me. "Everyone give him thread."

"Thread? Some thread . . . ?" The man stopped a limping boy with a bitten lip. The boy held out a paper wrapped with coarse black twine, but the man walked unseeing past him.

"Lots of thread." The old man waved his good arm angrily. "They thought he was dead, the cannibals, and they cut off his ear."

When I reached field headquarters, I found Diaz's aide, Lieutenant Urdapilleta, a grimy young man with strange white patches on his face where sweat had rolled down from his forehead. Diaz was *there! there! there!* he screamed over the boom of the howitzers, pointing in all directions, handing me a pair of field glasses. I tied up my horse to an empty wagon and climbed into the back of it. For a while I could make out only patches of smoke-obscured color through the glasses, but suddenly I focused them in on a patch of gaudy orange I had noticed earlier on a bluff across the stream. It was a huge tent, streaming with flags, and an officer had just come out and was looking down at the battle raging in the stream, his eyes shaded by his hand. If he had spoken I think I could have read his lips, but my fingers shook, and I was suddenly focused on a running soldier in a uniform tattered to no-color. His arm, which ended in a bloody stump, was uplifted, his mouth shaped to a scream.

A shell exploded close by, sending clods of dirt against my face. My horse reared up violently, shaking the wagon; then, as I had not taken time to tie him securely, he jerked free and bolted into a cloud of smoke.

I ran into the smoke after him, and for a moment even glimpsed him ahead, pawing the earth nervously like some ghostly unicorn. But then the smoke closed before my face. I sucked in a huge mouthful and doubled over, coughing.

A ragged line of men suddenly appeared before me, firing rapidly at a clump of foliage. Little pieces of shell speckled the air. I found that I was running toward the white swarm of men in the stream, and checked myself so violently that I fell to my knees. I had slipped on blood. The grass was oily with it. A dying man, still wearing his tall leather *morrione* although blood streamed from his neck, staggered toward me with his arms out, calling "Maria! Maria!" He wanted to hug me, but his face, gouged like a cheese, frightened me so much that I shoved myself up and ran in a crouch toward some underbrush. I crashed through stinging nettles and dropped to my stomach in the mire. I didn't lose consciousness, but a few minutes passed before I began to feel the limits of my body again. My hands burned. I sat up, edging the nettles out of my skin with my thumbnail, and for the first time thought about my position. While on a horse I had felt invulnerable: not from death, but from emotion. If a shell had exploded beside me I would have blazed up in a thousand unrecognizable pieces, or if a bullet had smashed my heart I would have disappeared from myself. As an actual event it was nothing; what I hated was the intellectual perception of such an event and the consequent throb of emotion it produced. Sweat, stammering, trembling—all of these things I had experienced, of course, but without having to attribute them to a cause. They were as natural as sleeping. If I began to trace the trembling in my hands as I squeezed out the nettles, back through the nerves dangling like marionette strings from my brain, I would lose control of myself. I could feel the rash bubbling under my skin. Old memories washed with strange vividness across my eyes as a corre-

lative to the horror of the present. I saw my grandmother lying in her graveclothes, her dyed black hair
encircling a head that had turned to skull years before
her death; my father, striking my cheek for forgetting a
passage of scripture, while my cousin Calvin, his hair
slicked back, smirked in the doorway; the ponderous
King James Bible my father used to read nightly to my
mother as part of his effort to stamp out any taint of
Catholicism she might have inherited; while my grandmother, pretending as always not to understand English,
stitched handkerchiefs in the corner. Then I saw my
mother's wasted, dying face, and my own face, equally
pale, adjusting my wedding veil over my braids in the
pier glass because I was too cowardly not to marry
Calvin, my father's choice. But the rash, my curse, had
also been my revenge, for he had turned from my body
in horror, barely consummating the marriage. I remembered the stiff black bombazine I had worn to my
father's funeral, which Calvin had performed, his hands
already trembling from the drink he had turned to in
the small New York State town he had been assigned to
as pastor. I buried my face in clean, sharp-smelling
leaves. Now perhaps Calvin was out there in the midst
of that smoke, and might materialize before my eyes; or
I would materialize before his eyes. Actually, the shock
might be Calvin's.

A variation in the din about my ears startled me.
Through a gap in the leaves I saw a group of soldiers
running in my direction. As they neared the underbrush
where I crouched, frozen, they wheeled about and
began firing at a blue blur close on their heels. The
Allies must have crossed the stream. I kept low and
crawled over a little behind the trunk of a tree, for

bullets whizzed into the leaves around me, shaking the nettles like snow. The Paraguayan soldiers were far outnumbered. Through the smoke I saw a rank of Argentinians. They were calling out, "Surrender, you dogs! You fools!"

Only four or five Paraguayans, blood pouring from their buckling legs or disfigured heads, were still shooting. Their red shirts made clear targets. The Argentine soldiers, dense around them on three sides, stopped firing a moment. One of their officers shouted hoarsely, "Surrender, you devils! Don't you see . . . ?" But he crumpled suddenly from a Paraguayan bullet. My throat constricted, and I realized that I too must have been screaming "Surrender!" into the noise. The Argentinians, in a deafening rage of musketry that forced my head into the mud, must have shot them all in a few seconds, for when I looked up in the momentary silence—I called it silence, although the background roar of battle was immense—they were twisted on the ground. The Argentine soldiers kicked the bodies aside as they wheeled off to the left.

I crawled out from the underbrush. The smoke was so thick that I didn't know which way to turn. I could hear firing all around me. Occasionally, ghostly figures appeared and disappeared, sometimes close enough to touch. Then, after a pause in the firing, the air cleared a little, and I could make out the green of the trees. A group of officers on horseback galloped past. I jumped back to avoid them and fell on a jagged tree stump, scratching my arm. I heard someone call my name, and suddenly General Diaz was pulling me to my feet, shaking me as if I were a watch that had stopped. His black horse pawed the ground behind him.

"A message." I was surprised to find myself whispering, but my throat ached from the smoke. I reached for the collar of my blouse where I had pinned the sealed paper, and handed it to him. As he opened it, I saw blood on his cheek, as if he had been grazed by a bullet; the cheek underneath was blue and swollen, and his left eye barely opened.

"This is blank, Mrs. Companion." He showed me the plain scrap of paper, the seal broken. "There's nothing in it. Where did you get it?"

"Lopez," I said hoarsely.

He groaned. "Get away from here—do you understand? Go that way." He gave me a shove into the underbrush. "Run, do you hear?" I turned a second to look back. He was already on his horse, but watching me. "Run!"

I fought my way deeper into the brush until I came to a trail where the prints of the barefoot soldiers who had defiled down it that morning were deeply impressed in drying mud. Here I ran for almost a mile, once leaping over a dead soldier swarming with big ants who had managed to crawl or stumble that far. I emerged into another jungle clearing crowded with wounded, where I spotted the telegraph equipment set up on several cracker boxes. Lieutenant Cela was arguing with three field officers who had bloody rags tied around their heads or arms. "The line's cut, I tell you!" he kept shouting into their exhausted faces. "I don't know what's happened to Bruguez or Diaz. I don't know anything."

"But Bruguez wasn't there," one of them, a major, kept repeating. "I pierced through the lines and Bruguez wasn't there. I had no support. Bruguez—"

"Major Olabarrieta, I said I don't—"

"Bruguez wasn't there," the major repeated dully. "We had to fight back through all those Brazilians again. I have eleven men left!" His voice rose suddenly, almost to a shriek. "Eleven wounded men, out of a whole regiment of cavalry! Where's Bruguez?"

"Major, I don't know, I said. The lines—" Lieutenant Cela spotted me and pointed. "Ask Señora Companion. She's been out on the field."

Olabarrieta and the other officers turned to stare at me.

"I saw the 25th Battalion destroyed. I don't know whose . . . "

"It's Casares," one of the officers groaned. "New recruits." He turned away, coughing blood into his hands.

"But Bruguez . . . " Major Olabarrieta grabbed my hand pleadingly. A long gash oozed blood from his forehead to his chin.

"Major, I don't know."

"He wasn't there." He pressed my hand tightly, peering into my face as if I had lied. "I pierced through the lines, and Bruguez never came. I had no support. I had to fight those Brazilians over again. . . . They burst out at us on all sides . . . !"

"Major!" someone shouted up from the mass of wounded sprawled across the clearing. "This boy knows! Ask him. He's seen Bruguez."

A young boy, thirteen or fourteen, limped toward us, a rag tied around the calf of his right leg. He carried as trophies, besides his own musket, a lance, a sword, a rifle, a dark blue poncho of heavy wool, and a small cannonball. He dropped the cannonball in the dust, but put his mud-caked foot on it to mark it as his own property.

"Bruguez was lanced through the shoulder," he babbled excitedly. "They've taken him back to Paso Pucu."

"Where was he?" Olabarrieta screamed at the boy, wringing his hands before his face as if he would like to strangle him. "I had to fight through all those Brazilians again!"

The boy turned white and clutched his new weapons to his chest, rubbing the rifle's shiny metal nervously with his thumb while glancing down at his cannonball as if he feared Major Olabarrieta would steal it. One of the other officers pulled Olabarrieta back, whispering that he had to report to Lopez before Bruguez claimed that it was he, Olabarrieta, who had not come with support. Sighing, the boy threw his poncho on the ground, sat down, and rolled the cannonball between his legs.

Something snatched at my ankle. I glanced down and saw an old man who had torn off his shirt to make a bandage for his leg, but he had fallen back exhausted in the dust. He made incomprehensible sounds in his throat and pointed down the length of his body. Up until now I had tried not to look at the wounded, for there were too many hundreds of them in the little clearing. I knelt down beside the man and began to roll up his trouser leg, almost vomiting at the red upheaval of muscle. The bone, like a piece of white bark, protruded at a weird angle. I hadn't the slightest idea what to do, except perhaps to tie the shirt he had feebly pushed at me around the place where the bone showed. I couldn't roll the trouser leg up any further, but I had the impression that the wound slashed all the way to his groin. I tried to lift his leg to get the shirt under, but he screamed. The pain seemed to clear mucus out of his throat, for he began to talk in a high, sharp voice about a black horse, then abruptly fell silent, his eyes closed. I glanced helplessly at Lieutenant Cela, but he was fiddling with the telegraph equipment, his back toward me. The boy was alternately stroking his cannonball with a kind of awe and adjusting the rag around his own leg. Already there were gnats mixed in the gobbles of congealed blood along the old man's leg. I tried to lift it again, but his high-pitched scream frightened me. I laid the shirt over the wound and tucked it in. A few seconds later the blood had soaked through. I was pulling down his trouser leg when the boy, glancing over at me, said softly, "He's dead."

"What?"

"See?" He pointed at the man's mouth, where a froth of green had appeared. I put my hand against his bare, bruised chest but could feel nothing. I sat back against a cracker box.

"After I rest," the boy said, "I'm going to give this to Marshal Lopez." He was rubbing spit onto the cannonball to make it shine. "Perhaps he'll make me a corporal."

"And then what will you do?"

"Why, I'll go back to the trenches, of course."

"Aren't you afraid?"

He looked around, frowning. "No."

"Where are you from?"

"Asunción. I worked on the palace."

"The new palace Lopez is building? Doing what?"

"On the stone—a soft stone from Empedrado. We drilled it, trimmed it . . . we couldn't lift it, though."

"We? Did a lot of boys work on the palace?"

He turned the hilt of his sword over so that it caught the sun. "Yes."

"You don't sound happy about that time."

He shrugged. "There wasn't much to eat, only a little mandioca or chipa."

"There's not much to eat here."

"No. But the army gets . . . well, things." He touched the sword.

"Do you expect to win this war?"

He looked at me blankly. "Of course."

"Are you badly wounded?"

"A scratch. I won't get the black horse, though."

"What black horse?"

"Lopez has promised a black horse to anyone who personally kills a general."

"Did you try to kill a general?"

"I never saw one. There was too much smoke. Then I was shot, just as I dreamed I would be. Only in my dream I was shot in the head, like this—" He demonstrated by knocking his fist against his forehead. "I didn't get any ears, either." He pulled a small knife out of his pocket. "I told the others I'd get some ears to hang outside the barracks."

"Molly!" Across the clearing Doctor McPherson was waving to me. He was stripped to the waist, smeared with blood and dirt, but I recognized the oilcloth cap protecting his bald skull. When I reached him, I saw that he was having difficulty breathing, and his hollow chest moved up and down rapidly. "You've got to get me some more bandages. I've been trying to use their shirts, but they're so muddy, I'm just infecting the wounds." He was almost sobbing as he put his trembling hand on my shoulder to steady himself. "I don't know how long I can take this, Martha. I'm sorry. Molly. My poor wife—" He peered into my face as if trying to trace some resemblance. "Please, go back to camp. See what you can do."

"All right, Doctor. I'll hurry." I squeezed his hand. On the far side of the clearing I saw an opening and plunged down a narrow path barely wide enough for a single person, where long, thorny runners tripped me or spiked branches tore at my face. Through the foliage I got occasional glimpses of flooded lowlands or *bañado*, fields of treacherous smooth mud and stagnant pools. After an hour I spotted the deep blue of one of the lagunas and realized that I was completely lost. The underbrush thinned. I shook some of the thorns and burrs from my sleeves, then spotted an abandoned *capilla* I hadn't known existed. A few wretched huts of wattle and dab, or warped wood with zinc or straw roofs, surrounded a church on a small hill. The church had once been whitewashed but was now spotted with ugly grey stains. A few blue tiles still remained in the cornice. It was quiet except for the peewits, furiously warning of my approach.

The single street leading up to the church was dry, cracked mud, although the central gutter still appeared damp and foul-smelling from the last rain. A hairless dog with a triangular face slunk out of one hut, whined once around my ankles, then bounded off in a curious, lop-sided gait, fat ticks shining on his long ears. Sarsaparilla tangled over many of the huts and had grown over open doorways. Behind the church I could see that a little orange grove had receded back to jungle, for scarlet lianas twisted from tree to tree. All the people who had lived here—men, women, and children—must have been swept into the army. I kicked an iron cooking pot with my foot, frightening the lizard sleeping under it. A

colonnade surrounded the church, and after reaching
the top of the small hill, from where I was glad to see
the telegraph poles of Paso Pucu and even one of the
watchtowers farther away at Humaitá, I sat down in the
shade to rest, my back to the cool, age-darkened wall of
the church.

In a few minutes the high iron door of the church
opened and a man came out. He wore a lilac *kepi* with
gold braiding, a blue frock coat, and long riding boots.
At first he did not see me, but merely stood in the doorway, partly obscured by shadow, biting his thumb as he
looked down at the empty town.

I held my breath. Under my hand, which was pressed
back against the wall, a little fragment of stone broke
off. I knew that if he moved a step forward into the sun I
would see his earlobe, still ragged from his fall on a
horseshoe as a boy. I couldn't speak. I waited until his
glance followed the skim of a hawk from a tree to the
left horizon, then fell on me.

"Molly!" His voice broke harshly. He grabbed his big
adam's apple as if he were choking. "Who sent you
here?"

"Sent me?" I leaned forward. "What do you mean?"

"Who sent you over here? Bliss?"

I shook my head. "You knew I was in Paraguay, then?
They told you?"

His lip twitched, but he didn't answer. The sun glared
full on him now. The bones in his face seemed to have
shifted over the past years, like a glacier, leaving his expression strangely unfamiliar to me; or else it was the
skin, eroded, revealing the shapes of the bones for the
first time. I felt as if I had just twisted a telescope out of
focus; or, rather, it had been dimly out of focus all along,

and now the clearest image had leapt forward. I felt confused. I knew he would be changed, but not so much. Yet I couldn't say where the difference lay. He had always dipped his lids over his eyes that way, looking at me. The chewed earlobe was the same. His large, twisted nose still broke his face into two equal parts, the skin slightly discolored, like a cut peach bruising in the air. The sun emphasized new lines, but that wasn't it, either. Nor was it his new, ugly way of biting his lip.

"So now you've smelled me out." A sudden breeze lifted his hair, longer and greyer than I remembered. I could see the pink of his scalp through the thin strands. He had just shaved, for his jaw had a raw, bluish look, and blood oozed from a small nick on his chin. He laughed. "You came all the way to Paraguay. What for?"

"I wanted to see you again."

"What for?"

I looked away. "I don't know. To see you, I guess. To understand it."

He squatted down against a column opposite me. His boots shone, and there was a suggestion of lace on his shirt. In my dreams he always wore rusty black, his cold, freckled white hands fumbling at my buttons. The hands were still white, but thinner, with strange stains along the fingers and black crescents under the nails. One knuckle was terribly swollen.

"I was a coward."

"That's not what I meant."

He spat. "I ran, Molly. And it wasn't any Christian revulsion to war, either. I like war, I've discovered." He laughed. "But out on the field I couldn't take it; I vomited under fire, if you can believe that! Once I hid in

the woods with a flask of brandy. Then, finally, I ran
from the field in full view of my whole company."

"That's when you deserted."

"Deserted." His yellowed teeth clipped his lip again.
"Oh, I was wild afterwards on the ship, cursing God!"
He laughed, but pressed his hand against his heart as if
it had begun to beat too rapidly. "I got drunk every
night. I was going ashore at Rio; then I decided, Hell,
hell's what I want. The most remote place I could think
of, where I still might survive, was Paraguay."

"I got your letter."

"Did you?" He coughed. "A year later, I suppose.
What an ass I was to write to you. That's when I told you
I was getting into the tobacco exporting business and
would be back in a month with a fortune! Ha! If I'd
made a fortune I'd never have gone back." He stood up.
"But every fortune in Paraguay is stamped 'Lopez.' I almost ended up in prison for operating without a govern-
ment permit. Luckily they hired me as an engineer for
the railroad." He looked down at me, gnawing at the
knuckle that was puffed like a small cauliflower. "Did
you wait?"

"I needed money. I went to Aunt Susan in Boston and
persuaded a newspaper to let me do some articles."

He shrugged, a sudden, hostile expression clamping
his face. "The new Margaret Fuller." He grabbed for
my wrist, pulling me up. "Let me show you something."

He shoved me into the church. I was blinded both by
the sudden watery dimness of the interior and the shock
running up my body at his touch. The sharp smell of
gunpowder, however, was unmistakable, and as he
nudged me down the main aisle of the church, I gradually perceived that the crude benches of the worship-

pers were either upended or stacked with barrels and muskets, and that the altar had been turned into a chemist's table. Over the altar—with its glass tubes and capsules, zinc boxes and vials of what looked like acid, wads of cotton wool, copper wire and scissors—hung a cross with a nearly life sized figure of Christ attached. The hands of the figure were broken. It had been torn off the cross, dressed in the baggy pants and scarlet shirt of a Paraguayan soldier, and roped back in place. The gaudy pink-cheeked face was still contorted in the O-gape of agony, but a cigar butt had been stuck between the parted lips.

"Here's what I do, in *this* war." He picked up a little glass capsule off the altar. "This is sulphuric acid. You pack it in a little chlorate of potash and sugar, wrap it in cotton wool . . . a fuse."

I looked around. Two windows of buckled stained glass pierced the wall on either side of the crucifix, sending down shafts of rose light.

Calvin brought the swollen knuckle to his lips again. "When the war started, they forced me to work with Kruger, a munitions expert for the Confederacy." He set the capsule down carefully. "He was blown up."

"He's the one who tried to steer a torpedo raft close to the fleet."

He took off his kepi and flung it at a pile of old clothes in the corner. "He was crazy."

"So you make the torpedoes and the hand grenades, then?"

"And the case shot." He pointed to some awkwardly sewn leather buckets. "If you can call it that—those, filled with bits of scrap iron. But you know all about that." He grinned. "Bliss told me about your job."

"Why are you so isolated here?"

He swept his hand around the church, over the barrels of gunpowder. "Isn't it obvious? I could blow up a city." He came closer to me, his voice dropping to a whisper. As he passed through the shaft of rose light, his face shone like a saint's, then darkened into slabs of shadow as he touched my shoulder. "I didn't do it, you know." He glanced up at the crucifix. "You thought I did, didn't you?"

"You seem so changed," I murmured.

"That fellow's only the bad thief, now. Appropriate. So I let him be." His fingers tightened on my shoulder. "What did you want?"

My breath came hard. "Just to see you again."

"And now?"

"And now? Nothing."

"Just nothing? Aren't you going to plead with me, like a good wife?"

I looked at him coldly. "No."

"Aren't you going to plead that I come back with you? Reform? That I take your scabby body in my arms again, kiss your bumps?"

His words went through me like needles. I could feel my arms growing hot under my tight sleeves. Nevertheless, I said calmly, "Back with me? How? Aren't I as trapped here as you?"

He dropped his hand and moved away, frowning. "You always want *me* to end things. You want *me* to say it." He picked up a coil of copper wire and began to wrap it around his finger. "I should have been a priest, not a soulless Methodist minister." The wire was gradually cutting off the blood in his finger, turning it purple.

He watched it. "One of those masked Jesuits in a black gown, like Lopez's secretaries."

I swallowed hard and moved behind the altar so that I did not have to see his finger. "What's this?" A few links of a massive chain were coiled in a corner.

"We're going to stretch a chain across the river, to stop the fleet. That's only a small part of it. They're still working on it at the foundry."

I laughed at him across the altar. "Those ironclads will break it in two!"

"No." Both hands were in his pockets now. The copper wire, twisted out of shape, was back on the altar. "I'm going to attach torpedoes all along it. They won't dare ram it."

The gloom of the church oppressed me. "I think I need some air."

He shrugged and followed me back outside to the steps, where he sat down, his face broken into deep lines that made him look like an old man. He pulled a turnip out of his pocket and chewed off a bite. "Sit down. I want to talk to you."

"What about?"

"I think you know."

I watched his stiff blue jaw. "About your marriage?"

"I'll go through with it if I have to." He laughed. "Hopefully, I won't have to."

"Bliss and McPherson said you had a plan to escape."

"I do. You're going to help me. I'm going to assassinate Lopez—that is, you and I are going to assassinate Lopez."

I stared at him. "What?"

"There's a general who'll help . . . who'll take over

the country. Naturally, I haven't let those cowards Bliss
and McPherson know anything about my real intentions
yet."

"Isn't there an easier way to get out of Paraguay?"

He brushed away the bee that had landed on his
sleeve. "That's not why I'm doing it."

"Why, then?"

He positioned his boot carefully over a large ant hill in
a crack of the step below him and ground it flat. A
stream of red ants rushed madly to the left. "You won't
understand, probably. I need to prove something about
myself."

"You're a man of God. Or were."

He laughed. "It is expedient that one man shall die for
the people and that the whole nation perish not."

"Calvin!"

He turned on me, the planes of his face twitching. The
sun had flushed his skin red; and drinking, I realized
now that I saw him in open light, had broken the veins in
his nose and enlarged it further. "I was a coward, don't
you see? A deserter, traitor. . . . Now I have my
chance. I can end this war single-handedly, Molly." He
stood up, pulling me with him, then jerked his fingers
away from my arms distastefully. "I shouldn't have told
you yet." He spat at the passing line of ants, catching
several in his glob of saliva. The other ants circled
around. "You're weak-minded."

"Just don't involve me in murder," I said. My skin felt
clammy, as if I were wrapped in wet flannel. "Why don't
we just steal a boat?"

He laughed. "Romantic!"

"What general?"

"I'd better not tell you that."

I felt a little dizzy. "Diaz?"

He shrugged. "I can't say. But this general will take over the country and end the war. Think of all the lives saved."

"No." I turned away. At the foot of the church steps an army of caterpillars was descending the trunk of a Casuarina pine in a solid phalanx. I watched them for a moment. "I think it's wrong."

"Wrong!" Abruptly he grabbed me by the shoulders again and swung me around to face him. His nails bit into my skin. "I spent a few years turning the other cheek, and where did it get me? A miserable congregation in a cold valley where a bunch of farmers—louts—gossiped if I had a nip of whiskey or looked at their pretty wives because my own wife . . . and now, I'm to stand meekly by while Lopez starves or tortures me to death, or better yet"—he laughed, drops of spittle hitting my face—"I blow myself up for the cause like Kruger? Ha!" I tried to jerk away, but he held me tighter. "You want to die here, sweetheart?"

"No." I saw my tiny image flickering in his eyes. "Why don't we steal a boat, then?"

"You know it's impossible. There's no easy way out, Molly. When you hear from me again, you'll do what I say." He smiled. A sore on the corner of his lip cracked and seeped blood. "You're getting old, Molly. I see lines in your face."

I wiggled away from his grip, which had slackened. "No wonder."

I looked back at him once as I hurried around the church. He was wiping his nose again, laughing. In the marsh I stopped by a pool of water. My reflection shimmered beneath the fine net of insects hovering just above the surface. I felt as if the real world existed back of the pool, that I had once stood on the other side, fallen in, and had emerged, dripping and bewildered, here. The firing had all but stopped in the distance, and the rightful sounds of the marsh emerged in strange trills and rushes. A bird with a musical twitter flew from a nearby branch, startling me. His wings shone black. Surely he was some enchanted prince searching for his princess, who had turned into the ugly frog mouthing upward in the pool. The frog seemed to suck my reflection off the surface; then I realized that the light was fading. If I didn't hurry, I'd be lost in the jungle at nightfall.

# Four

It was completely dark when I finally found the small cemetery outside Paso Pucu. It was on a hill, which I decided to climb to get my bearings. A rough gravel path led up to the iron gate, which hung ajar, rusted. A number of expensive telescopes had been set up there so that Lopez could view the war without any danger. I heard voices and, oddly, some wild strains of music that must be floating up from the camp on the other side. As I entered the gate and glanced across the field of tombs in the shape of little pink and blue stucco houses to where a few stone angels loomed against the sky, I saw a huddle of figures against the far wall. At first I thought they were wounded soldiers who had taken shelter from the fine mist, but as I approached they wheeled on me violently with their rifles. They seemed to be guarding three women who sat together on a flat tombstone. Two of the soldiers recognized me, for I had been all over the camp, and lowered their weapons.

"Please, Señora!" one of the women screamed. "Help us! Can you help?"

"Shut up!" A fat soldier hit her in the face with the butt of his rifle. She sprawled back on the tomb, sobbing.

"What is this? What's going on?"

"Please go away; this doesn't concern you." A young lieutenant who seemed to be in charge pointed down toward the camp where bonfires blazed. The music, drifting up, was louder now. I felt confused. The woman who had spoken to me was stuffing her hair into her mouth in an attempt to stop her sobs and was looking at me with wild wet eyes. The second woman, muffled in a cape, kept her head down. The third woman had matted grey hair standing out like snakes. She obviously did not know where she was, and twisted her head this way and that in a frantic yet mindless rhythm.

"I want to know what this is."

"Señora, I order you—!"

The girl who had spoken first sobbed out. "I want to go home."

"Why can't she go home?"

The lieutenant looked up from the lantern he had just managed to light. "Because she's from Corrientes. She was trying to cross enemy lines." He spat in the girl's face, and his saliva ran and dripped over her lip. She did not wipe it off. "She's a little slut, an Argentine. She followed the army while we were victorious, and now that things are rough, she wants to go back. Lopez will peel every inch of flesh off her back."

"Why don't you just let her go?" I said softly. "There's so much confusion. What harm?"

The lieutenant, whose face was swollen with anger like a block of wet wood, laughed. "It's even worse." He

72

kicked viciously at the other, muffled woman, who fell over in the mud like a doll. For a moment it seemed incredible that she should be so easily knocked off balance; then I saw, under her red skirt, the black iron fetters.

"Pancha Garmendia!" the lieutenant said, watching contemptuously as the Corrientino girl helped her up from the mud. "Lopez would decimate the army if Pancha Garmendia escaped."

The Corrientino girl stood up, shaking back her wet hair. Her eyebrows were sharp and glossy from the rain, which was falling harder now. "She's almost dead!"

One of the soldiers flung out his elbow to strike her breast, but she saw him and ducked quickly down on the tombstone. She put her arm around Pancha Garmendia, whose head was uncovered now, and whose skin, in the dim lantern light, shone white as paper.

"Can't you see—?" I began, but the lieutenant, at my first words, turned abruptly away and began to whisper rapidly to one of his soldiers.

"It was the old woman," the Corrientino girl told me sadly. "We were all right, hiding here, but she started singing—bim bim something—and looking up at a stone angel she thought was Lopez. I tried to stop her; I put a handful of mud in her mouth, even, for the soldiers were coming through—but she choked, terrible, and I had to slap her breath back into her. They heard her cough." She pulled the hood up over Pancha Garmendia's head again. The lantern, which one of the soldiers was trying to protect with his poncho, reflected off her wet face like a mirror.

"You should go," she added after a minute. "I thought you might help, but I see you can't."

"I'll try. I'll speak to Lopez, to someone . . . "

73

The old woman next to her suddenly clawed at my arm. "Lopez is drowned." She leaned toward me, panting. "I saw his soul—turned to stone, to stone—!"

The Corrientino girl pushed her away. "She kept following us, shouting that about Lopez being drowned. . . . She saw me unchain Pancha from the tree where they keep her like a dog, you see. I had to take her with us. She's Pancha's old duenna, only she's crazy now."

"Aren't the mad good luck?" Pancha Garmendia pushed back her hood. The skin over her thin, aquiline nose was almost transparent. Her eyes glittered feverishly. "Aren't they?"

"Sometimes, Pancha," the Corrientino girl hugged her tightly.

"Do they want me to dance again, Rosalita?"

"No, Pancha."

"I lost my soul, too. For one moment, one moment— my bones were hurting like green twigs; the music wouldn't stop—for one moment I didn't believe in God, Rosalita. My soul flew out of my mouth."

"No, Pancha, no. It's there. I can feel your soul." Rosalita grabbed for the girl's hand. "Feel it, Pancha, feel it." She pushed Pancha's hand against her breast. "See? Throbbing." She dropped the hand suddenly, her face quivering, and turned away.


By the time I reached camp, the rain had let up. The bonfires were out, but the bands, which had been silent awhile, started up again with loud, rousing, victorious music. I passed one huddle of wet, exhausted men who were playing fiercely on charangos and hand-harps in the light of a few sputtering rush candles stuck in the mud before them under clay hoods. Paso Pucu had

74

rapidly become a large town of huts thatched with grass or covered with raw hides. To the left a high earthwork had been built to protect Lopez's new villa from shelling in case the enemy fleet should ascend the river Paraguay and take Curupayty, which would put it behind Paraguayan lines. I could see many lights in that direction. To the right, also blazing with light, were the hospitals, and beyond them, down a guarded path through the swamp, was the prison compound where the soldiers had taken Pancha Garmendia and the other two women. I had never been allowed to visit the prison, but according to the hiss of rumor that occasionally broke, even from the tight, nervous mouths of the Paraguayan soldiers, it was not for captured soldiers, who were often lanced outright, but for traitorous Paraguayans who were shipped downriver by the hundreds from Asunción.

I hesitated. I was wet and streaked with mud. My hair had fallen out of its chignon into a tangled mess. Lopez would laugh at me in this state. Or my appearance might be considered an insult to his dignity. Also, I needed to get some advice before I mentioned Pancha Garmendia to him; I had heard tales of a priest who had prayed for her openly and had been rewarded with a hot branding iron in his mouth. I started down the muddy street. Doctor McPherson was probably at the hospitals, thinking me dead because I'd never returned with the bandages, and although he might give me good advice, he'd be unable to do anything himself. The only other person I might trust was General Diaz. At the next corner another band was playing. Two of the musicians, in a stupor, had dropped back against a barracks. I almost tripped over one, who jerked back his leg, clutching his harp against him with bleeding fingers. He sighed, beginning to play in a desultory fashion, his eyelids twitching shut at intervals. A strange, faint burning smell had replaced the damp smell of rain and mud. The streets, although dark except for a few torches at the corners or rush candles burning in occasional doorways, were surprisingly crowded. I jostled past women with buckets and stacks of bandages, dancing sentries, soldiers with bound arms or heads, singing off key, and boisterous groups of drunken officers with their arms around each other shouting "Viva Lopez!" or "Victory! Victory!" A grinning soldier with a small dead pig under his arm stumbled against me, almost knocking me into the slick mud. Through the doorway of one hut, partially closed by palm fronds, a naked woman lifted her legs. Small wet dogs growled over bones or scratched their sharp ribs against poles. Now I heard some of the soldiers yelp angrily; the phrase "burning them" struck me from several sides. I was beginning to notice the smoky odor again, but I kept on until I reached an open area near headquarters where all was dark. Looking up, I saw the strange constellations wheeling overhead. They made me dizzy, but I knew they were stationary, and that it was only my throbbing pulse that made them seem to swim, as I recalled the brutal red hands of a soldier pushing Pancha Garmendia down the hill. For weeks I had ignored the fact that Lopez kept her chained to a big tree on the edge of the camp, and I felt ashamed that it was someone else, not I, who had tried to help her escape. I had kept away from that area so as not to be distressed. I had a sudden image of the dying man with the gouged face staggering toward me, his arms out. I looked hard at the stars again. Was that Centaur which Doctor McPherson had pointed out to me? I couldn't find the Southern Cross, for my eyes were blurry, as if filled with tears; yet when I touched them with my fingers they were quite dry. I hurried over to Diaz's hut, built against the stockade wall that surrounded Lopez's villa. If he wasn't there, I would wait up for him all night if necessary. "Yes, burning them like pigs!" Someone's high, clear voice rang in my ears as I entered, surprised at the canopied bed, with posts carved into bulging frogs, that almost filled the small, empty room. The stiff brocade canopy pressed against the straw roof. A candle guttered on a chest beside the bed. I sat on the high-backed cane chair that filled the remaining space between the bed and the door. The sheets on the bed were yellowed and stained, and a few ants crawled desultorily up and down the wrinkles, but nevertheless the bed looked inviting. I could see the indentation of Diaz's head in the round bolster pillow, and grease stains from his hair. In my own hut I had a hammock and a straw pallet infested with various insects. How nice to lie down in a real bed and sleep away this nightmare!

I had just leaned back against the cane chair, which cut into my neck, when the scrap of carpet over the doorway was torn back. Diaz, sallower than I remembered him, his uniform splattered with mud, stared at me with confused eyes. He swayed against the wall.

"Are you hurt?"

"No, no." He sat down heavily on the bed, the springs squeaking under him. "Mrs. Companion, what are you doing here?" His eyes, still confused, touched mine. He brushed his hand along his trouser leg in embarrassment.

"I'm sorry; I shouldn't have come now." I stood up. "I feel better now. I was upset; I thought . . . "

He straightened himself. I could tell he was weary.

Nevertheless, he smiled politely. "Perhaps I can help?"

I turned away, choking, pressing my nails into my palms for support. "I hope so. I don't know . . ."

"You've smelled the bodies?" he asked softly.

"What bodies?"

He hesitated. "That smell. They're burning our dead—the heathens."

"Oh, God." I put my hands over my face. "But they're talking about victory out there!"

He coughed. "Lopez lost half his army. But you're right. It's a victory—don't ever suggest otherwise." He added softly, "What do you want, Mrs. Companion?"

"It's Pancha Garmendia." Once I had gotten her name out, my voice grew clearer. I concentrated on Diaz's shoulder, where an epaulette had been ripped loose, so I did not have to watch his sad, swollen face. "Another girl tried to help her escape, and now they've both been dragged to the prison camp. I'm afraid they'll be killed."

"That Argentine girl, Rosalita? She spoke to me once about Pancha. I warned her." He leaned back on his elbow, his eyes flickering shut. "What do you want me to do?"

"Can't you help them?" Diaz's mouth opened slightly, and I was afraid he had fallen asleep. I put my hand against his cheek, which felt hot. "General?"

He jumped and sat up, trying to smile. "Forgive me, Mrs. Companion. I'm very tired. What did you say?"

"Is there any way to help them?"

"No."

My voice rose. "No?"

"Mrs. Companion—may I call you Molly? Molly. Or have I been calling you Molly?" He stifled a yawn. "I'm

sorry; I'll be able to think better tomorrow." He flashed
me a quick, embarrassed look. "You see, there's another
woman whose life I'm presently trying to save."

"Who?"

"You."

I said stiffly, "You think I'm in danger?"

"You had proof today. That message."

"But why?"

He shrugged, beginning to unbutton his uniform
jacket. "It's impossible to say 'why' with Francisco. And
it's impossible to do anything for Pancha. She won't be
killed. They'll simply beat her and chain her to the tree
again. Lopez likes to ride by and look at her, you see."
He took off his jacket. Great bruises covered his arms.
He saw me staring and smiled slightly. "Not very pretty.
I was knocked off my horse several times." He sighed,
continuing, "When Lopez was a young man, Pancha
refused to be his mistress, so her humiliation is a matter
of dignity for him—a matter of state. Now, Rosalita will
be brutally executed, no doubt. However, speak to
Madame Lynch. She may be able to do something about
Rosalita, if you rouse her pity."

I said bitterly, "She has pity?"

"Don't underestimate Madame Lynch." Diaz pursed
his lips. "At least she has a reasonable imitation when
it's convenient." He lay down, closing his eyes." "I'm
sorry. I'm too exhausted to have any feelings now."

As he turned his face to the wall, I stumbled outside
again, covering my nose with the tail of my skirt so as not
to breathe the terrible air. When I reached my own hut,
I found Monkey-Snout sitting cross-legged in the doorway. He scrambled lithely to his feet when he saw me,
bowing. "Señora, I have a gift for you."

"Yes?" I pushed back my red carpet door and saw that a good wax candle, not a smelly tallow dip, burned on the cracker box in the corner. "Thank you. The wax smells sweet."

He had followed me inside and now unbuttoned a large pocket under his arm, which I had mistaken for the bulge of a tumor. "This is what I promised you." From his pocket he pulled a large piece of white lace so beautiful that I gasped. The threads were knotted into intricate swirls of flowers. He flung it on my hammock.

"It's more beautiful than a spider web!"

He shook his head. "Once I found a skeleton in the jungle that the spiders had dressed with their webs. The dew covered the strands, so that each glittered. I have seen nothing so lovely."

"It's strong lace." I touched the threads. "It doesn't look that strong."

"Sometimes, in the villages, the women will hang up the corpse in a hammock of lace, so that the ants keep off until the coffin's ready." He ran his finger through his grey hair, which hung from his face like the tail of a mule. "A widow usually buries her husband in her wedding veil."

"What if the woman dies first?"

"Then she is buried in her wedding veil."

We both turned at the sound of a step outside, and a soft curse. Porter Bliss poked his red face in the door. "Molly? I've got to see you."

He looked hard at Monkey-Snout, who bowed. "Senora, there's a good-luck charm woven into the lace for you. Keep it always. Or bury a loved one in it, to protect his journey."

Monkey-Snout brushed like a wisp of smoke past Porter Bliss, who wore no tie or collar; his shirt was

open halfway down his chest, and his feet were bare. He
carried a basket with a lid tied down with strips of
leather. He scowled at me. "I was hoping you'd be
alone."

"I am now. What do you want?"

He whispered, "I've seen Calvin. Just now."

"Yes?"

"Don't look so damn blank." He set the basket on the
dirt floor and sprawled in my hammock, pushing aside
the lace, which I caught up and held against me. "He's
told me everything—about how he saw you today, and
how you'll help." He whistled softly. "So it's an
assassination."

"That pleases you?"

He bit at his drooping mustache. "Immensely. I've
dreamed of killing Lopez. Only I'm the first to admit it—
I'm a coward. I was afraid to move alone." He looked
nervously at the basket. I thought he was about to prod
it with his toe, but abruptly he tucked his foot in the
hammock. "What a horrible death, too."

"What death?"

"Snake bite—only, no ordinary snake bite. This is a
jararaca peculiar to the jungle. It causes great pain and
paralysis before death."

I said quietly, "In that basket?"

"Yes."

I pushed at the air with my hand, squeezing my eyes
shut. "Take it out of here."

"Oh, no!" He laughed. "You'd better get used to it,
Molly. It's going to spend the night with you."

"It won't!" My voice rose uncontrollably. All of the
horror I felt at the events of the day now focused on
that thing in the basket. "Get it out of here, Porter."

He pulled a gold watch out of his pocket. The chain

81

hissed over his fingers as he opened the face. "It's only a few hours until dawn. You'd better get some sleep." He jumped out of the hammock. His breath was strong with rum; his mustache, flecked with dried lemon pulp, quivered as he leaned toward me. "Here's what you'll do, then. Go visit Madame Lynch around eleven in the morning. Lopez is usually making his rounds then. You'll pass the open window to his office as you walk behind his villa to the orchard house where Lynch lives. You'll be out of the sentry's view on that side for just a moment. Open the basket, if the room's empty, and drop the snake in the window." He slapped a mosquito. "Then go on and visit Lynch as if nothing had happened."

"Why don't you do it?"

"Because it would look suspicious. You've often been to visit Lynch."

"What if the snake bites me?"

"Then you'll die." His lip twitched. "So you'd better be careful, eh?"

"How do you know the snake will bite Lopez?"

"Because at noon he locks himself in his office for an hour before luncheon. Don't worry. The jararaca is easily upset, and has been known to bite some victims a dozen times, even after they're dead." He bit his own finger, grinning, showing me the white fang marks in his flesh. "Death is excruciating, although almost instantaneous."

"Calvin gave you the snake?"

"Yes. He caught it just this evening." Bliss sucked his lower lip, staring at me. "You'll do it?"

"I don't know."

Bliss puffed his cheeks with air, then blew it out, his

fingers curling into fists. "If a word about you were dropped in Lopez's ear—"

"Are you threatening me? Don't."

"For Christ's sake, Molly! Isn't it obvious? Someone's got to kill Lopez. It's a duty! These people are all under his spell." He bit off the tip of his thumbnail with a tiny crunch. "We've got to save these people, Molly. It's not like we've asked you to shoot Lopez point-blank."

"Just drop the snake in his office." I fell into the hammock, burying my face in the lace I still clutched to my breast. "I see."

"It's simple."

"Go away, Porter."

I could hear him grinding his teeth. "Are you going to do it?"

I didn't answer, and after a minute I had the impression that he was gone. The new wax candle had almost burned down and was hissing as it threw long, wavering shadows up the reed walls where green beetles glinted; then I imagined that the hissing was coming, not from the candle, but from the basket on the ground. I thought I saw the basket jerk, as if the snake had coiled and leapt in his confinement; but then the candle sputtered out, leaving me in darkness.

# Five

I carried the basket with the jararaca on my way to visit Elisa Lynch the next morning. Outside the stockade walls some soldiers had begun an impromptu circus. Three clowns in white nightshirts tumbled around in the drying mud while the circle of soldiers whistled and applauded. The clowns had painted their faces red with berry juice and splashed their cheeks with black ink. They did handstands and awkward somersaults and attempted a pyramid by standing on one another's shoulders. The top clown tumbled off but seemed unhurt. Then they threw buckets of water at one another, or at the audience, sometimes goading a soldier into chasing them into the circle while the whole crowd roared. After a while they parodied the battle, two clowns marching around with captured Brazilian or Argentine drums and bugles, playing them for the sake of noise only, while the other clowns pretended to shoot

them with broomsticks. The crowd threw their hats up
with wild cheers. One of the "dead" clowns jumped up
and hurried back, leading a dog on a long chain. A band
had appeared at the edge of the crowd and played
while the clown, with a stick, ordered the dog, who
wore a green felt vest, to rise on its hind legs. Gro-
tesquely, it began to turn around and around, its paws
extended as if embracing a partner. The clown flicked it
down with his stick. Three of the Golden Combs leapt
into the circle, while the soldiers clapped and stamped
their feet; the women wheeled in a dance, holding
hands, round and round. Each had a white oleander in
her brown hair, beads, and a scarlet skirt, but each face
was hard-set as wood. On they whirled as if their feet
were shod with hot iron. Their faces haunted me.

Then a monkey in a pink dress, with a bow around its
neck, appeared on a horse. The horse trotted gently
around the circle, while the monkey clung nervously to
its neck, its little head darting back and forth. The
soldiers hooted. General Bruguez, whom I suddenly
noticed sitting on a crate at the edge of the crowd, one
arm wrapped in bandages, raised his free hand. "Loose
the dogs!" he screamed. A pack of hairless brown dogs,
straining on ropes, were brought up and released. They
tore madly toward the horse, barking, snapping their
immense white teeth; terrified, the horse reared on its
hind legs for a moment, then kicked in what seemed all
directions at once. The clinging monkey chattered in
terror. The dogs attempted to leap up the side of the
horse, growling and barking, for the monkey, nearly
catching its little pink dress in their teeth. I closed my
eyes, feeling sick, expecting any moment that the
monkey would be torn to pieces by the dogs.

A great cheer rose. When I opened my eyes, I saw the monkey riding expertly on the back of one of the dogs, while the others followed docilely around the ring. It had all been part of the trick. Bruguez had the monkey brought to him and cradled it like a baby with his good arm, letting it chew his ribbons. I hurried past, not wishing him to see me with the basket, although I was not going to do as Porter Bliss and Calvin demanded. Near dawn I had made my decision. I would speak to Elisa Lynch about Rosalita and Pancha Garmendia. If she promised to help, I would release the snake in the marsh; if she refused, only then would I consider dropping it in Lopez's window.

Elisa Lynch's house was in a small orchard behind Lopez's headquarters. A pretty garden had been planted around it, and a real mahogany door with an ornate brass handle had been fitted into the whitewashed adobe. This was open today, and sunlight streamed inside onto the Oriental carpet that led from the hall to the parlor. An old woman, her face covered with a shawl, dozed on the doorsill, her blue-veined bare feet stuck straight out before her. She roused at my touch and wordlessly beckoned me into the parlor, where a snowy-haired man I had never seen before, in a civilian frock coat and patent leather boots, sprawled on the divan, his handkerchief to his nose. He snorted at me but did not say anything or remove the handkerchief.

Along two walls of the parlor, from ceiling to floor, dozens of wicker cages filled with multicolored birds were piled one on top of the other. I sat down, the basket on the carpet beside me, watching them. Canaries, apricot-colored, pale blue and white, and solid

white, hopped their constricted dance. There were canaries in ordinary shades of yellow as well, and tiny
green parakeets. Looking closer, I saw some little birds
that resembled sparrows; also grey birds with dark grey
heads and red beaks, and a few larger dark grey birds
with red heads and throats. All the birds began to sing
or trill, and I felt as if I had entered a magic jungle.

"Wisner?" Elisa Lynch appeared at the door in a pale
yellow dress; brown silk boots glinted under the bottom
flounce as she walked. "Where did you come from?"

"The boat landed at Humaitá an hour ago." The man
on the divan talked nasally, with a heavy accent, keeping the handkerchief in place. Under his shaggy white
brows he watched me curiously.

"This is Mrs. Companion; I've mentioned her in letters. Molly, Wisner de Morgenstern, my dear old
Hungarian friend."

I smiled at him.

"Is something wrong with your nose?"

"It's melted, Elisa. I made the mistake of going into
the boiler room on board the steamer, and when I
looked in the glass later . . . " Slowly he removed the
handkerchief. His nose resembled a candle stub, with
pink teardrop globules along the sides. "It's wax, you
see," he said to me. "I have to be very careful about
heat or it loses shape."

"He was shot in the face many years ago," Elisa Lynch
added softly.

"In the Napoleonic wars, to be exact." He sighed.
"For years I lived only at night, avoiding my friends and
my family and especially my fiancée. I had rooms in
Venice. Then one day I saw an advertisement for glass
eyes and mammarical balm, cupping glasses, that sort of

thing. And wax noses! Since then I've lived in the light again, but, like Cinderella . . . " He shrugged. "I must avoid heat. I've got several extra noses with my luggage on the steamer. I didn't realize what had happened until I looked into your glass, Elisa. I'm glad the children aren't around." He put his handkerchief away. "Do you mind for the present? Am I too disgusting, Mrs. Companion?"

"Not at all. Why did you come to Paraguay? Why didn't you return to Hungary, then?"

"My little property in Hungary was confiscated. I no longer had an income. Then the revolutions of '48, you know. Europe seemed dead, decaying." He glanced over at Elisa Lynch, who was nervously picking up and replacing the figurines on a table, her head cocked at the increasingly loud noises from the soldiers outside. "What's wrong? What are they doing out there?"

"It's a circus." She looked at him hard.

"I see." He coughed. "Don't let it disturb you."

"How can I—!" she broke out violently, then clapped her hand over her mouth. "I'm so stupid; I'm so stupid." She paced around the room for a minute, then wheeled on me abruptly. "Do you know that once I was with a circus? If Francisco knew, he'd laugh so! I told him I was the wife of a surgeon in Algeria in those years. But I was married to a ringmaster. I used to eat spiders."

"Elisa, calm down." Wisner grabbed for her hand and covered it with his huge, vein-gnarled fingers. "He *won't* find out."

"Eugenie," she sobbed. For the first time I saw tears in her eyes. "Now Carlota . . . "

He shifted his stout body awkwardly and pulled her down beside him. I remained standing, biting my knuckles, embarrassed. "That's all past, those bad days," Wisner went on, then added in a low voice that he didn't intend me to overhear—but he was probably slightly deaf—"Someday they'll both tell catty stories about Empress Elisa . . . "

"I used to watch Eugenie go by in her gold carriage. I stood on the pavement, with a shawl over my head, that poster of me with spiders in my mouth smeared vulgarly on the very walls she passed."

"It's over, Elisa."

She jerked away from him. "I'm sorry. I shouldn't have got so upset. I've been having bad dreams lately." She shook herself, looking at me. "Please forgive me, Molly. I'm not usually so hysterical." Abruptly she began to rummage in a drawer of a Chinese cabinet. Her left hand drummed on the red-lacquered piano next to it which some soldiers had found one day in the woods, she had told me, abandoned by wealthy Argentine refugees in the early days of the war. "I want to show you these. What do you think?"

She had taken out a stack of sketches. The first sketch showed a woman in a white dress crossed with a sash from shoulder to waist. She was standing at attention, with a rifle in one hand. The dress was drawn in great detail, but the woman's head was only a scrawl of lines. The second sketch showed a woman kneeling in pantaloons, firing at some blurred figures in the distance. A baby in a basket hung from her back. The other sketches were of various details: a plumed helmet, a cartridge belt, embroidered capes, gloves, a flag with an intricate insignia resembling a spider. I looked up, puzzled. She was holding her face rigid, as if for a portrait, and I could see all the planes of muscle under her skin. "The Marshal has made me a lieutenant colonel. But it's not public yet."

I handed back the sketches, and she passed them to Wisner. "You're organizing a regiment?"

"The women want this—they've come to me. But the only weapons that can be spared now are lances." She leaned toward me, lowering her white lashes. "In Buenos Aires, they call me an Amazon, don't they?"

"Yes, I've heard that."

"There's a legend among the Guaraní—a woman who kills will turn into a lizard." She pulled out another sketch from the cabinet. It showed the same woman standing at attention with her rifle, only instead of the shapeless lines for a face, a lizard's head, hugely out of proportion, with sharp black scales and round, staring lidless eyes had been drawn on top of the body.

"These are interesting, Elisa. Yes, yes." Wisner had pulled out a small pair of silver-rimmed spectacles, which he held carefully in place over his nose as he looked at the sketches. "Did you know I'm writing a book, Elisa? Perhaps I may use these."

"What sort of book?"

"About earthworks. It's a new strategy, Elisa. I believe war may well be different in the future—wars of entrenchment, not pitched battles and sieges." He replaced the spectacles in his pocket. "It's because of breech-loading and couchant drill. You wouldn't find those old Romans on their stomachs, eh?" He rose ponderously to his feet, his round belly swaying like a pudding beneath his green-striped waistcoat. "I've got to get to my luggage, Elisa. General Diaz promised to show me the trenches, and I can't go like this." He pinched his soft nose and picked up a big-brimmed straw hat. "A pleasure, Mrs. Companion. Elisa, perhaps you'll give an old man some tea later on, eh?" He chuckled, putting his finger familiarly on her cheek. "Empress, empress," he whispered, glancing at the green parrot on his perch in the corner as he loped out of the room.

Elisa Lynch sat down across from me, brushing the fair hair back from her face. She seemed to have recovered herself completely, although she was pale and kept picking at a loose thread on her dress. "Wisner's been a good friend to me. I haven't had many friends here." She sighed. "When I first came to Paraguay, I was pregnant with my first child and very frightened."

"It's so far away."

She nodded. "Yes, and then there were the women in Asunción, waiting to make fun of me. They're so moral here, the rich ones. It's not like Paris. They're so stiff, so hypocritical. Just like in Ireland. I'd forgotten about that kind of people during my years in Paris, you see." She pressed her lips tightly together for a moment and her nostrils flared. "My aunt used to tell me about hell. According to her system, I'm there."

"That was in Ireland?"

"Yes, I used to dream of being eaten by harpies. They were scaly, but with feathers over their throats, and enormous beaks. She used to embroider them on aprons." She shuddered. "She had this book of hideous lithographs, a prayer book, written by some priest—oh, well, I'm boring you."

"What was it like to live in Ireland?"

She rolled her lower lip over her teeth. "I remember these dark cottages, all black inside from smoke, with rush lights burning while my mother—I think it was my mother; my memories are all muddled, because she died

so early—stitched until she had to put cold compresses
on her eyes." She sighed, opening her eyes wide so that
they appeared lidless because of her pale lashes. "I was
lucky. An old uncle took an interest in me, after my
mother died, and sent me to boarding school in Dublin.
They beat me, but I learned."

"When did you go to Paris?"

"When I was seventeen—I ran away. My old uncle
took more than just a fatherly interest in me, it turned
out." She laughed a little, shaking her head. "I woke up
one night and he was stroking my legs. He had a fetish
about my calves . . . if I showed him my legs, he'd give
me a coin; two if he could touch them. After I had
enough money, I took a boat to France. On the boat I
met M. Quatrefages, my husband."

"I didn't realize before today that you had been married," I said. "I thought 'Madame' was a courtesy."

She said shortly, "He left me." She looked at me.
"What about your husband?"

I hesitated. "He disappeared."

"Were you glad?"

"I think so." I added carefully, "I'm looking for him."

"I will look for Jacques Quatrefages in hell," she said
bitterly. "Because of him, I am a woman who may never
marry." Abruptly she added, "Why did you come to see
me, Molly? You seem nervous."

"It's about Pancha Garmendia."

"Oh, please!" She half rose, her hands spread before
her face, not touching it, but forming a web with her
fingers between me and her eyes. The veins along the
backs of her hands strained sharply. "Don't say any
more, please!" The rigidity suddenly left her fingers,
and she dropped her hands. Her eyes were again wet.

"Please don't speak of poor Pancha. It's dangerous, Molly." She flushed. "More so than you think. As a joke, Francisco called our firstborn 'Pancho.' He was baptized 'Francisco,' after his father, but as the priest poured the water, the Marshal said 'Little Pancho,' and he claims the baby's arm withered—right there before his eyes. A curse." She rubbed her forehead. "Yet my baby was born with a withered arm, Molly." She closed her eyes. "But he claims Pancha Garmendia put a curse on our child, which is why he keeps her chained like that—only of course that's not the real reason."

We were both silent awhile. The nervous birds chirped and trilled at intervals, and their gaudy plumage as they fretted back and forth in their cages made me a little dizzy. Finally I said, "There's another woman who tried to help her escape, named Rosalita."

Elisa Lynch sighed. "Frankly, Molly, I know all about this. General Diaz came to me this morning. I told him I'd try to help her." She spread her hands out, palms up. "*Try* is all I can do."

"I understand." I watched her averted face, the lashes spread like tiny fans against her cheekbones. She had powdered the area below her clear eyes heavily, for veins had surfaced and broken in a faint blue wash. I was considering what to do with the snake in the basket, which was partially hidden by the hem of my skirt, when we both turned at a stir in the hall. Lopez strode into the room. He was dressed for riding, in white trousers and a tight blue jacket. General Diaz followed, the side of his face swollen even more than yesterday. But he wore a clean uniform, and he grinned when he saw me, his one open eye luminous.

"Inocencia's driving me crazy." Lopez pulled out his

handkerchief, wiping the sweat off his steaming round face. His mustache glistened. "Here's another letter Wisner brought down."

Elisa Lynch took the crumpled lavender sheet from his fist and spread it over her knees. "What does she want now?"

"Read it. She wants five lengths of satin, five lengths of silk." There seemed to be a certain smug approval behind Lopez's irritation with his sister. "She's a fool."

"I thought she might want Calvin Ferris back in Asunción."

"She hints at that." Lopez ground his teeth. "She has no conception of war, of sacrifice. Jose? You know what Ferris wants?" Lopez gave a harsh laugh. "He wants my soldiers to save their piss in cans, so he can turn it into saltpetre. Now there's a wedding gift for Inocencia!" He glanced at me, flushing slightly. "For gunpowder."

Diaz laughed. "That's clever. He's a clever man."

I stood up, holding the basket with the snake gingerly away from me. If I was ever going to drop it in Lopez's office, this was my opportunity. I had to decide quickly. "Will you excuse me, your excellency?"

"Of course, Mrs. Companion." Lopez bowed elegantly over my hand, leaving a little round wet circle where his lips brushed across my skin. "What's that?"

I said numbly, "What?"

"What are you carrying?"

"A basket."

"A basket?" He turned to Diaz as if I had told a joke. "She says it's a basket, Jose."

Diaz laughed, but he must have sensed my distress, for after the laugh his face settled into severe lines. He shook his head slightly as if warning me.

"What's in the basket, Mrs. Companion?" Lopez put his hand on my arm.

"Bread."

"Bread?" Lopez pursed his lips. "Good. I'm hungry. Give me a piece of bread, Mrs. Companion."

My heart beat loudly in my breast like some strange wing. Finally I said, "It's not really bread, Marshal. I was lying. I'm sorry."

He looked at me sternly. "What is it?"

"A snake."

"A snake!" Lopez's teeth gleamed. He chuckled, patting my arm. "Oh, it's a snake now, is it? Let's see."

"It's a poisonous snake, Marshal. I don't dare open the basket."

Lopez grinned over his shoulder at Diaz, who stood unsmiling by the window, rubbing his hand along his thigh uneasily. "She says it's poisonous."

"Perhaps it is." Elisa Lynch spoke crisply. She moved over so that her green parrot fluttered from his perch to her shoulder. She folded her arms.

"Nonsense."

"Please, Marshal," I said, a catch in my voice. "It is poisonous."

"You think I'm afraid of a snake?" Lopez flushed, his voice rising. "Give me that basket. Is this some kind of joke to show me as a coward?"

"I found it in my hut, Marshal. I think it's a jararaca." I gave him the basket and stepped back. "I was going to drop it into the marsh."

"*You're* afraid of it." Lopez watched me step behind the divan. "That doesn't mean *I* am."

"Please, Marshal!"

"Francisco!" Elisa Lynch's voice quavered. "I think

you should believe her. I don't think this is a joke."

Lopez snorted, cutting the leather strips on the basket with a small knife he pulled from his pocket. He opened the basket and grabbed the long speckled brown snake by the neck, holding it up. The snake writhed through his hands, attacking his throat. It moved with a hiss, its long tongue flashing out momentarily as its fangs dug into Lopez's skin. Elisa Lynch screamed, and the parrot spun in dizzy loops up to the chandelier. Diaz leapt toward the snake with his sword out, but before he could hack it, the long brown body coiled up from Lopez's arm and bit him again on the cheek. Lopez fell back on the divan, whimpering, while Diaz chopped off the snake's head where it had fallen on the Oriental carpet; a colorless fluid seeped out of the snake.

Elisa Lynch patted the wound on Lopez's neck with her yellow skirt. I watched the two smaller red marks on his cheek spurt blood, waiting with horror for the pain.

In a few moments Lopez pushed Elisa Lynch away. "I'm all right."

"Jose, you'd better go for Doctor McPherson." She dropped her bloodied skirt. "Tell him to hurry."

"No, Elisa. I'll be all right." Lopez, his face smeared with blood, turned around to smile at me where I stood trembling in the corner. "See; it wasn't poisonous."

I said hoarsely, "It was."

"No." He bent over to observe the snake's body, then glanced at Diaz, who had turned pale and stared dumbly at the blade of his sword. "You were frightened, Jose?" Lopez toed the dead snake. "You thought you were saving my life? For that I thank you. And you, Mrs. Companion, for trying to protect me with your little lie."

Lopez sat back. "I feel weak. It was the shock. I didn't expect it to attack like that." He stood up, licking blood off his fingers. "I'm going to rest, Elisa."

"Let me call the doctor."

"It's Jose who looks pale, eh, Jose? Why don't you take Mrs. Companion fishing? You mentioned it to me."

Diaz said stiffly, "I told Wisner I'd show him the trenches."

"Send Urdapilleta. You wore yourself out yesterday. Besides, those trenches aren't a pretty sight. They're still bringing up the wounded."

Diaz nodded. "Mrs. Companion?"

Outside, the sun blinded us both, and we stopped for a moment to shade our eyes. Diaz pulled his sword out of the scabbard again, shaking his head over the traces of the snake's colorless fluid.

"Will Lopez be all right?"

"Molly, that was a jararaca, the most poisonous snake in South America. You were right."

I caught my breath. "Then he'll die!"

"But he didn't." Diaz replaced his sword, taking my arm. "He should have died instantly, but he didn't. He didn't die."

The river rolled swollen under the late afternoon sun. I sat quietly in the canoe with the bamboo pole between my knees, watching yellow ropes of muddy water twist and dissolve into the deep grey permanent water below the surface. Diaz watched me under his half-closed lids. Even when his pole bent and he brought up a flashing fish, momentarily upsetting the delicate balance in the canoe, or tilted his flask of rum to his lips, he was watching me. We kept near shore, weaving in and out among low-hanging trees, sometimes edging out toward the main current, sometimes cutting into little inlets where a profusion of butterflies, driven up by the increasing heat, would flutter around our heads, lighting on our hands and poles. Some butterflies had black wings inlaid with red centers or purple centers or yellow centers. Others had black and white wings, or red or blue speckles. One, landing on my finger, had mosaic wings of blue and grey; yet others glinted brown and pale pink, or dark blue, or brown and gold, or speckled dark blue edged with dark blue. Here was the enchanted forest. I forgot about fishing to watch them, and Diaz stopped his paddling, watching me. Several butterflies lighted on a half-eaten plum Diaz had tossed into the bottom of the canoe, and their wings pulsated slowly as they sucked it.

"They're waiting for you to die." Diaz laughed, pointing at two pale yellow butterflies, small as flower petals, pulsating in a pool of sweat at my wrist. "I've seen corpses covered with butterflies."

An orange butterfly as large as his hand lit on the edge of the canoe. I looked up to see a little green butterfly dance past, then realized I was actually seeing the jungle through its transparent wings, which were edged with gold and partitioned by delicate black lines. After a while the swirling colors made me dizzy, and I was glad when Diaz paddled out of the inlet again, under glossy trees weighted down with vines and mosses. We floated into other inlets, sometimes encountering butterflies again, other times only hot silence broken by the gunfire call of caracara birds, whose pink and blue beaks warned of our approach. Once in the distance I saw a small deer drinking, but with the next splash of Diaz's paddle it had blended subtly into the underbrush, and I was not sure. Perhaps it was an illusion. I glanced up at the palm leaves overhead, chewed to tatters by voracious insects.

"You're dreaming, Mrs. Molly Companion," Diaz said suddenly. "Your worm's been eaten off long ago."

"I don't care. Let's move into the sun again. I don't like these dark places."

After a few strokes the sun was steaming over my face again. Sweat trickled along my neck.

"Do you think it was a miracle?"

"Lopez?" I watched his face. "I don't know." He frowned. I saw nothing in his face but genuine puzzlement. Idly he scratched his belly. "It's hard to say. I know *you* don't believe in such things, but . . . no, it's not likely. But that snake was poisonous, Molly. And Lopez lived."

"Strange," I said.

"You're strange," Diaz added abruptly, then flushed. "I mean, I don't understand." He swallowed hard, looking at the paddle he held in midair. "I'm sorry."

"How am I strange?"

He looked at me eagerly. "You're not strange. But I can't talk with you very well."

"Yes, you can."

His mouth opened, but he only wet his lips, then sighed. "Oh, no. I know about Yankee women."

"What do you know?"

"What there is to know. How they are." He groaned mockingly. "What you can't do with them. Even married ones with no husband."

I thought of Calvin, of the way his scalp was surfacing under his thin, oiled hair. I had trouble breathing. "It's not that," I said slowly. "I have a rash, you see."

He looked at me stupidly. "A rash?"

"You wouldn't want me." I looked at the water, frowning at a bit of weed floating past.

"Let me understand." He cleared his throat. "You have no Yankee morals about being with me. It's merely your rash?"

"Yes."

At first he giggled; then he began to laugh, slapping his leg until the canoe shivered ominously. Nevertheless he leaned toward me, cupping my face, nuzzling his hot, sour mouth all over my stiff lips. Then he looked at me, still laughing.

# Six

Across a wide grassy space stood the tree where Pancha Garmendia was again chained. The undersides of the leaves turned up silver in the stiff wind. From this distance she was only a shadow, but I could imagine her peaked white face with great vividness. I didn't know how to help her. The Argentine girl, Rosalita, had not been executed; but she had been beaten, Diaz told me, and would stay indefinitely in the prison camp, where she might eventually die of neglect or starvation. I forced myself to look away. There was nothing I could do now. Diaz had shaken me by the shoulders to emphasize that fact, telling me how much Lopez distrusted me. Although I was yet in no immediate danger, I made Lopez nervous, and he would prefer me dead. I must be very careful not to give him any pretext. I sighed, entering the purple swamp where a little parakeet called a Penelope bird darted from a bush, flapping his wings helplessly against the invisible air, which brightened as if shot full of silver wires. The long grass along the path where I walked bent flat. The coquito palms thrashed over my head, fronds spinning off like scarves. Wind in the sunlight always made me nervous. If accompanied by clouds and rain, it seemed natural, as if caused by the clouds, but wind through clear air was inexplicable to me. As God punished the earth by flood, my father had told me, so he punished the planet Saturn by wind. Those colored rings were successive populations blown off the surface, condemned to circle forever in a whirl-wind. As a child, I had imagined children, dogs, porches, rocking chairs, pickles, coins, church steeples, and cows spinning wildly about; the children were crying, trying to touch the fingers of their mothers, who were con-stantly blowing past them, skirts ballooning like clothes on a line. I used to take no comfort in rainbows, for al-though they promised an end to floods, I felt they hinted at Saturn's fate. I stayed on the path a long time, until it suddenly petered out in the orange grove behind the abandoned capilla. Here I could hear the Brazilian guns, for the trench at Curuzu, right below the fortifications of Curupayty, had been under heavy bombardment for a week. I splashed some greenish water on my face from an old well. A ragged cat with rust-colored fur and white paws darted, mewing, from under a board. Then I circled slowly through the orchard around to the front of the church. Calvin sat on the steps, peeling a potato. He frowned at seeing me, wiping the snot from under his nose with his sleeve.

"You're late." He bit the raw potato with a crunch, chewing while he spoke. "Why didn't you get here sooner?"

"It's hard to get away unseen." I sat down on a lower

step. He had been drinking heavily. Even this far away, his breath smelled sour; an empty bottle rolled gently back and forth on its side as the wind touched it. "You make a pretty bridegroom."

He reached for the bottle, saw it was empty, and flung it down the hill into some weeds. "What went wrong, Molly?"

"The snake bit him. He got a stomachache."

"Mithridates!" He jammed the potato violently into his palm. "It should have been so simple."

"He's having the snake gilded and put in a reliquary, now that he's confirmed that it *was* poisonous."

"Christ!" He flicked a piece of corn from between two teeth with his fingernail. "Now we've got to start all over."

"Just shoot him," I said bitterly. "That's what they did to Lincoln."

"That's suicide. Why get yourself hacked to pieces?" He glanced at me. "Unless you're feeling noble, Molly. I'll get you a pistol."

"Thanks, no."

"Then I'll get General Caxias to do it for me."

"The Brazilians? How?"

He stroked his chin. "I was in Asunción two days ago, to see sweet Inocencia." He smirked at me. "Washburn's back at the Consulate. He says the Emperor of Brazil purchased some new long-range artillery from the United States, and they'll bring it into play on Lopez the next chance they get. Naturally, he's not informing Lopez."

"Washburn's in on this, too?"

Calvin nodded uneasily. "He's on the side of civilization."

"He's the United States Consul. He's supposed to be neutral."

"Don't be naive."

I stood up. "If you have his help, you don't need mine. I don't like this, Calvin. Let's concentrate on getting out of here. Yes, Lopez is a tyrant, but—"

"But why don't we hold an election?" He sucked at the potato. "You think your friendship with Madame Lynch will save you for long? I wouldn't trust her. She's got her own skin to look after, and her bastards'." He looked at me closely. "You've spent a lot of time with General Diaz lately, too. Just remember, Lopez has executed three generals in this war already. Did you know that?" He added coldly, "I'm still your husband, Molly, no matter how often you get Jose Diaz to kiss your ugly skin."

I picked a petal from a ragged sunflower, biting my lip. A week ago in Diaz's bed I had whispered to the blue-jawed image of Calvin that rose in my mind, "I divorce you, I divorce you, I divorce you!" That was the way Moslem men got rid of their wives, Richard Burton had written. But now Calvin had reached out to claim me again. "Your husband," he had said, and in his yellowish eyes I saw the belief that this was an ultimately compelling command. Calvin had often used that other command: "Your father." Under my sleeves I felt my skin prickling; the rash Diaz thought barely noticeable was rising again, rooting up from somewhere deep inside me to bloom across my breasts and down my legs. The tie I had thought severed forever by the act of making love to another man had been reasserted. It was the same tie that had dragged me crazily to Paraguay.

"What am I supposed to do this time?"

"Keep me informed for the present. I want to know if Lopez plans any kind of attack. He usually puts up a tent on the field, out of range of the guns." Calvin laughed. "This time he won't be out of range."

"How will they locate the tent? It's usually under a tree, camouflaged." I shook my head. "If Brazilian balls start exploding in Lopez's vicinity, how long do you think he'll stay put?"

Calvin chewed his lip. "I've got to think about this. They'd have to hit him the first time, or he'd be back in Paso Pucu before you could wink." He sighed. "Too bad he's so cautious. Caxias himself has an orange tent you can see for miles." He grabbed at a spider that had swung by on an invisible piece of web. "You might as well go back. You'll hear from me, Molly."

As I reached the edge of the swamp, I heard singing. An old woman was pulling white flowers off a small gnarled tree that resembled dogwood. She stuffed them into her apron, singing "bim, bim, bim," and when she turned, startled, to see me on the path beside her, I recognized Pancha Garmendia's old duenna. The soldiers had released her from the prison camp at the same time Pancha had been chained back to the tree. Her job was to feed Pancha, who was only allowed to eat what the old woman herself cooked and brought; the old woman, however, remembered Pancha only fitfully, and the other women had to trick her into taking stew to the girl, who otherwise would have starved.

Abruptly upon seeing me she let the flowers scatter into the mud. "Here's Mariscal Lopez, Señorita." She giggled, clutching at her black skirt. She pulled a gilt picture frame of some sort out of a big pocket and held

it out to me. It was not a painting but a mirror. Most of
the silver had worn off the back, and my face threw an
indistinct shadow on the glass, except for the reflected
corner of my lip. "Once I saw his face here," she added
sadly. "Now he's gone." She took back the mirror and
held it up, squinting. "But I can see his eye. He
drowned."

"Have you taken Pancha her dinner today?"

A gleam of interest crossed her clay-colored face. She
bent over, grabbing up the flowers she had let drop. "I
was going to make her a soup of flowers, Señorita, to
make her beautiful again. She dances too much." She
put a flower to her nose, sniffing. "Don't you think she
dances too much, Señorita?"

"Yes."

"Silly girl." The old woman let the flowers fall again.
"The young men will think you're a flirt, Pancha! That's
what I told her. But she won't listen." She turned her
back, reaching up for a high blossom.

I grabbed her by shoulder blades so sharp and bony
that I imagined a pair of wings had been broken off her
once. "Señora, let's go get Pancha some stew. Come
with me."

She insisted on putting more flowers into her pocket,
along with the mirror. Then she followed me like a blind
woman out of the swamp, her shawl completely over
her face. We passed the field where young girls practiced throwing spears. Straw had been stuffed into
crude bundles resembling soldiers so they could knock
off worn Brazilian caps or pierce the paper hearts
pinned to the dummies' chests. The old woman, hearing
their voices, pulled off her shawl; catching sight of one
of the dummies, she shrieked "Pancha! Pancha!" and

ran fiercely toward a tall girl who had just thrown her spear, beating at her face with gnarled fists. The girl shoved the old woman to the ground. Another girl with three fat braids down her back pulled the old woman to her feet, shaking her. "Pancha's hungry, you old bitch! I'm going to make you feed her." She dragged the old woman in the direction of the kitchens, where the kettles boiled night and day. I hurried on to Paso Pucu, surprised to see a huge crowd of soldiers outside the stockade. They made way for me quickly, averting their eyes. In the front of the crowd, a few women crouched with their skirts over their faces, rocking back and forth on the balls of their feet.

A shot startled me. A soldier standing stiffly by himself against the stockade wall fell in a heap. The scene, which had been a confused mixture of faces and uniforms, suddenly focused. Two soldiers dragged the dead man away to a heap of naked bodies where they stripped his uniform off and threw him into a fire. The straw brought a touch of greasy smoke across my face. One of the women in front of me, with a wild wail, threw herself in the dust. Another soldier, flung against the stockade wall, straightened, saluted, then fell like a corn-husk doll. The woman on the ground twitched as if she too had been riddled with bullets. The soldiers standing around me had tight, shut faces and looked at the sky or at their hands each time the shots rang out from the firing squad. Two of them lifted the weeping woman, making a basket with their hands, and carefully carried her to the back of the crowd, while others tossed gifts into her lap—bits of tobacco, chipa, oranges—anything they happened to have in their pockets as she passed.

I tried to turn away, but the crowd was wedged too deeply around me; one cavalryman absentmindedly stroked his horse's flanks, while a boy beside him had his head down, delicately braiding the tail. Up in the tall mangrullo at the corner of the stockade I thought I glimpsed the sparkle of Lopez's uniform.

"Fire!" General Diaz screamed, his voice breaking. I had not seen him until that moment. He stood behind the firing squad in full-dress uniform. I closed my eyes, but his image was imprinted on my lids. More shots followed. When I looked, another dead body was being dragged to the heap beside the fire, where arms and legs, smeared with blood, stuck out at odd angles. Two priests, one swinging a censer from which oily smoke ascended and the other sprinkling holy water from a gold orb, chanted Latin in high falsetto voices. "Fire!" Diaz screamed again, and I pressed my hands against my ears. I had been naive never to imagine him in such a situation. I could almost hear Calvin laughing. Another dead soldier was stripped, and then it was over. Like a fist opening, the crowd dispersed. I ran from the stockade, trying to escape the smoke, which settled thickly into my lungs and throat as if the souls of the burning soldiers clutched at my breath.

I imagined the cool dimness of a room where white stucco walls sweated humidly, and I hurried across the camp to the new church, where the whitewash still had a sharp, clean smell. Here the Bishop preached his garrulous sermons to the officers on Sundays, and Lopez told dirty jokes to the common soldiers from the steps afterwards. The high windows were set with clear glass, so the sun fell in white strips over the carved kneelers brought down from some older colonial church in Asunción. At first I thought I was alone, but a head popped up from behind the massive altar with its candelabra and canopy of misshapen angels. I recognized Bishop Palacious. He beckoned me as I stood hesitating at the door.

"You startled me. I thought . . . is it over?"

"Yes." I walked slowly down the aisle, wishing I were alone. "What happened?"

"Lopez decimated the 10th Battalion." The Bishop had a huge gold monstrance in his hands that he banged down on the altar. It was shaped like a star, with a small hinged door in the center for the host. "There was a skirmish this morning and they ran."

I sat down on the altar steps. "The 10th Battalion had never been in battle before."

"But they ran. Every tenth man was shot. The officers drew pieces of grass to see who would die." The Bishop, with a soft rag, polished a chalice. "I'm going to offer a mass for their poor souls."

I stood up, looking at the altar top more carefully. The white lace cloth bristled with chalices, some plain gold and some jeweled. There were salvers, silver reliquaries, censers with long brass chains, crucifixes with grotesque ivory Christs pinned to the smooth metal, rosaries of pearl, ivory, lapis, emerald, and crystal; spread out next to the tabernacle were big rings with ruby crosses, small carved boxes, tiny statues of the Virgin with turquoise eyes, and anonymous saints wrapped in satin cloth seeded with pearls. Three crates on the red carpet before the altar seemed to contain similar articles, for a plaster head of Christ peered at me with an onyx eye.

"What is all this?"

"The treasure of San Lorenzo. I ordered the monks to send it here for safekeeping."

"Isn't San Lorenzo in the north, though, away from the front?"

The Bishop winked. "Looters."

"Looters?"

"Actually . . . " The Bishop held the chalice up to his face, grinning at his distorted reflection; his mouth stretched and pulsated like a long worm as he gummed his lips, and his nose flattened enormously. "I don't trust the monks of San Lorenzo. They have a reputation for preferring the temporal to the spiritual."

I brushed away a fly that was attracted to the sticky sweat on my face. "Did the Allies take Curupayty?"

"Pôrto Alegre—a pig, but a brave pig, they say— marched through enfilade fire from the trench at Curuzu this morning, taking it by surprise, and got around its left flank through the lake." The Bishop held the chalice under his chin for a different perspective and stuck out his tongue. "That's when the 10th Battalion retreated, leaving the artillery. They say two soldiers rushed each other so fiercely they were each stabbed by the other's bayonet." The Bishop set the chalice back on the altar, patting his heart. "Pôrto Alegre *could* have taken Curupayty then, but you know these pigs; they're lazy; they like to wallow in certain glory." He shrugged. "Are you afraid of frogs, Mrs. Companion?"

"Frogs? You mean ordinary frogs?"

He nodded. "I need someone to help me get those frogs out of the baptismal font."

"What are frogs doing in the baptismal font?"

"Stupid children! They should all be in the trenches."
He stepped behind the altar and came back with a
bucket and a big long-handled net. "Some tale about an
enchantment. They thought holy water would break the
spell."

We walked toward the back of the church. The baptismal font was a large cistern with two stone cherubs
crouched on the sides. Their wings peaked over their
heads, and their faces resembled dogs' snouts. I remembered an old fairy tale. "Do frogs turn into princes here,
too?"

The Bishop, with a deep groan, lifted the heavy lid.
"Into crocodiles, more likely." He banged the lid down
on the tile floor with a sharp crack. "Do you see them? I
have to perform a baptism this afternoon."

A bubble appeared and a frog surfaced. The Bishop
twirled the net nervously in his fingers, looking at me.

"Do you want me to do it?" I took the net. He immediately stepped back, his hands clasped behind him. I
dipped out the frog, which thrashed wildly, its legs
caught in the woven string. "Put him in the bucket."

The Bishop stepped further back, shaking his head. I
untangled the cold blue frog and threw him into the
bucket. Swishing the net back and forth in the water, I
tried to locate another, but only water and weeds
trickled through. The Bishop came closer and peered in.
"That bubble?"

"Nothing. The others might be dead. The net's not
long enough for me to touch the bottom. . . . This is a
strange font."

"It's a well. We blessed it and built the church around
it."

I kicked the bucket. The frog leapt halfway up the side; the Bishop, with a tight squeak, scurried away. "Get rid of it!" He crossed himself. "Wait—!"

"I'll toss it into the marsh."

"No, you can't just . . . it's Christian now."

The frog stretched its long body, preparing to leap. I put my scarf over the top of the bucket. "What, then?"

He teetered from foot to foot, clawing at his cassock. "I don't know. But you can't just . . . I don't know."

"Do you want to keep it?"

"No! Find someone who wants it. Find it a home." He reached into his pocket for a gold coin, looked at it, hesitated, then reluctantly held it out. "Here. Give them this."

I waved the coin away, intending to drop the frog into the marsh anyway. "Surely they'll do it out of Christian charity."

He screwed up his lips, but nodded. "And tell them to name it." He danced a few anxious little steps, glancing back at the altar. "Hurry."

I went out into the steaming sun with the frog, who shifted this way and that in the bucket, tilting it against my skirt. Somewhere a lone harpist played, the notes floating almost tangibly through the thick air. I imagined each note turning into a dying bee, spiraling lower and lower through the grove of trees where I paused. It was September. Each day turned a little warmer. Far in the distance, like summer thunder, the guns of the fleet boomed. I thought of General Diaz, remembering, in an odd, visionary way, the time I had peered through a rip in a tent at two boxers in Boston edging around each other in a delicate, expert dance. Although their taut, misshapen faces terrified me, I admired the gracefulness of the preliminary movements. At that moment some ladies in pink dresses came along and I turned my back on the rip; but the dull, sucking blows, then later the whistling cheers and catcalls of the gentlemen spectators, rang in my head for weeks, making me ill. Yet this was far more real. I winced as the image of General Diaz behind the firing squad rose again in my mind. The frog thumped hard in the pail. I shook myself and was about to dump him out when I felt a light touch. Monkey-Snout stood behind me, his papery face wrinkled in a smile.

"That frog is for General Diaz."

"Diaz?"

He flicked off the scarf, grabbed the frog tightly in his good hand, then buttoned it into one of his many pockets. "A frog placed in holy water overnight by a child will tell the future. This frog is for General Diaz." He beckoned me, his ragged sleeve fluttering. "Come."

The air inside his hut, four poles covered with reeds and a corrugated tin roof, was the consistency of mustard because of the heat and the way the sun fell through the reeds in yellow stripes and speckles. Also, some sweetly nauseous weed burned in a clay dish. Diaz sat on the floor, his arms folded, his eyes closed. Thick beads of sweat, appearing in the strange light like globs of wax melting off his sunken face, dripped down his nose and forehead. He lifted his heavy wrinkled lids as we entered. I felt myself flushing.

"Look." Monkey-Snout pulled the frog roughly from his pocket, dangling it by one leg. "And the third person for the circle, a female, for good luck."

I sat on the ground next to Diaz, who glanced at me mournfully but said nothing. I pressed my hands to my

115

ears, for I kept hearing him scream "Fire!" I could not associate the violent military figure that rose in my mind with the man who had slept with his face against my shoulder.

Diaz squeezed the moisture out of each side of his mustache and ran his fingers around the collar of his uniform. Monkey-Snout pulled out a tiny knife—or perhaps it was only a sharp stone, for his quickness made it difficult to tell—and slit the frog's belly. He put the frog on its back in the burning dish of weeds, where its legs twitched spasmodically for a while, and sponged up the blood and mucus with a rag. He lit a match, placing it upright in the frog's belly like a candle, where it quickly guttered out. Then he dug his fist into the frog, tearing out some of the organs, which he gave to Diaz, who must have been instructed in the ritual: he immediately flung them onto a large palm leaf in front of him, wiping his hands on his trousers. For a long time Monkey-Snout peered at the pattern of organs on the leaf.

"Touch something." Monkey-Snout looked at me.

"What?"

"Anything. Put your finger somewhere on the frog." I could not make any sense of the blob of shapes and mucus before me. I touched a little knot which might have been the heart.

"Now, General, turn around."

Diaz turned his back to the palm leaf.

"What do you see?" Monkey-Snout shook his hands in the air.

"Nothing. The wall."

"Close your eyes. Now what?"

"Some dark shapes and lines."

"See!"

"Some men, falling. No, just some shapes. Maybe guns." His voice broke. "I keep thinking about . . . "

"What?"

"The executions. Lopez ordered them; I didn't—"

"Tell us about it."

"This boy was eating an orange, right before. I could hear him sucking it. Then he was called. He threw the peel on the ground, stepped on it . . . . I saw him spit out a pip just as I yelled 'Fire!' I don't know, I . . . "

"Now. Reach behind you and touch."

Diaz awkwardly jerked out his arm, crabbed his fingers over the floor until he found the palm leaf, and touched part of the frog. Then he turned around. For several minutes Monkey-Snout frowned over the pulpy mess, which was beginning to attract tiny bugs that traveled together like a web.

Monkey-Snout looked up after a while and asked softly, "What do you wish to know?"

Diaz swallowed hard. He swatted at a drop of sweat on his cheek as if it were a mosquito. "About my death."

"If you know that"—Monkey-Snout looked at him— "it won't make any difference. No bargains."

"I just want to know, to prepare myself. If I'm going to die of torture, disgraced—"

"You'll die of battle wounds."

Diaz sighed. He put his head in his hands. "Thank God." After a minute he looked up. "You're not lying?"

Monkey-Snout shook his head. "Any more questions?"

"Nothing." Diaz laughed. "In battle? Ha!"

Monkey-Snout flung the rest of the frog onto the palm leaf and rolled it up carelessly. "You didn't ask when."

"God, no!" Diaz stood up, stooping because of the

hut's low roof. "I always thought I'd die in battle, honorably." He slapped Monkey-Snout on the shoulder, glancing at me. "Lopez was looking for you earlier, Molly. Better walk with me over to headquarters."

Although the sun was still harsh, it felt cooler outside after the stifling closeness of Monkey-Snout's hut. Diaz took deep breaths and kept shaking out his long limbs like a swimmer emerging from the water as we crossed the camp. Once he squeezed my shoulder, but he seemed too tired to speak. I stole glances at him. In the bright light I saw the weariness in his face, and something else—a hardness I had not noticed before.

Dozens of men worked in Lopez's compound on a heavy scaffolding erected high over one side of the villa. Some men, bare-chested, were sealing the beams with pitch from several cauldrons that bubbled at the side, and others brought in carts and wheelbarrows of dirt. Seeing my puzzled look, Diaz said, "Another earthwork. A badly fired shot from the fleet fell in here last night— a freak shot, really, but Francisco's going to make the place really secure. It'll be thirty-six feet thick at the base."

An ugly voice screamed, "All right, move, move, you bastards!"

I turned. General Bruguez and several soldiers carrying rifles came through the gate of the compound behind us. Before them, they drove three emaciated men whose bare arms and legs oozed with sores. Their shaggy hair and black stubble beards had erased all their features except for pairs of wild eyes. The shortest of the three had a little bundle clutched to his chest. Another, who limped, had a band of iron around his right leg.

"They've escaped, they claim," Bruguez shouted at us. "They were captured by the Allies at Uruguayana, they say, and it took them this long to escape. Cowards!"

Diaz shrugged. "Well, they made it back. Give them some meat."

Bruguez, his thick chin shaking like chicken fat, laughed. "These traitors, cowards? They'll be flogged to death. Lopez's orders."

"What orders?" I asked.

"They should have escaped before, if they were patriots. Gobbling Allied food, Brazilian pig meat." Bruguez prodded one of the men with his sword hilt. The man flinched, gurgling inarticulately in his throat. "Look at them!"

"They were prisoners," I said. "They escaped when they could."

Bruguez spat in the face of the man with the leg iron. The man kept his head down for a moment, then suddenly exploded at Bruguez, his hands curved into claws so tight the veins stood out like ropes. "Mother kiss your ass!" he screamed. "Traitor, grafter—!"

Two soldiers butted their rifles into his belly. Bruguez, sweating heavily, wiped his brow with a yellow silk handkerchief. "See! See what they are, Diaz!" He glanced to the left at a boiling cauldron of pitch. "Toss him in!"

One soldier threw down his rifle and grabbed the man by the arms, pinioning them. Another picked up his feet.

"For God's sake!" Diaz screamed. "Stop!"

The two soldiers, holding the man like a hammock between them at the edge of the cauldron, paused nervously, glancing between the two generals. A breeze brought the smell of pitch sharply to my nose. Up on the scaffolding the workers were frozen, watching.

"Put him down!" Diaz pulled out his sword. "Put him down or I'll run you both through."

"Dip his ass!" Bruguez pulled out his own sword. "Dip his ass or *I'll* run you through!"

The man with the leg iron squirmed in a last attempt to escape. The soldiers had difficulty holding him. The old man who had been about to stir the pitch with a sticky black paddle dropped it and backed off, knocking over a can of nails that clanked and rang as they spilled out against one another. The soldiers swung the man with the leg iron back and forth between them, faster and faster, like a twist of rope. "Eeeh! Eeeh! Eeeh!" the man screamed in spurts. At the top of the arc they let him go. The momentum was too great, however, and he flew entirely over the cauldron, tumbling in a heap on the other side. Diaz ran over. The man's head was twisted back. I could see the blood frothed on his lips.

"You've broken his neck." Diaz stood up and walked past Bruguez, replacing his sword. "Bury him, you pig sucker."

"He's too lucky." Bruguez spat in the direction of the other two prisoners, who cowered together against the stockade wall. "What have you got there, hey?" Bruguez pulled the little bundle out of the short prisoner's arms, tossing it on the ground. He kicked it open with his boot. Inside shone a harmonica. "Play it! Go on, you bastard." Bruguez spat at the harmonica. "Let's hear how you traitors play, eh?"

Trembling, the man stooped down for it, wiping it off on the side of his trousers. Bruguez elbowed him in the ribs. "Hurry up!" The man stumbled, holding his side.

He blew into the harmonica, making harsh, shrill sounds at first; gradually he got control of himself. I recognized the tune about the monkey and the silver comb. The music floated eerily on the still air. Very gently, the old man who stirred the pitch placed his hat over the dead man's face.

"Let's go." Diaz took my arm, whispering. "As long as we're here he'll keep it up."

We went into the antechamber of Lopez's villa. Two soldiers on guard in the dim, uncarpeted room clicked to attention. "Is he back?" Diaz asked. The soldiers nodded. One rapped on the door. It was opened by a brown-skinned young officer with a forelock ruffled high like the plume of a bird. He kept rubbing his hands through his hair. "Announce us, Saguier."

Saguier closed the door. "It didn't go well."

"Should we come back?"

"No, he wants to see you. Señora Companion, too."

"What didn't go well?" I asked.

"Lopez had a personal interview with Mitre this afternoon. It was kept secret." Diaz added softly to Saguier, "Their terms were unchanged, then?"

"Absolutely, sir. Lopez must leave the country before any peace talks." Saguier sighed. "He's furious. Be careful, sir." He disappeared behind the door for a few minutes, then opened it a crack, beckoning us. We went inside. Lopez sat at his desk, his boots propped up on the edge, sucking on the corner of a book out of which he had ripped most of the pages, which were crumpled into balls around the room. Elisa Lynch, dressed in black silk, sat stiffly on a chair by a bookcase, her hands on the shoulders of her oldest son, Pancho, as if to restrain him. Pancho, dressed in a miniature uniform, kept clenching the fist of his good arm, muttering "Papa! Papa!" to himself, or else "Those pigs, pigs!" I couldn't tell which. On a divan across the room, their backs to the curtained window from which I could still faintly hear the harmonica, Lopez's two brothers, Benancio and Benigno, sat in civilian clothes, one in a lilac frock coat, the other in a red tunic. Lopez himself wore a uniform frock coat, without epaulettes, but with a row of medals pinned across his chest. His scarlet poncho was tossed over the back of his chair.

"The toad! The old toad!" Lopez shouted at Diaz, flinging the book behind him. It crashed into a portrait of Napoleon in an ornate gold frame, rocking it crooked on the wall. "Those long white hands of his! I'd like to break his knuckles." Lopez drew a circle in the air above his head. "He wears an old black hat with a big brim. The President of Argentina! Ha! Thinks he's Don Quixote, does he?" Lopez kicked a porcelain shepherdess off his desk. The head, breaking off soundlessly as it hit the carpet, rolled against Pancho's boot. Pancho stepped on it, grinding the glass to pieces into the carpet. Elisa Lynch pushed him away from her and drew in her skirt. "Then Flores came, that bandit." Lopez growled. "I told him the war was all his fault."

"What about the Brazilians, Caxias and Polydoro and Pôrto Alegre?" Diaz broke in calmly.

"Caxias wouldn't come, the wretch." Lopez poured some brandy into a glass of water before him on the desk. "We exchanged riding whips; that's all it amounted to. Hey, Benigno!" Benigno, who had the riding whip across his knees, rose and gave it to his brother. The two resembled each other closely, except that Benigno was taller and had waxed his more fashionable mustaches to thin points. I sat down in the nearest chair. Diaz remained standing, his arms folded across his chest. "Look at this!" Lopez cracked the whip across his desk. Everyone in the room, including Elisa Lynch and her son, winced. "Mine had a gold hilt. This is a common cavalry whip. Those Argentines are misers, Diaz."

"And the Brazilians smell," Benancio said timidly. It was odd to hear such a small voice coming from such a fat man. Benancio was a balloon image of his brothers, all their features distorted and smeared over his aspic-colored skin.

"Shut up, Benancio. You don't know what you're talking about." Lopez turned his twitching face toward his brother. "They say you take five baths a day, you big blubber!"

Benancio's round eyes winked. Without moving, he seemed to collapse inside himself, like a snail. "They're going to give me the *coup de grâce*, Diaz. Bah! Mitre!" Lopez turned to Elisa Lynch. "*Quoi qu'il soit intelligent, il ne sait rien.*"

She nodded, smoothing a fold of her dress. "Attack."

"What about that other trench along the bank at Curupayty?" Lopez jumped up abruptly, twisting the riding whip in his fingers. Everyone stood up also, according to the new custom. "Is it done?"

"Almost, your excellency. It's nearly two thousand yards long now, and the new platforms for the guns are finished." Diaz coughed. "This ploy of yours—to talk to Mitre—will give us the time we need. Pôrto Alegre won't take us by surprise again."

"How many guns?"

"Forty-nine, and two rocket stands—thirteen of the guns for the river-battery, the rest for the trench."

"Who commands the river-battery?"

"Captain Ortiz."

"Put that coward from the 10th Battalion, Major Sayas, in the river-battery. He may as well die usefully." Lopez paced around the desk. "What about the remainder of the 10th Battalion?"

"Drafted into other corps."

"Good. And the abatis?"

"Thin, but finished. There isn't time to sharpen the branches. We've just felled the trees."

"So it's a strong position, then. The trench will run all the way from the river to Laguna Lopez?"

Diaz went over to the huge wall map and traced the line of the trench with his finger. "When it's done, all the way. After that, to attack us will be suicidal."

"Fools." Lopez flung away the riding whip and rubbed his hands slowly together as if he were working in a lotion. He looked around the room. "Get us some wine, Benancio. Why are you all standing there with such sullen faces?" He frowned. "You think we'll *lose?*"

"Impossible!" Benigno cried aloud, pulling out his watch. "If you'll excuse me, your excellency, the boat for Asunción? The wedding gifts you asked me to take to Inocencia?"

Lopez shrugged. "Get out."

The two brothers hurried away together. They seemed to be holding their breath. Lopez turned to me. "Well, you weren't here when I needed you."

"I'm sorry; I didn't know."

"I wanted you to transcribe the meeting in English. I wanted the United States—and Queen Victoria, the whore—to know what scurvy wretches these Allies are, about their plotting. Well," he added, scowling at me, "you'll see what cowards they are, then. You're going to be out on the field, Mrs. Companion, in the thick of the battle." His lip twitched sarcastically, and I thought of the blank scrap of paper that had almost got me killed before. "You're my war correspondent, remember?" He touched my cheek. "Have you ever met Mitre?"

I shook my head.

"He has lice in his beard!" Lopez laughed heartily at his joke. The colored ribbons on his chest fluttered. Diaz laughed, too, louder even than Lopez, but his eyes bored dark and steady when I glanced at him. Lopez went over and kissed Elisa Lynch on the head. " 'Attack,' she said. Did you hear her, Jose? 'Attack' in that sweet, low voice. Madame," he said, taking her hand, "if you weren't already my mistress and the mother of my four children, I'd . . . " He pulled her into his arms, hugging her tightly. She was a head taller than he and had to stoop a little—I imagined the cramp in her knees under her black silk—to put her head on his shoulder. He caressed her back, his fingers twitching up and down. Pancho turned away. Lopez was whispering into Elisa Lynch's ear. I looked at Diaz. He nodded, and we both quietly left the room, followed by Saguier, who closed the door behind him. Benancio was in the antechamber with two bottles of wine.

"Better not." Saguier put his finger to his lips. Benancio, sighing, folded up on a bench, popping the cork from one of the bottles. He tilted it down his throat.

Diaz and I went out into the sunlight. "I've got a lot to do," he muttered, not looking at me but quickly moving off, as if something he didn't want to see might be reflected in my eyes. I watched him cross the compound. He had a swaying gait, his legs bowed from riding horses. I followed him at a distance, noticing that the dead prisoner had been carted away but that the harmonica, smashed almost flat, gleamed in the dust.

# Seven

In the twilight the trees across the plain formed several huge masses, tinged blue near the top where they blurred into the darkening sky. When I glanced over my shoulder, the lights of Paso Pucu twinkled as if it were a real town of neat streets and hedges, not a squalid camp where soldiers turned restlessly in their hammocks, dreaming of tomorrow's battle. Doctor McPherson kept his big, rather flabby hand on my arm so that I wouldn't trip. Bliss strode ahead, every now and then pulling out the handkerchief he kept stuffed between two buttons of his brown frock coat, to blow his nose. They had come for me on Calvin's orders. Tomorrow Lopez planned a surprise maneuver to force the Allies into a suicidal attack. He had erected a small tent under a tall Guasü tree on the plain where he would have the illusion of participating in the battle and at the same time be well away from the Brazilian artillery. It was our job,

Bliss said, to make sure that the new long-range artillery guns had a clear target.

Calvin was waiting at the tent, which was covered with leaves and moss, holding a lantern that gave off a milky light. He wore a putty-colored frock coat too short in the sleeves; he swung the lantern up high, so that moths fluttered about his exposed wrists, as he said bitterly, "You were supposed to keep me informed, Molly."

"How could I? Lopez doesn't tell me anything."

"There's General Diaz—if it weren't for Bliss, I might have missed this particular chance."

"I haven't seen General Diaz for days." I sat down in the long grass beside some tin cans that glistened as if they contained liquid. "What are these?"

"Paint."

Bliss straightened the gilt tie pin that pierced his stained cravat. "You're going to paint the tent?"

"Of course not. Do you think I'm a fool?" Calvin spat close to my hand. "I'm going to paint the tree red."

"The tree?" McPherson craned his neck and stepped back, almost losing his balance. "How can you paint a tree?"

"Just the top leaves, so it won't be noticeable to Lopez—but the Brazilians will see a tree with a red top. They'll fire."

"Brilliant." Bliss reached up to pull off a leaf and chewed the tip suspiciously. "They won't know what it means, but it will be a target, and they'll keep firing until it's down."

"Lopez may be the first Paraguayan to die tomorrow, if we're lucky." Calvin set the lantern down by the paint. "All right, Molly, start climbing."

"What? Why should I?"

"You're the lightest; otherwise I wouldn't have bothered with you tonight. You're the only one the upper limbs are likely to hold." He pointed at McPherson. "Then you, Doctor, halfway up. We'll have a relay and pass the paint up. Bliss, you'll be in the lower limbs. I'll hand the paint to you and stand guard." He looked at the lantern. "I hope that doesn't attract any curiosity, but we need it. I'll keep it on the far side of the tree so it won't be visible at Paso Pucu." He moved the lantern, then beckoned me. "Come on, Molly. You used to be good at climbing trees."

He made a step with his hands. I placed my boot on them sharply, making him grunt, and grabbed for a limb, the bark burning my hand. I scrambled up. The moon had appeared, and enough light washed across the sky so that I could distinguish the dark shadows above me and pull my way from one branch to the next. I thought of the time I had thrown black walnuts at Calvin as a child; when he had tried to climb after me, he had fallen and bruised his forehead. Now I could hear Doctor McPherson beginning to climb, cursing and thrashing and ripping off leaves. The branches began to tremble and sway under my weight. I wedged myself securely between two crossing branches, not daring to go higher. The wind rocked me gently. Through a curtain of leaves the stars shone with bright intensity.

"Molly, are you there?" McPherson grunted.

"Yes."

He dropped his voice to a whisper, but I could still hear him distinctly as his voice rose, disembodied. "Christ! If I'd only been able to picture myself like this on the boat from England! I would have drowned myself." A wheeze threaded his words, and he ended with a fit of coughing.

"Are you all right?"

He gasped for breath. "I'm dizzy. I don't like heights."

"McPherson!" Bliss's voice sounded far away. "Here's the paint, now. Lean down. There. Got it?"

I climbed back down a branch, so that Doctor Mc-Pherson would not have to strain, and took the can of paint carefully from him, trying not to let it slop onto my skirt.

"Molly! You've got it?" Calvin's voice rose hollowly. I saw the glow of the lantern far below me. "Try to get the leaves on this side—the outer leaves."

I climbed a little way out on a branch, but there was nothing to support me while I painted. "I can't!"

"You've got to!"

"This is crazy!" I crawled back to the main trunk, where it crooked to the left, and wedged the can of paint carefully. Then I saw a slightly lower limb that was thicker and had-a bulge at the end. The paint can had a brush in it, tied to a long paddle; I straddled the limb and worked my way down it with the paddle, which I thrust out before me, splashing the leaves with paint. "Someone's got to help me," I called down. "Someone's got to hand me the brush."

"McPherson!" Calvin yelled. "Go higher."

I heard McPherson groan again, then felt the end of my limb tremble as he reached it. "Careful, Doctor. Do you see the paint in that crook? Here's the brush." I leaned back, holding it out. "Dip it in."

In the dark he was only a shapeless bulk, but I felt him grab the brush. He handed it back. I swished out at the leaves again.

"Are you getting the outer leaves, Molly? Pull some of the little branches in toward you."

I leaned forward and pulled in some clumps of leaves, painted them, then let them spring forward again, spraying my face with paint. I worked for an hour, eventually locating another safe branch where I could reach a larger section of the tree. Paint dribbled from my hands and face, and I felt it soaking through my skirt to my legs. Below me Calvin's lantern grew paler. A white mist was rising from the ground.

Suddenly Calvin's voice hissed up, "Freeze, all of you! Someone's coming."

His shadow flickered momentarily as he extinguished the lantern. The white mist grew more visible, for the moon reflected off its surface as it rose slowly higher, like water, around the tree. Sometimes the winds parted it, and it tumbled over like rolling steam, revealing a black fissure of earth. I moved back beside Doctor McPherson, who wheezed asthmatically, his hands pressed in a cross against his chest. Then I heard faint singing.

"It's that old woman," McPherson whispered.

"Bim, bim, bim!" Her voice began solemnly, like a chant; next, rising quicker and livelier, it broke into further repeated bursts of "bim, bim, bim"; then her voice subsided, and she trilled unintelligibly again as she turned off into the swamp. Perhaps, far away, Pancha Garmendia also listened in the darkness.

When I reached my hut, after scrubbing my face and hands with Calvin's turpentine until my skin burned, I found six pink candles burning in a candelabra on a cracker box beside my hammock. There Diaz was sprawled in a red silk dressing gown embroidered with

131

big silver palms, clutching an empty brandy bottle. The swelling of his face had receded, so that his cheekbone was now only slightly discolored. When he heard me enter, he fluttered his eyelids several times, as if emerging from a dream.

"Ah, at last." He sat up, almost tumbling out of the hammock. From where I paused I could smell the brandy on his breath. It had trickled down his lip, matting his beard. "I wanted to talk to you about London, Molly."

"I told you I'd never been to London."

He squinted at me. "Did you? Why is part of your hair red?"

I turned to the shiny piece of metal I had hung on my wall for a mirror. Several strands near the front brushed my shoulder, stuck together with red paint. I rummaged in my valise for a pair of scissors and, without answering Diaz, hacked the pieces out.

"Your beautiful hair," he said fuzzily. Then he eased himself down to his hands and knees and crawled toward the fallen locks. "Give me that beautiful hair, Molly." He began stuffing hair into his dressing gown pocket. "Help me up, will you?"

I helped him to his feet, and he put his arm around me, his head on my shoulder. "I brought you some brandy, Molly, but I drank it all." He pushed back my hair, pressing his lips against my ear. "I want to go downriver to London. I told Francisco, 'Francisco, when the war's over, make me your ambassador to Queen Victoria.'" He hiccuped loudly. "And you'll go with me."

"Yes."

Suddenly I realized that I was supporting his whole weight. He had passed out leaning against me. I lowered him to the pallet on my floor and covered his bare feet with straw. I lay down beside him with my head against his chest, but the beating of his heart reminded me of the drums that would be beating in the morning, and I sat up, shivering.

From the mangrullo the smoke swirled over the plain like a low snowstorm. Sometimes with my field glasses I glimpsed the advancing ranks of Allied soldiers—most with puffing rifles, but some burdened with fascines of rushes and canes to fill the trench, others with scaling ladders. Many had saucepans hanging from their belts, and the joke, according to Lieutenant Lescano, an aide-de-camp of Lopez, who had been ordered to accompany me on the field, was that they intended to sup at Humaitá. "Their own blood for soup," he added gleefully. "Their own livers for a bit of meat."

Because of the smoke I could get no sense of the shape of the war from the mangrullo, although Lescano said the Allies were pouring ahead in four columns, two toward the center, one toward the left, and one toward the right along the riverbank. The Brazilians had not yet brought forward their new guns, for I still saw Lopez's tent across the plain, although from this angle I could not see the red leaves of the Guasü tree. Lescano kept pointing his finger, pretending to fire as if he were a little boy. He had thin black hair plastered tightly to his bumpy skull by sweat, and large, intricately coiled ears stuffed with yellow wax. His fresh trousers were stained with urine around the crotch as if he had lost control of himself in the excitement.

"We must go to the river-battery, Señora Companion. The Marshal ordered me to take you there."

I nodded, handing the field glasses to one of the three soldiers stationed in the mangrullo. I felt numb. I knew Lopez hoped I would be killed today, although I doubted if he himself knew why he wanted it. He was sending me to the most dangerous part of the battle, for no reason. I didn't have the strength to protest. I kept remembering Diaz's heartbeat, and before climbing down I took a last look around the area, hoping to glimpse his regimental flag. Behind me stretched the green of swamp and jungle; several other mangrullos rose above the trees in an uneven line to the fortification at Humaitá; occasionally a signal flashed by mirror. Telegraph poles with protruding lightning conductors stretched in radii from Lopez's villa toward Humaitá, toward Tuyucué, the river and Curupayty itself. The whole area between Curupayty and the new Allied position at Curuzu had the unreal quality of a dream; sometimes a palm or a candelabrum tree emerged from the grey haze, or the scarlet blossoms of a liana appeared and disappeared in a rift of smoke. Carefully I climbed down the rickety ladder, and we took a short path through the swamp, which led directly into the smoke. The roar of gunfire increased. We came upon a group of cavalry. Some men lolled on the grass drinking *caña;* others danced about or stroked their nervous horses. One soldier took a nimble leap, landed on his palms, and walked around a tree with his feet in the air. Nearby a band of musicians played, the music drowned out so completely by the barrage of artillery that the musicians seemed to be a mime troupe, their fingers working delicately over the harps, their faces heavy and sad. A young lieutenant dashed up on a black horse, spurs flashing on his bare feet. "They're falling by the thousands!" he screamed when he saw Lescano. "Thousands! Thousands! We've only lost a handful!" He rode off in the direction of Paso Pucu. "It's the 8-inch guns," Lescano tried to explain, screaming over the noise of exploding canister-shot. "They're in such a position to rake . . . you see . . . !" He gave up, shrugging, laughing. The soldiers back of the lines had shiny looks in their eyes, or mouths that trembled toward a smile at the edges. A few had painted their leather morriones red, white and blue; one hat even had an apple painted above the tricolor band, and another a target. Up in the sky above the river, bombs thrown by the Brazilian fleet exploded in beautiful patterns, so that the soldiers often turned excitedly to one another, pointing. "It would almost be a consolation to be killed by one!" Lescano screamed into my ear as the sky glowed with a shower of red lights.

As we approached the river-battery by a roundabout way, I gasped to see General Diaz, his uniform spattered with soot and mud, a streak of blood along one cheek. He rode past, his face set, not noticing me. I watched him until he disappeared into the smoke, my heart pounding. All over the battlefield the soldiers were shouting about the inexplicable risks he was taking, as if he thought he was immortal. I had been asleep when he left my hut this morning. For a long time, until Lopez sent Lescano to fetch me, I had sat moodily digging at the stubs of the pink candles with my fingernail.

As we approached the river-battery, a tall soldier with a blackened face leapt at us, knocking us over. "Keep down!" he yelled, gesturing. All the men here crouched behind the parapet, only leaping up occasionally to fire with their old flintlock muskets or load the guns in the battery.

"What is it?" The noise was so great that Lescano mouthed the words to the soldier.

"Battalions. Chaco." The soldier stretched his mouth elaborately. In a momentary lull he added out loud, "Two battalions were landed across the river in the Chaco. And the fleet . . . !"

"That's Sayas." Lescano pointed to a man who had just stood up. "He's got to prove he's not a coward today, after what happened to his 10th." Lescano crawled on his hands and knees toward Sayas, who rose in silhouette against the glowing red sky. Bullets sang past like invisible insects. I decided to stay where I was. The ground shook as the big guns fired again. Suddenly the gun right next to Major Sayas exploded, the muzzle cut halfway up the chase. A pillar of flame crackled. I saw Sayas rise a few feet in the air, twist over backwards, and land on top of Lescano, who, screaming, pushed the flaming man off him. Two nearby soldiers rolled Sayas in the dirt, putting out the fire; but when they turned him on his back, his face was missing. Lescano, gripping his head in his hands, jumped up, screaming. He began to vomit. "Get down!" several soldiers yelled at him. A bullet struck him in the back of the neck. He toppled over, his head crashing on Sayas's chest.

Instinctively I started to run toward him. The tall soldier grabbed my ankle, pulling me on top of him. "Get out of here!" he screamed. "He's dead." He pushed and elbowed me until I began to crawl away, choking on the dust and smoke that swirled in patterns before me. I looked back once, to see the sky lit scarlet with tiny dancing lights. The guns in the battery fired. I crawled forward until I was long out of range, deep in pampas grass, my face ruffling against the silvery tassels, trying to wash away the vision of the explosion that kept recurring before my eyes. When I stood up, I was well back of the battery on a marshy path that cut close to a pool of viscous black mud. A vampire bat, stirred up by the gunfire from his daylight sleep, dipped overhead. I found myself a hollow in a thicket of bamboo and crawled in, holding my shoulders tightly. I had another vision of Major Sayas's body tumbling over in the air, flames running up and down it. Then I heard General Diaz screaming "Fire!" I covered my ears; deep inside my head I heard his heart beating as if I still lay against his chest. Hours went by. Except for occasionally standing up to uncramp my legs, I did not move until the sound of gunfire dropped to a distant rumble, and a deepening of the green around me indicated that twilight was beginning its rapid fall. Then I headed back to Paso Pucu by way of the cemetery hill. Two officers were up there looking through the mounted telescopes. One, his arm in a sling, I recognized as Lieutenant Urdapilleta, Diaz's aide-de-camp, so I walked to the gate.

"They've retreated." He waved his good arm when he saw me. "Even the fleet has gone downriver, hey, Quinteros?"

Quinteros nodded. He was fat and resembled a stuffed bear because of the wildness of his beard, which spread over his cheeks, almost to the eyes, it seemed, and over the buttons on his chest. "And we've lost fewer than fifty men." He turned back to the telescope. "The 12th

Battalion has gone outside the trenches for the spoils. They're lancing the wounded."

"What?"

"Only those who can't walk." Urdapilleta's little white face puckered. "It's only humane. We can't feed or cure them. Usually we can barely nurse our own wounded."

I shuddered and began to wander around the graveyard, my arms folded tightly together. Against the far wall I saw a pretty tomb with a mosaic of red tiles across it by way of a slab, and a wooden cross with an illegible name carved deeply into the bar. I pulled up a strand of sour grass to suck, remembering my mother's tale about how graveyard grass tasted like blood. Finally Urdapilleta walked over, pushing his curling dark hair out of his eyes.

"They do the same."

"I suppose."

He sighed, shifting his arm painfully in the sling. "I feel like you, though," he said in a low voice so that Quinteros couldn't hear. "I'd have bad dreams if I were in the 12th Battalion."

"Have you seen General Diaz? Is he all right?"

Urdapilleta nodded. "The risks he took today were amazing, but he's all right. God was on our side." He grinned, indicating his arm. "A bullet grazed me. It could have killed me, but it didn't. Of course, you've heard about Lopez?"

"No, nothing."

His eyes opened. "Another miracle, Señora Companion. Lopez had just ridden a little way from field headquarters when there was an explosion. Apparently the Brazilians have some new long-range guns." He ran his

good hand through his crinkly hair, clicking his tongue.
"The tent and the big Guasü tree were blown up, but
not a soul was hurt. The tree had sacrificed itself for
Lopez—there was blood all over the leaves, Señora."

Quinteros had come up behind Urdapilleta, fingering
the little gold cross around his neck that protruded
through his beard. "Lopez is sending one red leaf to
every village in Paraguay and has made this day a holy
day forever."

I shivered, turning away. Darkness had been falling
imperceptibly all along, so that the men's faces were
beginning to swim milkily before me. When I looked
down on the plain, I could see the flicker of tiny fires
where a few soldiers had bivouacked for the night.
Somewhere down in that darkness Pancha Garmendia
slept on the hard ground, and once again the guilty
thought crossed my mind that I must help her. But I was
so afraid. I murmured good night to the two lieutenants,
who wandered back to the telescopes, focusing them
now on the stars appearing like confetti across the sky. I
picked my way down the hill to Paso Pucu; moonlight
glinted white off the stones, and the shadow of a dog
rolled distinctly across the sandy track. I had reached
the edge of the camp when someone tapped me on the
shoulder, and I turned to see Monkey-Snout, his thick,
ancient skin puckering nervously about the eyes and
mouth.

"Señora, the doctor—please come."

"What is it?"

He tugged at my sleeve. "Please come. He tried to kill
himself."

"McPherson?" I ran to follow him, for he was already
hobbling ahead, his grey trousers slapping together.

When we reached McPherson's hut near the hospital, where oil lamps threw long yellow beams from the narrow windows, and men whimpered or coughed or cursed at an occasional violent shriek from some dying neighbor, Monkey-Snout pushed back the piece of worn carpet hanging over the doorway and waved me in with his curved little fingers.

Doctor McPherson was lying on a cot, his eyes closed, a wax candle burning on a cracker box beside him. He stirred as we entered, his eyelids flickering momentarily.

"Martha?" He sat up. "Oh—go away. Unless you want to do it."

"Do what?"

"Shoot me. In the heart."

"What are you talking about? What's wrong?"

He put his face in his hands. "Martha."

"Your wife?"

Monkey-Snout picked up a crumpled piece of paper from the dirt floor. "Señora, it was this."

I sat down next to McPherson on the cot, smoothing the paper. It was from Lopez, although written by one of the Jesuits who served him as secretary. I moved a little down to the candle, trying to decipher the spidery writing. "You're to write a letter to *El Semanario* declaring your wife, Martha McPherson, an enemy of—a traitor, an inhuman—what *is* this?"

He lifted his head. His eyes, crisscrossed by wiry red lines, were sunken deeply in the surrounding flesh. "It means she's dead."

"But why?"

"God knows. For some silly, innocent remark. When someone deserts, or surrenders, or even—God help him—gets captured by the enemy, their relations are forced to write letters declaring them pariahs—but this, I never expected . . . she was so ill. Martha . . . " He began to cry, hoarse, dry sobs that racked his body in violent spasms. "Poor Martha. I never got home to . . . to . . . " His voice disappeared.

Monkey-Snout, who had been crumbling some dried leaves in the corner, came over with a tin cup. "Make him drink this, Señora."

I tried to pull McPherson up so he could drink, but he threw me off. He clawed at the blanket on the cot. I was afraid he was going into convulsions, but finally, with a wheeze, he stopped.

"Doctor, drink this."

"It will make you sleep," Monkey-Snout whispered in his ear.

McPherson sat up, breathing heavily. He looked keenly at Monkey-Snout. "Is it poison?"

"It will make you sleep."

"I want poison."

"Doctor, she may be alive." I touched his shoulder. "You may be able to do something."

He grabbed the cup, almost spilling it, and drank hastily. "Never." He choked. "She's dead, dead. I tried to shoot myself, but goddamn it to hell, the powder was wet, and now he's hidden the rifle. . . . I was going to step on the trigger with my toe." He laughed, sticking out his right foot, which was bare. "My toe."

"Lie back. You need a rest."

He shrugged but stretched out on the cot, a little calmer, propping his head against the woven reed wall. A white spider scurried away. He held up his right hand. The cuff of his shirt was dark with blood. "Don't ask me how many bones I sawed through today. And tomorrow Lopez wants me to cut open that poor bastard sent down from Asunción and find a tongue in his chest instead of a heart—to prove his miracle!" Wincing, he put his hands over his face again. "How long before I sleep? I feel like I'm going to puke. Why not let me die?" He smiled slightly. "I'll do it tomorrow, then."

"You'll feel better tomorrow, Doctor."

"Maybe *you* will. I won't. I can't bear it here, you know. Without Martha . . . " His voice sputtered drowsily. I looked at Monkey-Snout, who was sitting against the far wall, his bent little legs drawn up.

"I'll watch him, Señora."

I unfolded an extra blanket over McPherson. His skin, faintly blue, was bathed in a cold sweat, but he seemed to be sleeping peacefully. Beside the candle he had placed his wedding ring. I picked it up and was trying to slide it back onto his hairy finger when he suddenly roused up, grabbed my hand, and viciously gnawed it like a piece of meat. I shrieked. The ring dropped onto his chest.

In one swift movement he cupped the ring, flung it into his mouth, and swallowed it. His throat fluttered, but he didn't choke. His skin seemed to grow bluer, as if all the tiny surface veins were breaking.

He raised himself on one elbow. "I can see the future now, you, every star. Martha? Martha?"

"Doctor, are you all right?" I put out my hand to touch him, but he made a blind swiping movement in the air.

"No, it's too dark," he whispered. Then, shouting, "Martha? No, I thought they were stars, but they're just maggots, aren't they? The maggots in my brain. I'm dead."

142

I turned to Monkey-Snout. "What have you done to him?"

"What he wished."

"You've killed him?"

McPherson flung himself off the cot, flat on the ground, and began licking and eating clumps of dirt. A second later he lifted his head. "I'm burying myself, Martha. See, I don't need you. God, it's dark. I see those worms; those red ants are getting in my ears, but you, now—!"

"What have you done to him?" I screamed again at Monkey-Snout. I was afraid to touch McPherson. He clawed fiercely at the dirt, stuffing great handfuls into his mouth.

"He wished to die, Señora." Monkey-Snout still sat calmly against the wall, although his eyes twisted in sympathy. "This way he doesn't sin."

"But it's murder!" McPherson's sprawled, crablike body, one foot booted, the other bare, jerked violently and was still. I knelt down. No pulse beat in the wrist. When I rolled him over, his face, streaked with red dirt, had deepened to purple, as if the blood ran loose below the surface. A grubworm, uprooted by his nails, crawled along his collar.

"He's dead." I put my hands over my mouth, for I could feel the sweet sickness welling back of my throat. "You've murdered him."

Monkey-Snout stood up, nodding imperturbably. "But he's innocent, Señora. Thanks to you, he did not die in absolute despair."

"You killed him."

"He wanted to die, Señora. I know him well. Without his wife . . . " He shook his head.

"But he's dead."

"He wished to die, Señora." Monkey-Snout's voice was slow and patient, as if he were explaining something to a child. "But it's a sin to kill oneself, to despair. So I fetched *you*, Señora."

He put his crooked little hand on me. The cuticles of his nails had grown up so thickly that the nails were hardly visible. The missing fingers ended in white scar tissue. I shoved him away and ran to the door, beating the carpet awkwardly. It snapped back in my face, and it seemed like a long minute before I could escape into fresher air, which I gulped greedily, filling my lungs as if I had just surfaced from thick salt water.

# Eight

All night the women, their white blouses wavering like ghosts in the dark, rebuilt the two rows of huts the Allies had fire-bombed at dusk. The Brazilian General Caxias had marched part of his army of thirty thousand the long way around by the bank of the Paraná, crossed the Bellaco at Paso Frete, and marched to Tuyucué. After a brief skirmish with the Paraguayan vanguard, he had encamped almost within range of the guns of Espinillo, on the side of the enceinte opposite Curupayty. The huts at Espinillo had been flamed as a gesture for morale, and the damage observed by three huge Brazilian balloons. Lopez intended that a strange cry should go up in the Brazilian camp at dawn when the first sentries saw the huts intact again; it would be further proof of his omnipotence. He had ordered me to climb the nearest mangrullo just before dawn so that I could observe the commotion for *El Semanario* and for the three new weekly papers I now also worked for—the *Centinela*, a Spanish-language paper with texts of mythological Allied documents I invented myself under Lopez's direction; the *Lambaré*, a Guaraní-language paper containing stories about brave soldiers; and the *Cabichuí*, patterned after *Punch*, full of bad jokes that I collected from the officers about lizard-tailed Brazilians and pig-nosed Argentinians. When Lieutenant Cela wasn't operating the telegraph, he made woodcuts of these creatures with a knife, carefully emphasizing the scales and curlicues, the long donkey ears protruding from smooth foreheads, the hands curling into claws, the venomous snakes emerging from mouths, or the feathery necks and huge eyes on stalks.

The Brazilian pal-tents swam up gradually in the dawn mist, and I thought of my plan to escape. At last I was going to help Pancha Garmendia. I had discovered a canoe hidden in the woods along the river Paraguay. The Paraguay swept down into the Paraná, where the Brazilian fleet had anchored after the unsuccessful attack on Curupayty. It would be a difficult journey, for both rivers were high, and the Paraguay was beginning to rise over the carrizal, the wide reed swamp along its margin. The river was full of debris, however, and, as dangerous as the logs, rafts, uprooted trees, and *camelotas*—torn fragments of bank that swept by like floating islands—might be to navigation, they would provide a kind of camouflage for the canoe. We could keep low, and watchers would assume that the canoe had torn loose somewhere far upstream.

The canoe was in a little inlet that led under trees thick with fragrant air plant into a passage, almost obliterated by high water, that cut through the carrizal to the river. Since I had a fair amount of freedom to roam the camp and the outposts, to watch occasional skirmishes and ride with the cattle-raiding parties, it had not been difficult for me to stock the canoe with food, water, and the file I would need to cut off Pancha Garmendia's fetters. I expected that the river current would sweep us around toward the Paraná, and then it would be a question of how to hail the fleet before they suspected we were another torpedo canoe and opened fire. Another dangerous place would be the Paraguayan fort at Curupayty, where we would have to pass under the guns and duck the iron chain, loaded with torpedoes, that stretched across the river near that point.

However, I needed some kind of diversion to focus the attention of the whole camp; except for the occasional explosion of a torpedo boat on the river, or the peculiar report of the guns at dawn, where each blast echoed like rolling fire, the camp had been quiet since last week's battle. I was hopeful that this new move on the part of Caxias would provide me with an opportunity. From this mangrullo at Espinillo I had the best view yet of the Allied forces. In the hazy morning light I felt almost as if I were in one of the Brazilians' big balloons, floating dreamily over the terrain, for the mist swirled low to the ground around me, conveying the sense of motion. I could not make out the Oriental army under General Flores—rumor had it that the small force of gauchos had melted back to Montevideo—but the Argentine camp of hide huts was clearly visible to the left of the neat rows of Brazilian tents, as were the disordered wagons, tents, and cattle of the camp-followers and traders. As the mist drifted away—into the cracks of the earth, it seemed—the soldiers in both camps stirred:

the Brazilians, mainly Negroes, in fatigue suits of brown drill; the Argentinians in uniforms of wild improvisation, composed of yellow ponchos, with pink trousers or dark trousers or striped overalls, or knickerbockers and gaiters; half the soldiers wore riding boots, the other half were barefoot or in sandals. A few black women moved around them in big mushroom-shaped straw hats, selling small shiny articles out of baskets. The sentries must have noticed the new huts, for a few officers gathered on a short hill with their telescopes; but there was no flurry of excitement.

In a little while the flags were hoisted up, but only to half-mast. A gun fired in the air from the Argentine camp and was answered by the Brazilians.

"What's going on?" I asked the yawning sentry, who had rubbed his eyes so hard with his fists for the last hour that the whites now flushed pink.

"Something." He lifted his field glasses. The Argentine gun fired again and was answered by a gun in the Brazilian camp. "They're firing blanks . . . strange. Somebody must be dead."

"Somebody important."

He nodded. "I'll flash the news." He tilted the huge mirror into position. I climbed down the mangrullo and started the long walk back through the marsh to Paso Pucu. The hot early sun steamed down, sending a trickle of sweat across my neck which I wiped off with my fingers, licking them for the salt taste. The Allied blockade was becoming more effective. The women who used to make salt from the river mud or wash the dirt under the smokehouse were now so busy digging trenches or weaving broadcloth for shirts and drawers that only the hospitals, and Lopez's private table, had salt. Halfway to Paso Pucu I sat down on a fallen log with my little writing journal—several bound pieces of cowhide scraped to a white surface—and jotted a few notes about the Allied astonishment at the magically restored huts. *Thousands of soldiers gathered; some ran forward, obviously trying to surrender to Lopez, but others pulled them back. One general fell to his knees, praying. The officers had a difficult time disbanding the frenzied men; a half-articulate cheer rose up from the enemy: Lopez!* I put the journal into my pocket and hurried on, past a group of soldiers who were boiling ashes and fat to make soap for their division.

"Mitre's dead!" A soldier waved his paddle at me. "Lopez says Mitre's dead!"

I waved back to him, surprised that word had traveled so quickly, and took a short cut through Piquete Bomba, a cavalry advance post where some inexperienced soldiers had once propped up their broken cooking pot with an unexploded 9-pounder shell and sent their dinner splattering to the treetops. When I reached Lopez's villa, I stayed well away from the pacing jaguar, chained to a stake in the ground, which had been captured in the Chaco by three young lieutenants yesterday and presented to Lopez as a gift. The sentry in the antechamber rapped on Lopez's door. Nervously I entered, my journal of facts ready. Lopez sprawled in his dressing gown on a velvet meridienne. He wore blue boots of soft leather decorated with a red pattern. Lieutenant Saguier stood behind him, trying to hand him a glass of brandy and water, but Lopez kept bouncing and rubbing his hands in his excitement.

"Mitre's dead!" He curled his hand into a fist when he saw me. "The war's almost over. You think those Brazil-

ians—those conscripts, those Negro slaves and Indians—
will fight alone? Ha!"

"How did he die?"

"Of fright." Lopez laughed. He grabbed the glass finally from Saguier and gulped noisily. "My little trick
worked. When he saw those huts, with freshly thatched
roofs, his heart stopped."

I said carefully, fingering my hide journal, "Are you
certain it was Mitre . . . ?"

I expected him to turn scarlet and throw his brandy
into my eyes, but instead he smiled. "Of course. I've sent
Bruguez to kidnap a couple of Argentine sentries. His
men have a way of creeping up through the brush, like
so—!" Lopez stood up and mimicked their tiptoe. "Just
like my fine new jaguar, my sleek Abe Lincoln." Lopez
squinted, curving his fingers into claws. "Does it offend
you that I've named my jaguar after your dead president, Mrs. Companion? It's because of that pig, that
great beast with a monkey's white brain, Washburn."
He sat down. Saguier poured him another finger of
brandy, which he drank straight. "He wants to visit the
camp, he says, to see if he can make peace—the pig! He
wants to spy!"

A rap on the door interrupted him. "General Bruguez," the sentry called. "With two prisoners."

"Let him in."

Bruguez, his skin greenish with exertion, puffed into
the room, followed by the two prisoners, whose arms
were chained behind them. Their shirts had been torn
off, revealing raw skin and bruises where they had been
kicked and pummeled. One, a tall, gaunt blond whose
hair looked like a wig, had a caved-in chest and
breathed asthmatically. His pale blue eyes switched

nervously back and forth between Lopez and Bruguez. Occasionally his tongue flicked out to lick his long upper lip. The other prisoner, a squat, dark Indian, kept his eyes on the floor, his lips pressed tightly together. His right ear dripped blood, as if an earring had been torn out of it. Bruguez pointed to the two men. "The pigs have been lying."

"But it's true!" The blond man spoke with a heavy German accent, close to tears. "Don Marcos Paz has died, not Mitre. Yah, it's true!"

Bruguez slapped him across the face with the palm of his hand. The man stumbled back, his eyes watering, an ugly red splash rising on his skin. "Liar!" He turned to the other prisoner. "Tell his excellency that Mitre's dead."

The man raised his black eyes momentarily. "Mitre's dead," he said in a flat voice.

"Jose." The German's high voice shook. "What are you saying? It's Don Marcos Paz, the vice president, who has . . . we both saw Mitre just this morning!"

"Flog that fellow," Lopez said in a cold voice to Bruguez, nodding at the German, "until he stops his foul lies."

Bruguez herded the two men out. I could hear the German sobbing in the hall. I glanced once at Lieutenant Saguier, but he kept his eyes fixed on the top of the curtain. Two days ago a commission of eight, led by Lopez's brother-in-law and treasurer general, Don Saturnino Bedoya, had arrived from Asunción to present Lopez with an offering from the citizens, a sword of honor, the hilt set with jewels, and a crown of gold laurel leaves. After the speeches and the blessing of the gifts by Bishop Palacious, Lopez had arrested his brother-in-law and drafted the commissioners into the army. No one knew why. Saguier picked up a silver letter opener and slit an envelope for Lopez, who stretched out full length on the meridienne, arranging some embroidered pillows behind his back.

"I'll go write this story for *El Semanario*," I said.

Lopez pursed his lips, then raised a magnifying glass to inspect the letter Saguier handed him. "By the way, Mrs. Companion, your friend Bliss has been arrested."

I paused at the door. "Bliss?"

"Yes. He turned out to be a spy for Caxias. He strangled Doctor McPherson, who was trying to warn me."

I took a deep breath, keeping my face immobile. Doctor McPherson had been buried up in the cemetery last week. A Paraguayan surgeon had carefully called it a heart attack. "Where is Bliss?"

"I've set him to work on a biography of Washburn." Lopez giggled. "In chains."

"Good day, your excellency." I shut the door. The sentry glanced at my face, trying to read Lopez's mood through it, but I had learned to keep my expression blank. Since McPherson's death I had focused on only one thing: my plan to escape. Outside the stockade I passed General Diaz, who was teetering back on a chair near his hut, surrounded by a small group of officers and soldiers sprawled in the shade of the carob tree outside his door. He had a leather bag of sugar lumps which he tossed one by one to the men, who attempted to catch them in their mouths without using their hands. Lieutenant Urdapilleta watched him with jealous eyes.

A sugar cube hit my arm. "Have you seen the promenade?" Diaz called.

I turned, surprised, for he had not spoken to me since the night I had found him drunk. "No—what's happening?"

"The Marquez de Caxias is promenading his army from Tuyucué to San Solano and back." Diaz laughed. "He's trying to scare us with his forces."

"He's got three times as many men," yelled one of the soldiers, who wore a high leather helmet faced with brass. "That means we're even!"

"What do we need guns for?" another soldier called. "Why not bows and arrows?"

"Why not *bodoques?*" The helmeted soldier pulled a clay ball from his pocket. I had seen soldiers shooting parrots with these balls and doubled-stringed bows.

"We could fight them naked!" Diaz stood up, flinging away the bag of sugar cubes. "Fifty naked Paraguayans could wipe out a whole battalion."

The men cheered, dispersing in different directions. I was walking away, too, when Diaz called, "Molly?"

"What is it?"

"Come here."

It was dim inside his hut; the oil lamp threw a white circle of light on the roof. I sat down on the rumpled bed. The sheets, torn in places, were yellower than I remembered and spotted with mangled ants that he no longer bothered to shake out. The smell of stale sweat made me slightly nauseous.

"I want to ask you," he said stiffly, still standing, his thumb under his belt, "not to look at me the way you look at me as if I've betrayed you."

"I don't look at you any differently than I look at anyone else." I forced myself to meet his eyes, which had brown bowls of permanent shadow below them.

"You make me feel bad."

I looked away. "You changed so quickly. You were so
. . . so solid before, and now all you do is drink, working yourself up into wild excitements . . . "

"You shouldn't care."

"I don't care."

"Good." He sat down at the other end of the bed, set-
ting off a tumult of bedsprings. His recent drinking had
collapsed certain muscles in his face, so that he looked
older. "You haven't been driven crazy by anything, have
you? You just watch crazy things. You ought to be crazy
by now."

"I'm lucky I'm not."

He sighed, scratching under his arm. "Tonight we're
digging a trench near Potrero Piris—right under the
nose of Caxias's left flank. That munitions fellow, the
one who's marrying Lopez's sister, is going to create a
diversion on Yataity Cora."

I stiffened. This might be my chance. I thought of
Pancha Garmendia huddled like a dog under her tree. It
was difficult to get the old woman to feed her anymore.
"Do you mind if I come? Lopez wants me to do articles
on everything."

"If you wish—" He looked at me wistfully. "There
was something I wanted to show you, Molly." He
fumbled under one of the pillows and pulled out a torn
leaf from a book. "Is this England?"

I looked at the sketchy map drawn on what must have
been the flyleaf of an old novel. Dampness had dis-
solved the inked names of cities. "Yes, that's England's
shape. That dot there must be London."

He nodded, replacing the map under his pillow. "I

was pretty sure. I found this in a dead Argentine's pocket. Maybe he was English."

"Maybe." I stood up. "How can the men dig all night, that close to the Brazilian trenches?"

He looked hurt that I had changed the subject. "By dawn it'll be deep enough for cover, and they can throw the earth behind them for a parapet." Absently he pulled a hair out of his mustache. "We need protection on that flank."

"But how can you dig so quietly? Spades clank."

He shrugged. "That's where the explosions help."

I moved to the door. "I'll come tonight."

"Come, then."

Outside, I took a deep breath of air, for I felt sad and lost. Some brown chickens with red heads scurried in front of me, making me stumble against a dirty sheep with a blackened rear. The sheep moved stolidly away. I shook myself and went on to the telegraph office. Two soldiers stood on guard outside the hut next to it, and between their legs I glimpsed Bliss's white face staring out at me, mouthing my name.

"Porter!"

The two soldiers blocked my way. "Sorry, Señora," they each said, almost in unison. "No one is to speak to him."

I heard chains clank; then Bliss's voice sounded spectrally from within. "Did you know Washburn failed out of fifty-three colleges, Molly?" His thin giggle made the hair rise on my arms.

I was not used to the jungle at night. Somewhere stars shone, but their pale light never penetrated the thick canopies of leaves and vines where I stumbled over roots and soft, nightmare mosses. Later, we had to crawl on our bellies in order not to be seen by the enemy sentries. The ground was still littered with cannonballs, cartouche boxes, bullets, and rusted guns from the last battle; I was continually hitting something sharply with my palm or knee and biting back a yelp. But the bodies were the turn of the screw. Although after each battle the Allies had burned the Paraguayan corpses in huge stacks, with kindling, many were still strewn in this no man's area of the woods, not decomposed but mummified. Once Diaz, his back to the enemy, had lit a match to show me. The skin was dried tight to the bones, brown and fragile. The closer we came to where the trench would be dug, the more of these corpses we came across, and sometimes, during pauses, when I peered ahead, it was impossible to distinguish them from the living men on their stomachs. Sometimes I brushed against bark, then, looking more closely, found my palm cupped around a skull. I was glad when the actual digging began, even though the silence seemed to magnify every clank of shovel on stone and every wheezy breath. Any moment I expected the Brazilians, whose campfires I could see in the distance, to attack. Diaz positioned the men along the length of the trench; put his favorite aide, Lieutenant Urdapilleta, in charge; then sent a whisper down the line that he would personally slit the throat of anyone who spoke. He crawled back to the tree I was sitting under. I had already told him that I planned to go back by myself, after seeing the operation, and I was a little worried that he would try to accompany me, or send an officer. But he quickly pulled out a flask of rum, took two healthy swigs, and stretched out comfortably. Some firing began in the distance.

"Bruguez," he whispered. "Part of the distraction. Do you want to go fishing again?"

I swallowed hard. Tomorrow I would be out on the river, but not with General Diaz. "Yes."

"Ah, good." I thought he was going to touch me, but he hesitated, settling back into the leaves again. It grew monotonous watching the men shovel. Rhythmically they threw the earth before them like black veils against the thinner black of the air. Occasionally pebbles or a metal handle gleamed as a light flared up in the Brazilian camp, which began to happen more frequently as the distant firing increased to a steady drone. Suddenly the whole area flashed bright as day. The men froze, each sharply illuminated. Diaz had raised his flask halfway to his lips and held it there as if turned to stone. A tremendous explosion followed. The earth shook, and I reached behind me to grab the tree trunk as darkness, like a tidal wave, washed back. "A torpedo," Diaz whispered excitedly, as the sound diminished to a low rumble. "Over a thousand pounds of powder. But I didn't realize there would be such a glare." He stood up, peering toward the camp, trying to determine if the Brazilians had spotted the diggers, which they *should* have, I thought, shuddering. If a torpedo boat or raft had been sent downriver with that much powder, the fleet would be nervous all night. I doubted if any of the Brazilian boats had been destroyed, for ever since Kruger had been blown up trying to navigate one, Calvin had left them to drift down, and they often ran aground. Still, after such a big explosion, the Brazilians would try to sink any suspicious object floating past. It would be especially dangerous to go down in the canoe tonight. Yet this might be my only chance of escaping camp undetected. I bit my knuckles. When Diaz sat down, satisfied that the Brazilians had been too confused and frightened to see anything, he offered me a drink. I accepted, grateful for the raw rum burning across my tense nerves.

In a little while, after I caught myself yawning, I tapped him on the shoulder and whispered that I was going back. He was asleep. For a long time I stared at the dark planes of his face, over which the night's shadows gathered like swirling thicknesses of black gauze. Then I kissed his cheek and crawled carefully over him. My eyes had thoroughly adjusted to the dark, so I could distinguish the watery darkness of air from the deeper, textured darkness of foliage. I belly-crawled a little way, until it seemed safe to stand. My legs trembled. I had a panic desire to run blindly ahead, but I forced myself to go one step at a time, my hands scissoring before my face to protect it from dangling vines and coiling, thorn-spiked branches. Insects whined and stung past my face. At one point the trail seemed to cut in close to the North Bellaco and the island of Yataity Cora, for the guns barked suddenly close; but it may have been the same strange atmospheric condition that caused firing to echo weirdly at dawn, for the sound diminished almost as rapidly as it had intensified.

The jungle thinned. I was on the marsh now, where it was even more important to stick to the trail, for deep black lagoons and smooth pools of mud that could suck up a horse pocked the seemingly flat plain. A low, waist-high mist swept in white tatters past me. I circled the camp. The high earthwork around headquarters resembled in silhouette some medieval castle, although by day it was a wretched mass of clay and stone. I glanced

at it once, then headed straight for the open field where
Pancha Garmendia was chained. She was asleep on the
ground, her tattered poncho pulled over her head, her
bare feet tucked under the skirt of her dress. The chain
was merely wrapped twice around a high limb of the
tree where anyone except Pancha, who was very weak,
could have undone it. The fact that no guard was ever
posted over her indicated that Lopez had no fear that
someone besides Rosalita might try to help her. The
chain made a dull, clanking sound as I unwound it, but it
was not dangerously loud. Pancha would have to coil it
around her neck until I found a safe place to file it off.
The chain connecting the fetters themselves gave her
little freedom to walk, and the iron was heavy enough to
slow us down considerably. I shook her, trying to wake
her without frightening her. She moaned, rolling over,
the fetters grating against each other. Her tight, drawn
skin reminded me of the corpses in the woods. I was
glad when she opened her eyes.

I put my fingers over her mouth. "Don't be afraid,
Pancha. We're going away."

I helped her sit up. Her arm, when I touched it, was
sharply thin, cold and dry. "Do you think you can walk
with this chain?"

She nodded. Her hair, which she pushed back from
her eyes, was greasy, tangled into hopeless wild knots.
"You're going to bury me in lime now?"

"No, don't be afraid. I want to get you away from
these people."

"I'm not afraid," she said dully. "I'll just dissolve,
easy . . ."

"No!" I shook her. "It's all right."

"Yes."

159

I took both her hands. "I'm a friend. I'm going to help you."

She looked at me. It was too dark to read the expression on her face, but the low, flutelike quality of her voice turned me cold. "They held a fish in by its tail, then pulled it out. . . . 'Like that, Pancha,' they said. 'First your legs, then each arm'—"

"No!" I hissed fiercely in her ear. I wanted to hug her, but I felt she would vanish, her body imprinted delicately on mine like a fossil shell. "Please don't talk about that. We're going to the water, to a canoe."

I helped her up, still uncertain as to whether she had heard me or whether her docility was merely complete acceptance of death. I had to keep one arm around her to support her, and even at that, each step must have been painful, chafing the raw wounds at her ankles. It seemed hours before we entered the relative protection of the carrizal, where the high, intertwined grass shielded us from view. Two dangers faced us. Many of the lower trails through the carrizal were now under water, and there was the ever-present danger of meeting a patrol of soldiers on those that were still passable. I had not been in the carrizal at night, either, and although a white moon had appeared in the sky, my sense of proportion was thrown off. A cypress loomed on the left instead of on the right; a log I had used to fill a bog hole was missing, and we sank almost to our knees in muddy water. A gun fired, impossibly close. I kept hearing voices ahead that I knew must be only the unintelligible chatter of parrots, yet I felt afraid. After a while I had to hang Pancha's chain around my own neck, for the weight of it was bending her over at a painful angle, and then we moved even slower—one united,

hobbled creature. I had left a large white stone in front
of the thin screen of reeds separating the well-traveled
trail from the hidden passage that led to the canoe, and
luckily the moonlight struck it just when I was turning in
another direction. Just in the last two days the river had
risen higher, for the passage was several inches under
water. I had taken off my boots at the edge of the carrizal, and I could sometimes feel the slimy dart of a frog or
water snake under my bare feet. I shivered a little as the
water grew deeper, for if we lost the trail we might
stumble into one of the deep lagunas intersecting the
area. At times, I knew, the whole carrizal was under
water. At that moment I spotted the dark shape of the
canoe, which I had tied to a clump of unusually sturdy
reeds. I had planned to stop awhile and file off Pancha's
chain, if not the fetters themselves, but the water was
now up to our knees, and the mud oozed threateningly
soft under our feet if we stood too long in one place. The
canoe rode higher than I remembered. It was difficult to
distinguish the trail from the lagoon itself.

"Wait here, Pancha." I wrapped the chain back
around her and splashed toward the canoe. Unexpectedly, I fell into chest-high water, sputtering noisily as I
regained my balance. Pancha shrieked. I got hold of the
canoe, swinging it back toward the shallow water. When
I turned toward her, she was standing exactly where I
had left her, but with her hands over her mouth.

"Can you get into the canoe if I hold it here? Be careful; if you step too far the water gets deep."

She had to drop herself into the canoe backwards, for
she couldn't lift her legs over. She remained crumpled
on the bottom while I got in, pulled the paddle from
under her, and dragged in the rest of the chain, which

she had left dangling over the side. I untied the canoe, and in a few swift strokes we were lost in one of the black channels of the lagoon.

In the canoe, for the first time since crossing the lines, I felt free. The lagoon widened, and I noticed a strong current underneath it, pulling us to the river. A breeze brought the smell of mimosa and orchids from one of the twisted black trees along the bank. Ahead, I thought I heard the river roaring past, but I may have imagined it, the way I had strained after the sound of the sea in a conch shell when I was a child.

After a while Pancha sat up, balancing carefully in the bottom of the canoe. "Are you taking me to dance?"

"No, to the Brazilian fleet. Don't speak so loud," I whispered, bending toward her. "Voices carry on the water."

"Is dancing sinful?" she whispered back. She looked genuinely puzzled. There were sores on her lips, probably from not eating properly.

"No. There's some food in that basket back there— some oranges."

She turned her head but made no movement to get them. "I can't sin anymore, anyway."

"Don't talk like that. Please, there's some salted fish, too."

She shook her head, let her poncho fall to the bottom of the canoe, and began to play abstractedly with the torn lace edging her chemise. "Last year the sun disappeared."

"You mean the eclipse? I wasn't here then."

"All the birds flew in circles. The crows flew north, too." She frowned. "I was feeding them, and suddenly it

grew dark, and they flew off. They used to come to my
fingers and eat my bread."

"Where was that?"

"Someplace. Corrientes, maybe, where Rosalita lives.
She would bring me meat, secretly, so I could give my
bread to birds. Anymore I don't."

"I didn't realize you had met Rosalita when the army
was in Corrientes."

She nodded, looking around her with growing
curiosity, although there was nothing to see but the dark
shapes of trees outlined by moonlight and the flash of
water from my paddle. "I don't have to dance?"

"Never again, if you don't want to. Lopez has been
dragging you from camp to camp, then?"

She didn't answer but dipped her hand in the water
and brought it up gingerly, crossing herself. She lay
back in the canoe, and after a while I thought her
asleep. Suddenly the current grew quite strong, and the
canoe leapt forward. I worked the paddle furiously but
found I had no control. The bank fell away. The moon
had slipped under a cloud, and now on all sides of us
black water rushed. When the moon reappeared, I
found that we were right in the center of the swollen
Paraguay, a black speck, turning up a froth of white
water amid all sorts of other ominous shapes. I took the
paddle in, for a passing log almost sheared it from my
hand. Sometimes the water appeared as a smooth black
sheet; sometimes it seemed to rush and leap forward. I
was helpless, much more so than I had expected. A lake
in a storm is wild, but there is no inexorable current
shooting you forward, and it is more a battle against
wind and the resultant waves than a battle against iron
water flowing deep below your perception. The sky

lightened. The moon faded against it, almost transparent, and I realized that dawn was much closer than I
had imagined. We had taken too long to cross the carrizal. Now it would be daylight when we passed under the
guns at Curupayty. A huge, uprooted tree floated past
us, leaving a damp green smell in its wake. The low cliffs
along the Chaco side of the river flushed with color:
first, shades of rose, then red, brick red, blood red. In
places the sandstone appeared soft and crumbling, in
other places hard as granite. A few lights gleamed,
growing dimmer as grey air washed along the shore,
picking out first the high fan palms, then the lower
hardwood trees. We ran by a crescent of island where
the trees were bound branch to branch with bush ropes.
I was straining my eyes toward the left shore, trying to
pick out early signs that the fort was near, when suddenly a monstrous object smashed down on the canoe,
upending it; a wall of water closed over my face. Pancha
fell on me, and somehow I grabbed her around the neck
with one arm, desperately fumbling for the canoe with
the other, although in a moment I saw through wet,
nearly blinded eyes that it was already too far away.
Pancha's chain dragged on both of us, and I had difficulty keeping our heads above water; already she
seemed unconscious. A bush scratched my face, and I
grabbed it before realizing that it was rooted in a moving bank. A camelota, I thought with relief, but for a
moment I was too tired to scramble up and, clinging
tightly to the bush, drifted with it. Finally, after an
effort that even at the time seemed unreal, and that
made my ears ring and every bone in my body strain like
wet wood, I heaved Pancha up onto the ragged bank
and crawled after her. Her chain cut across my face,
stunning me. For a long time I lay in some grass, unable

to move, until a cloud of sand flies attacked my bare feet, stinging me awake. Pancha was sitting up, breathing heavily, her face more glazed than usual. I looked around. We were on a torn bit of land, moving rapidly down the middle of the river like some prelapsarian raft. Dozens of gaudy parakeets and cockatoos fluttered and sang above us in a clump of graceful trees; between its canes and rushes, the camelota was luxuriant with water hyacinths and waxy white lilies. Through the trees on the left I saw the profile of the earthworks at Curupayty, fast disappearing; canoes—some decked out with greenery to disguise them as camelotas—cutters, small schooners and other little boats were moored along the bank, but none were launched, I saw with relief. We passed under the chain. Some of the leaves of the trees were torn off in its loops, but the momentum of the camelota continued; none of the attached torpedoes exploded. That was one danger past. I knew from the maps that the river swept around a bend at this point, although the carrizal was deeply flooded—water seeped through the friable banks easily —and appeared, in places, miles wide. At any moment the camelota was likely to break up into clumps of earth, or crash ashore in some inexplicable movement of the current. Still, there was a chance, if its clay was deep and thick enough, of riding it all the way down to Buenos Aires, where jaguars from a thousand miles upriver sometimes came ashore. However, by that point we'd probably be starved, I thought, looking doubtfully at the wild birds. I suspected I wouldn't have any luck catching them for food. I'd have to make sure the Brazilian fleet rescued us before we either slipped by them or were cannonaded as a suspect torpedo raft.

Pancha was pulling up the hyacinths and twining

them in her hair, which was frizzy and coiled full of
tangles that only scissors could get out now. By daylight
she looked terribly unhealthy, with bruised blue
patches on her skin, especially under her eyes, and
scabby areas of rash on her arms and neck. All the food
had been lost with the canoe. I would have to go fishing
today, after all, I thought, oddly remembering the
slightly sour smell of Diaz's body as I climbed over him
in the dark. I stared at the thick, muddy water, wonder-
ing whether I could catch a fish with the only hairpin
left in my wet hair. There were plenty of worms in the
grass, probably driven up by the increasing damp and
the erosion under the island. But there were no matches
for a fire. Everything on the island was damp. Beads of
dew hung on every reed or blade of coarse grass. It was
strangely peaceful. I had an almost overwhelming desire
to fall asleep, for the birds sang continually, like the
sound of rain falling, and the murmur of the rushing
river seemed to echo the rush of my own blood.
Pancha's hair was full of flowers now. She attached
them to every part of her dress that she could, even
poking the stems into the little area where starvation
had caused her flesh to recede from the tight fetters. I
watched her idly, trying to keep awake, for I knew if I
slept it would be for hours and I would wake to find the
island far below the fleet, or my body coiling underwater. Pancha stuck a final flower in her chemise, then
stood up, the chain wrapped around her neck—it, too,
decorated by a few flowers—and began dancing.

"Please, Pancha, don't!" I rose to stop her, but she
backed away, still moving awkwardly but rhythmically,
her wet dress flapping a little in the wind, the petals of
the water hyacinths fluttering or spinning away. It was a

quadrille. She hummed, her bound feet hobbling a little forward, a little back, the chain swinging in a long line across her body from neck to ankle. She lifted her hands, as in the ballet, and pirouetted, almost losing her balance as she came around to face me again, smiling. One of the sores on her lip had broken, leaving a trace of blood across her cheek.

"Pancha, please stop! You're too weak to dance; you don't have to dance!"

She moved away again, closer to the edge of the camelota, into higher grass where it was more difficult to turn. A frog, croaking, hopped away. Two lean water snakes flicked into the river. "Don't go so close to the edge," I called, afraid to go nearer because of the way she had backed off. "It's dangerous!"

She waved her arms out again, turning, turning. Suddenly she shrieked, and in a flash had disappeared from my sight. A large portion of the bank where she was standing had broken off. For a few seconds I stood frozen, a scream collecting in my throat like fragments of broken glass. I reeled forward dizzily, but it was too late. Far from my reach I saw her black hair spread on the water, hyacinths still entwined in the strands. The current sucked her under. A white swallow dipped as if to peck her eye, then wheeled back up to the sky. I watched him until he was a speck against the sun's glare.

# Nine

Another piece of the island broke off with a sucking sound; one of the thin trees leaned steeply, dragging its tasseled head in the water. Its roots bubbled up from the damp clay, and a fissure split even wider across the whole camelota. The tree went over, its white, dead roots upended like a nest of blind snakes, and that portion of the camelota crumbled away. I would never make it down to the fleet. Already the other trees bent askew as their roots, with deep, wet moans, strained from the soil under the water's immense pressure. The river current tended toward the Chaco side, and there was a chance I might swim ashore; but I knew I couldn't hope to survive in that dead, uninhabited area without food and water. On the opposite bank the water had seeped through to flood the carrizal, which here appeared as a shining lake beside the river, divided in places by long waves of high ground, the *lomas,* on which grew thorn thickets or high, reedy grass. Then, ahead, on the edge of the river I spotted several canoes. At this distance the men were only black silhouettes, but almost certainly they were Paraguayan soldiers out catching fish for breakfast. I hesitated a moment—after all, it meant returning—before yelling. My voice broke hoarsely. I seemed to swallow glass; then it rang out high and clear, disembodied. I waved my hands over my head. The parakeets in the bobbing trees screamed away. An ash-colored heron, hidden in the reeds, stumbled into flight, then some wild pigeons and swallows. I was nearly opposite the men before they heard me, for my voice seemed to be caught in eddies of wind and thrown back at me. At once two of the canoes shot out on the river, as if it were a race, and before I could catch my breath a short, bare-chested soldier in white trousers was helping me into the first canoe while the men of the second shouted encouragement. Dizzily I watched the camelota spin by in the current while the soldiers, with swift, practiced strokes, paddled toward the bank. Crouched down in the bottom of the canoe beside a wire creel full of long, silvery fish, still thrashing at intervals, was Monkey-Snout. He handed me a blanket which I wrapped around me, shivering, nodding thanks but unable to speak. My clothes were almost dry, but there was a chill like a pillar of ice inside me.

"They've been looking for you all over camp."

"I got lost," I stuttered. "Then the bank where I was standing broke off . . . "

He bent his lean, nut-shaped face closer to mine. "You must have been far upstream."

I shrugged, watching the approaching shore, where seven turkey buzzards—I counted them—roosted in a clump of dead, white trees. Behind the trees stretched the smooth waters of the carrizal.

"Also, Pancha Garmendia is missing."

"It was probably another miracle," I said, unable to keep a bitter edge from my voice.

He nodded. "Of course. I told Lopez that. She has not escaped, Great Father, but in the night an angel appeared—in a flash of light, blinding the whole camp—taking her with him."

I looked at him. His small brown eyes blinked flat and still.

"Already," he added, "a woman touching the tree where Pancha was chained has been cured of goiter."

When we reached the shore, I got out and stood unsteadily on the strip of sand where men from the other canoes were already cooking fish. Monkey-Snout must have told them something about me, for none spoke to me or approached me except to offer a slab of hot white *surubi* on a piece of bark. Monkey-Snout had a contraption of wood and wire in his pocket, and from the men's conversation I realized that he divined fish with it; they wanted him to divine salt, but he shook his head over and over, sadly, the louder and more excited they became.

I felt him watching my silence. I was sitting on a log, unable to speak, barely able to chew the fish, although I could not entirely explain my numbness to myself. It was not my usual ironic perception, creating a little rift between myself and my behavior in a personal situation. Shock, I thought; of course, I'm in shock. I concentrated on the texture of the fish, the way the fibers broke up in my mouth, and on the rough burn on the side of my tongue from the first bite. A file of ants trickled over my feet, and I shook them off. Above me, orchids and small pink bromelias trailed over acacias from bough to bough. The sun grew hotter, and when I shifted my feet on the sand, it burned pleasantly.

Monkey-Snout brought me *yerba maté*. "We can take you in the canoe to Curupayty, or you can walk back from here—this loma cuts between Laguna Chichi and Laguna Lopez to the marsh before Paso Pucu—you know your way from there."

"I'd rather walk."

He pointed behind me. "Keep on the high ground."

I drained my gourd, then wrapped the blanket over my head to keep off the sun and the periodic swarms of sand flies. Every possible access to the Allied camp was thoroughly guarded by a battery of guns or a well-defended trench, so I had no choice except to head back to Paso Pucu. The foliage of the loma, which rose several feet above the flooded water of the carrizal, varied from high seas of reedy grass to boskets of thorn trees or tall palms strangled with brilliant creepers. I was exhausted by the time I reached the camp, and trudged slowly past the long mud barracks with their thatched or corrugated iron roofs to the women's huts. The rising, sinking wail of the spinning wheel sounded a long way off. Outside the doors of many of the huts, old women with cigars in their mouths sat spinning or weaving at wooden looms; others had big pots of dye boiling, where the finished wool or cotton was dipped red or blue or yellow before being sewn into ponchos or shirts. Children were running about turning cartwheels, while young girls in torn blouses and yellowing petticoats bent over sewing. Other women scraped hides stretched on large frames to make them thin enough for trousers, or cut carpets, sent down from the Club National in Asunción and the railroad station, into ponchos, since the spinners and weavers could not keep up with the need. In the distance I heard the weird ring of the *túrútútú* horns, which meant the fleet was moving up to bombard Curupayty again; sometimes at night when they moved up it was pleasant to watch the shells' trajectory by the gleaming fuses. Always the first gun in the battery to fire back was "Christian," so called because it was made of melted church bells.

When I pushed back the faded carpet hanging over the door of my hut, I was surprised to find a girl swinging in my hammock. She sat up, stopping the hammock with her foot as I entered. I gasped, for a moment thinking it was Pancha Garmendia. Her long dark hair tangled over her shoulders; the clean white dress she wore only seemed to emphasize her blue, emaciated skin, every vein standing prominent in her neck and hands. Dark patches washed across her skin below her eyes and under her hollow cheekbones, as if she had fallen face down into her own shadow and some of it had permanently stuck.

"You've forgotten me," she said flatly. "I'm Rosalita, Pancha's friend."

"Rosalita!"

"They let me go today; I don't know why." She lifted her skirt away from her ankles, which were puffed, white and scabby. "Do you think those scars will ever go away? I wanted to dance, though. It's like flying to walk without irons. But I'm so tired." She lay back in the hammock, and I saw that she clutched a tricolored sash in one hand. "I'm to fight with a lance, they say."

I had a half bottle of wine that Diaz had given me, and

I poured her a glass. "Here, drink this." She didn't seem strong enough to hold it, so I tilted it against her lips.

After a few sips she turned her head away. "I have to go find the lancers. I have to train."

"You're not strong enough. Just stay here," I added firmly, trying not to show her my actual despair. "It'll be all right. They'll leave you alone now."

She shook her head. "I'm to train, they said, so I can die in battle. I think they forgot why I was there." She sighed. "Did they torture Pancha?"

"No. I tried to escape with her last night, but she drowned. We were on a camelota and a piece broke off."

She looked at me. "That's better, though . . . yes. You can't escape."

"I almost succeeded." I sat down on a crate. "They don't know about Pancha. They think she flew to heaven. The tree she was chained to effects cures."

She smiled slightly. "I had a dream about an angel— maybe it was her. I used to think I *was* Pancha, sometimes."

"Do you know why they released you?"

"They forgot. New prisoners kept coming." She coughed painfully, her hands clasped around her throat as if she were strangling herself. "I had a shelter made out of my shawl and some reeds." She removed her hands from her throat, looking at them. In the dim yellow light of the hut they appeared transparent, like aspen leaves. "They threw us scraps of meat, bones, a little mandioca or chipa . . . the irons were the worst. Some poor old men had three or four, and had to crawl like babies. Oh, my hands are so ugly."

"When you start eating better—"

"But I was lucky." She sat up, her hair falling over her eyes. "They only flogged me that once, and never used nails. . . . Others—" She turned her head away. "I don't want to think about it."

"Lie down. I'll bring you some food." I touched her shoulder. She lay back and closed her eyes. Her lids were thin and reddened, veined like the map of some strange terrain. I pulled my piece of mosquito netting over her and went out to the stew pots with a clay dish. When I came back, I woke her, forcing her to eat, although she had no taste for any food and kept wrinkling her nose. I watched until she fell asleep again.

Sometime toward dawn I was awakened by shouts; at first I thought soldiers had come for Rosalita, who still slept soundly in my hammock. I crawled off my pallet and stuck my head out the door. The bright moonlight crusted four naked soldiers with silver sparkles, as if they had turned to salt. I rubbed my eyes, thinking I was dreaming, almost expecting to see a unicorn sail down from the sky. The four soldiers did not vanish. "Señora Companion!" they cried. "Come quickly; it's General Diaz—!"

"What?"

"General Diaz has been hurt."

When I ran out, after dressing hurriedly, the four soldiers danced excitedly in a group of whispering women, who handed them shirts and drawers. One old woman with a dark simian face kept crossing herself on the nose, heart and shoulders, over and over. "General Diaz! General Diaz!" Every mouth babbled his name when they saw me. "He's asking for you, Señora Companion," a soldier shouted, hitching up a pair of tight leather trousers.

"How did it happen?"

The soldier shook away the two women smoothing his shirt. "He led fifty naked cavalrymen across the Estero." He wiped shimmering sweat off his face. On his left cheek two long hairs sprouted from a mole. "We fell on the rear of a sleeping battalion with our swords, until some other soldiers came up with guns. As we were riding off, the battery fired. A 13-inch shell burst overhead, almost cutting off Diaz's leg—you've never seen so much blood! The parrot-kissers!" He spat hard. "They've sent for the English doctor. Go, Señora."

I hurried across camp to Diaz's hut; everywhere moonlight laved the trees and shrubs. My hair flowed around my shoulders. I felt as though I were weaving through some medieval tapestry, a needle, pulling a silver cord. Or I was the heroic figure, the princess, repeated over and over in scenes of colored thread. But if I ever turned my head, everything would unravel behind me. My whole past suddenly seemed like ancient threads. As long as I looked ahead, I could *suppose* the embroidered scenes behind me: my father, with his stern eyes and rusty black frock coat; my mother, peeling apples in front of the fire while snow lashed against the shutters; myself, in an ivory silk wedding dress, my hair wound in eight braids, turning before a dim mirror, pretending for a moment that I loved the man I was about to marry because I was an orphan and he a strange, older cousin—strange because he had been away for several years—a minister like my father . . .

Now I could smell the tapestry burning, thread after

thread. The corrugated iron roofs of the barracks gleamed as if a mysterious snow had fallen over the jungle. Ahead, my tapestry stretched out of sight. But if I looked behind, I would see the heat moving over the cloth, the threads tinged brown before charring black. I shivered, caught in the grip of the fantasy. Some invisible birds high in a tree I passed under stirred like wind; ahead, I was glad to see torches and a crowd of men around Diaz's hut, for the sensation that nothing existed behind me had gripped me so strongly that I could feel fibers unraveling from my head, as if the fire had reached the heroic figure before the final actions of her life could be completed.

The men outside the hut silently let me pass. Many of them were bare to the waist, as if they had pulled their trousers on hastily, and several still had their swords out, swishing them over their heads restlessly as if the sky swam with ghosts. The *whish! whish!* of the blades sounded mournful. Lieutenant Urdapilleta knelt near the door, his eyes wet. "They've amputated his leg," he whispered as I grabbed the hanging carpet. He put his hands over his face, shaking his dark hair. "Oh, God, Señora! Doctor Skinner gave him half a bottle of whiskey until he started singing. Then he cut it off at the thigh . . . it took three men to hold him." He lifted his face, which gleamed silvery like a fish dipped out of the water, and held out his hand, bleeding slowly as if from a deep wound. "I had to bite myself to keep from screaming, too."

"Is it all right to go in?"

He nodded. "He passed out. I couldn't bear to look anymore, but I couldn't leave; I . . . " He buried his face again, sobbing. I touched him on the shoulder and went into Diaz's hut. He lay on his heavy four-poster bed, covered with blankets except for his head, which was propped on a pillow, his skin almost as white as the fresh pillow cover. Lanterns burned yellow and rose around him but seemed powerless to affect that color, as if the salt-white moonlight had bleached him forever. His lower lip was twisted back under his teeth, and he breathed in a ragged whistle, as if the blankets oppressed him. Both his beard and his hair were plastered down with sweat like pieces of felt. Skinner, the English doctor from Humaitá, whom I had never seen before although he sometimes rode over to visit Madame Lynch, nodded his tanned, gopher face with its triangle of front teeth and turned back to his instrument case.

The Paraguayan doctor, a plump young man with fuzzy hair, was washing the blood from his hands in a pan of water. "He called you earlier, Señora, many times. Now he's sleeping."

"Will he be all right?"

The young doctor frowned, his lips rounded in a nervous little O. He looked at Skinner, who said crisply, "Of course."

"Has Lopez been notified?"

"Yes." The younger doctor pointed to a long object on the floor behind him, wrapped in white linen, streaked with blood at one end. "He's ordered a small coffin, for the leg." He pulled over the cane chair. "He may be waking soon, Señora. Perhaps you will wait?"

I sat down. The chair was close to Diaz's face, so I could watch the prickling of his nose as he breathed. I remembered the night I had sat beside Doctor McPherson. I put my hand on Diaz's forehead, which burned under the cool film of sweat across it. At my touch he turned his head sideways, his lips moving with a sucking sound as if he were whispering in his sleep. After a while his eyes opened, but they appeared to be glazed hard as marbles, and I doubted if he was seeing anything. Some kind of clear mucus had gathered in the corners. He ran his tongue around his lips, which he must have bitten in his pain, for they were discolored blue. In a few minutes I had the impression that his eyes had focused, for there seemed to be light behind them. He pulled his long-fingered, calloused hand from under the blankets, scratching his cheek. A mosquito lit on his forehead. I brushed it off. The movement of my hand attracted him. He frowned, looking at me. "I meant to  .  .  . " His voice, deep and stony for those three words, disappeared in a soft gurgle of phlegm. Doctor Skinner walked over, buttoning his coat. "Don't talk, Diaz." He pointed his yellow, nicotined finger at me. "Don't encourage him, please."

"That orange; I keep  .  .  . " Diaz's voice rose and died again. He put his hand on his throat. "Some bran—"

"Give him a glass of brandy, Baltazar."

The Paraguayan doctor brought over a small glass, put his hand under Diaz's head, and poured a little brandy into his mouth. It seemed to burn the phlegm from Diaz's throat. "Where is it?" he asked me huskily.

I looked at him, puzzled, but Baltazar said softly, "Over there. Lopez has ordered a little coffin, General."

"I want to see  .  .  . " The phlegm caught him again. He coughed harshly. "I want to see it, Skinner!" he called to the other doctor. "Let me see my leg."

Skinner's peppery brows flashed together. He

glanced over his shoulder at the bundle on the floor. "You need to sleep, Diaz. I'm going to see if I can get some kind of pain-killing herb from that fellow—what's his name?—Monkey-something, they call him. We're out of opium." He picked up his case hastily. "Good night, Mrs. Companion. Don't let him talk so." He nodded at Baltazar; at the same time Diaz cried "Urdapilleta!" in a hoarse, pained voice. Skinner and Urdapilleta bumped against each other in the doorway, muttering apologies. I caught a glimpse of men and torches outside. Someone sang "Lord have mercy! Lord have mercy!" in a high, quavering voice. A couple of dead mosquitoes were stuck on Urdapilleta's still-wet face, which he wiped quickly with his sleeve before facing Diaz.

"I want to see my leg. I never expected . . . " Diaz closed his eyes, the lids fluttering like moths. "There's a big mosquito bite just above the ankle, and a blister under . . . " He sobbed suddenly, covering his mouth with his hand. " 'Fucking blister,' I said. How will I ride, Urdapilleta? Off at the thigh?" He turned his head away. I felt my eyes fill with tears, but unlike Urdapilleta, whose tears fell freshly over his cheeks, my tears always fell inside, drowning my mouth and nose with hot, salty water. Diaz clutched his blanket. "Let me see it."

Urdapilleta and Baltazar brought the bundle over to the head of the bed between them and laid it across Diaz; they unwrapped the foot, which was shriveled white, with streaks of dried blood over the stony, crooked toes. I turned away. Diaz sobbed, low in the chest at first, then louder and louder. Distressed, the two men rewrapped the leg and laid it back on the floor.

"General, General," Urdapilleta repeated insistently. "Two weeks. In two weeks you'll have a sword in your hand. In two weeks, General. You'll cut them up. General, no, in two weeks. Two weeks, General . . . " Finally he could bear it no longer and ran, hiccuping, outside.

# Ten

I dreamed about huge crocodiles swimming beside me
in clear water, occasionally surfacing, the water spraying off their long white teeth. Others nuzzled grey
snouts against my legs as I swam desperately on, my feet
lashing up and down in the hard, heavy water. Then I
was swimming with General Diaz, who kept sobbing
that his leg had been eaten and that he was about to
drown. He clung to my arm. Down in the mud a creature
stirred, some kind of scaly lizard with Doctor McPherson's head sprouting from the green body. Bubbles rose
to the surface from his mouth. Beside him swam a girl
with skin flaking off her bones like baked fish, and dark,
swirling hair. Pancha Garmendia. Slowly Diaz sank
under the water, pulling me with him. He rolled on top
of Doctor McPherson, who lashed with his forked tail
until twists of yellow mud rose in the water, blinding me.
When the mud settled, I saw that Diaz too had grown a

long grey-green tail. He swam rapidly toward me, flicking it like a whip around my body. He fastened his teeth in my neck, gnawing deeply until the water colored red with my blood, and I fainted, awakening in the hot, close sickroom, on the hard cane chair where I had fallen asleep, my chin, pressed against the reed wall, bitten nastily by the invisible insects breeding there. Doctor Skinner stood in the corner talking quietly to Lopez, who was closing the latch on a small silver casket set with several enamel pictures of the Virgin; she was rising to heaven, holding a baby, speaking with an angel and combing the hair that dripped from her gold halo.

When he noticed me awake, Lopez turned with a face paler than usual, as if he had scrubbed it too hard: "An infection has set in, the doctor says." He sighed, coming over to look at Diaz, who breathed with a high, whistling rattle, his lids closed, a wet rag on his forehead. Mosquito netting had been drawn over the four posters, and through the white gauze he appeared like a wax figure, except for one hand, which turned on the blankets as he slept. The blankets were pushed down almost to his waist; his nipples were shriveled grey bumps protruding through a mat of black hair. "Poor Diaz," Lopez said, touching the palm of his hand against the mosquito netting. "Sometimes I think—" He squeezed his eyes shut. They shone watery when he opened them. "He's more to me than my own brothers."

"There's not much hope, then?"

"No." He sucked on his lower lip. "Not with the infection, the doctor says."

Diaz stirred, suddenly opening his eyes. The hand turned over on the blankets again.

"He's been delirious," Lopez said softly. "Talking

about some orange, some boy he claims he killed. . . . We brought him an orange, thinking he was thirsty, but he cried and hid his face." Lopez put his nose against the mosquito netting. "Jose?" His voice stuttered. "Jose, can you hear me? It's Francisco."

Diaz moved his lips vaguely.

"Jose?"

"Put me in a boat." Diaz's voice bubbled up from a distance.

"What? In a boat?"

Diaz twitched his hand. "*Agua abajo . . .* put me in a boat. I want to float down to the sea, Francisco."

Lopez took a silver capsule from his pocket. "This is a piece of the cross of Saint Thomas, Jose." He reached under the mosquito netting, putting the capsule loosely in Diaz's open, unmoving palm. "I've never gone anywhere without it; I . . . I want you to have it, Jose. I'm praying for you, Jose."

"*Agua abajo,*" Diaz repeated. The silver capsule rolled from his palm onto the blankets. "I want to float into the sea, Francisco; I never . . . " His voice disappeared in a gurgle of mucus. He coughed, wincing. "I never saw the sea; I never went downriver like you, to see Napoleon. I used to hear about, about . . . " He swallowed hard, putting his hand slowly on his throat. "I want to float into London, to see the Tower and those bears . . . was it you who told me about those bears, Francisco, or was it Molly? Look at those sparrows!" He pointed beyond the mosquito netting. Involuntarily Lopez and I both turned. "English sparrows; see their green feathers?"

Lopez crossed himself. He knelt down at the foot of the bed, his face pressed against the sheets. His folded hands trembled. At that moment Elisa Lynch, a purple shawl over her head, pressed into the tiny room with a basin of steaming soup. Diaz, catching sight of her, began to twitch and chortle in his throat. I reached a hand under the netting to restrain him. His skin burned. "Victoria!" he croaked hoarsely. "It's Queen Victoria; look! Your majesty, let me . . . " He raised his head off the pillows, then dropped it back in exhaustion, his cheeks so hollow they appeared smashed in with a hammer. "Forgive me, your majesty; I wanted to kneel like Francisco." He closed his eyes. Elisa Lynch winced, spilling soup over her hands. She looked at me with wet eyes.

Lopez jumped up, pulling the bowl of soup from her hands. "Let me feed him, Elisa. He's delirious." He splashed soup over the front of his uniform as he swished away the mosquito netting. "Jose?" He dipped up a spoonful. I was afraid he would spill it over Diaz's bare chest, but he kept his hand steady, the bowl held away from the bed. I lifted Diaz's sweat-soaked head. He swallowed one spoonful of soup, but then turned his head away. "Jose? Jose?" Lopez rapped the spoon against the bowl. Diaz's chest trembled up and down delicately as he breathed. A mosquito buzzed in under the open netting. Lopez handed me the bowl and slapped it expertly between his hands. The sharp crack startled Diaz, who made an inarticulate noise.

" 'Attack.' Didn't he say 'Attack'?" Lopez grinned at me.

"I didn't hear."

"He said 'Attack'! Elisa, he said 'Attack'! When the Brazilians saw that horde of naked cavalrymen pouring down on them—" He grabbed Diaz's limp hand, squeezing it. "Five more men like Jose and . . . !" He pulled the mosquito netting back into place. He began pacing back and forth. Elisa Lynch sat on the cane chair, her chin on her hands, swishing her foot back and forth. As I set the bowl of soup on the floor, Diaz suddenly screamed, "No! No!" A shock ran through everybody in the room. Doctor Skinner put his face close to the mosquito netting.

"No," Diaz moaned. He waved his hand in front of his face, as if something were there. "Don't fire. No, not yet. Let me eat my orange." He closed his eyes. I covered my face with my hands but kept staring through my fingers, watching his ragged breath, in and out. Once he opened his eyes, but they were glazed and saw nothing. His chest heaved less rapidly; then it did not move at all.

"He's asleep," Lopez whispered.

Doctor Skinner reached under the netting for the limp wrist. "He's dead."

As I walked through the swamp, I glimpsed a red ibis on one leg in a pool of water. Lately the men had begun to shoot them with bodoques, although their flesh tasted pungently of ginger, and old superstitions were whispered around the table or campfire: If you ate an ibis, you could never be completely happy again; at a wedding the dulces would taste like ashes; at a festival the wine would turn bitter in your mouth; your lover's lips would sour your tongue like a rancid cheese. I had eaten an ibis and now believed these superstitions. Tomorrow Diaz would be buried in a huge, elaborate ceremony in the cemetery. Since yesterday morning, the gun "Christian" had fired every half hour. Instinctively I stopped under a fat, waxy palm; off my path to the left, black mud oozed with a nervous, sucking sound, as though the oily light streaming in patches through the trees were slowly evaporating it. The gun fired on time. Scissor-birds, ovenbirds, paddy-birds, I repeated to myself, although I had no way of telling what kinds of birds shook invisibly in the leaves above me or dipped a white or blue wing. I had moved in a numb, mechanical round since that moment when Doctor Skinner had drawn the bedsheet over the face I'd suddenly realized I loved. I moved deeper into the swamp, not really caring where the path led, since it could only wind within the wide enciente, emerging eventually at a trench or battery. The light grew greyer the deeper I went, and as a consequence the few patches of open sunlight dazzled my eyes. Wherever I looked, my sight was limited by the multitudinous tangle of trees and the thorny creepers and bushes submerging them, like barnacles crusting a ship's hulk. The air was so humid that I felt as though I were actually in the sea, making my way slowly over some ancient sandy bottom. I was drenched with sweat; my cotton dress stuck to my back, unpeeling painfully when I wiggled my shoulders. Insects trilled and pinged in a metallic counterpoint. A half hour later "Christian" fired again. A little space of strange silence followed the boom; then the insects resumed piping. I thought of Diaz's hand turning slightly as he slept. He had touched me so gently. "No, no, it's hardly noticeable; a few bumps; they'll go away." I had coiled back from him at first, projecting my revulsion into his every gesture; at the same time I had held the romantic fantasy that his love might eventually cure me. Now, inexplicably, the rash had disappeared. I was cleansed, like Job, at some whim of God, who had picked the very point when it didn't matter, when I would gladly have run naked before the whole horrified army.

Ahead of me on the path I heard heavy thrashing. Before I could turn and run, Calvin emerged, stooping, through a swinging wall of foliage. He didn't look surprised to see me. He had a pistol in his belt, a cartridge belt across his torn embroidered shirt front, and carried a new Spencer rifle. The purple kepi was pulled low over his eyes. He had not shaved in several days. My stomach tightened. I had deliberately avoided the capilla where he worked.

"Molly! You got my message, didn't you? Where've you been?"

"Yes. I didn't wish to see you." I brushed my hair from my damp forehead, looking at his shoulder, for his eyes shone excitedly as if rubbed with grease.

"Then you risked being blown up. I'm glad I caught you."

"Blown up?" I looked at his rifle.

"Don't go to the cemetery tomorrow. Be sick; anything. Understand?"

I shook my head. The smell of crushed leaves drifted in the warm air. "Diaz's funeral . . . " I stuttered.

"Tomorrow Lopez, his entire staff, and maybe a fifth of his army will be in that cemetery to bury carrion." Calvin stepped closer, lowering his voice. "I'm going to blow them all to shit."

I must have gasped, for he laughed, tapping me with the butt of his rifle. "I would have blown you up, too, Molly, except for this chance."

"All?" I found my voice, but my mouth felt dry. "There'll be several thousand people in that cemetery tomorrow. You're crazy."

"The charges are laid. General Bruguez will—"

"Bruguez!" I turned sharply away from him. *"He's* your traitor? That pig!"

"Of course he's a pig. Lopez is a pig."

My lips moved numbly. "You can't blow up thousands of people. It's one thing to kill Lopez—"

"Is it? So now you approve of that, huh?" His brown teeth flashed. "What's the difference, Molly?"

"Calvin!"

"It's a moral question, Molly. You were always lousy at them." His face twisted. "You never shed a tear when your father died, but you wore black for a year." His knuckles tightened on the rifle. "You married me, but you never loved me; not one iota. . . . I always knew that. But I loved you, Molly. Don't look at me that way; yes, I loved you until I hated you, but you never loved me. But you didn't have the guts to say so; you didn't have the guts to say, 'Calvin, I hate you; I'm leaving,' even when I started drinking and my hands trembled before sermons, and I couldn't do it because of your rash; there was no chance of children. That's why I went down to the war, Molly, in the first place; to give you your chance." He pinched the cloth of my sleeve, careful not to touch my skin. I was too frozen to move. "The only reason you followed me to Paraguay was your damn rigid sense of—" He broke off, releasing my sleeve as if it were a snake. "I don't know."

"Sense of what?" I faltered.

"Responsibility. But it has nothing to do with me, has it? Still, the old drunk's your husband, after all; even more important, he's your cousin, the man your father chose for you, the man just like your father. You always hated him, too—"

"Shut up!" I put my hands over my ears.

"You're soulless, Molly, absolutely soulless."

I took a deep breath. "I came to Paraguay because I wanted to see you for one more time, to be completely free of you forever."

"You'll never be."

"I am. You can't tell me what goes on inside me anymore, because you're wrong. I'm nothing like that."

"You're like *that*—whatever you think I mean by *that*—exactly. Now go back to Paso Pucu and get sick."

"Do you think I'm going to let you—?"

"Of course." He held out the rifle. "If I thought you had the courage to stop me, I'd shoot you. But you don't. Lopez would never believe you weren't implicated. He'd *kill* you, and anyone who had anything to do with you. You know what a monster he is, Molly. Christ, there's a rumor now that he's arrested Inocencia, his own sister! And what about Bliss? How long before he arrests *me*, Molly? And you?"

"Bruguez is a monster, too."

"Bruguez is a puppet. You slip him on like a glove and wiggle your fingers."

"And maybe find you've strangled yourself. What's Washburn doing, meanwhile?"

"Someone has to be in the capital. Now get out of here, Molly. Get sick! Stay away from that cemetery, whatever you do, unless you relish exploding into bits, with your feet on one side of the river and your hair and fingers on the other." He laughed, rubbing the muzzle of the gun with his soft, stained thumb. "Now get. I might decide to shoot you anyway."

I turned and hurried down the path. Under the thick film of sweat that covered my skin, goose bumps pricked. I tripped over a snakelike grey root, falling to my knees. It was a moment before I could stand again, for a wave of nausea caught me deep in the stomach, traveling rapidly up to my throat. I closed my eyes. Because of the sharp sunlight, black shapes danced on the insides of my lids, causing macabre visions, as if the tunnel down to my imprisoned dreams opened a crack. A thin, strange cat of red and orange velvet whirled past amid a cloud of spiders. Diaz's white, fleshless fingers reached up from a hole. Calvin took off his black hat to show me the whiskey bottle balanced on his bald spot. I shook myself, dusting off my hands as I got up, readjusting my eyes to the violent white sun. The velvet cat recalled some recent dream. I passed into a corridor of heavy green shade, trying to remember: The cat had attacked me when I reached toward it in the dream. A stinging pain ran up my arm. It was Calvin's cat; that was it. But the cat was Satan. I remembered pleading with Bishop Palacious for some holy water so I could drown the creature, but Calvin kept it locked in his room with gunpowder. I didn't understand the dream, or remember all of it, except that I had awakened that morning with unpleasant feelings.

When I emerged on the marshy plain before Paso Pucu, I carefully circled the cemetery on its little hill. The tiny, colored houses and usual stone angels stood in silhouette against a sky washed colorless by the heat. Calvin was going to blow it up. Weeds shifted and clicked dry stems against the iron railing as I passed by. A lone soldier manned the telescopes. He waved at me as I looked up, his white trousers puffing in a breeze that crossed the hill but did not dip into lower areas. I imagined the explosion, the ground breaking open in a black geyser of dirt, the yellow bones of the dead spewing out amidst the torn, twisted bodies of the living, who had one single bird's-eye view of the whole camp as blood poured from their thighs and stomachs and their sight darkened. I saw Doctor McPherson's skull and covered my face with my sleeve. Yet it was impossible to inform Lopez. On that Calvin was quite right. I too had heard the rumor that Lopez had arrested, or was about to arrest, his own brothers and sisters. Once I had even heard him speculate that his mother was a spy. Elisa Lynch had laughed—only she could laugh at him—until he turned shamefully red, but nevertheless . . . He would torture me. I would be forced to provide the names of innocent people like Rosalita, Lieutenant Saguier and Doctor Skinner. I would kill Calvin. I would take a gun and crawl through the jungle tonight. I had a vision of the jungle at night—a black, breathing wall, laced with spiders and poisonous orchids. Yet I had been in the jungle before at night. I looked at my hand, brownish-yellow from the sun, the ragged nails crusted with dirt. I would use Diaz's pistol, which Lopez had given me. I would pull the trigger, like so, the barrel against Calvin's sleeping head. I imagined the soft red and white mucus, shivering. What if I couldn't find him, anyway? Or if he had laid a time charge and events had slipped out of his control? Was that possible? I would go to the cemetery tomorrow in my hot, black bombazine. Standing by the grave under an old parasol, I would glance around at everyone's face, a little ironic smile on my own. At least I wouldn't spend the rest of my life tortured by guilt. No, I would run screaming from the cemetery at the last second; everyone would turn, astounded; I would be halfway down the hill before it exploded. A boulder would crack my head open.

I hurried past a cornfield where women with baskets

on their arms slowly gleaned the dusty stalks for forgotten ears. An honor guard of the women lancers would precede the coffin. That morning the girls had been washing their white dresses; as I entered the women's village, I saw the dresses hanging on a rope between two trees, ballooning with air, so that they might have been worn by invisible women. Rosalita sat on a big log outside my hut, sewing a sleeve in a cotton shirt. She looked up, smiling, when she saw me. She had washed her hair and it hung blue-black over her shoulders.

"They said I should sew. They said I wasn't strong enough to train, yet." The needle gleamed in her hand. "They've given me a hut, too. Somebody died of chain. A lot of people are dying of chain, the sergeant said. For a while she said all the women had to stay in the village because of chain."

I sat down beside her on the log. Once again the cemetery exploded in a vision, the gravestone angels flying headless to the river.

"What's chain?"

"What?" I shook myself. "I'm sorry; what did you say?"

"What's chain?"

"Lopez has forbidden anyone to use the word 'cholera.' He doesn't want to start a panic."

She blinked. "In the prison they say 'cholera.' . . . Oh, I've stuck myself." She put her thumb in her mouth for a second. "What's wrong?"

"Nothing."

She drew in her breath, hissing. "They're going to arrest me again?"

"No, no. Of course not. I've been having a lot of bad dreams, that's all."

She tacked her final stitch and shook out the shirt. "Dreams tell the future, if you dream them near morning. Did you dream near morning?"

"I don't remember."

"What was the dream?"

I shrugged. "Oh, I don't know."

"Last night I dreamed I was on fire; I was trapped in a huge flame." She turned her arm over, looking at it. "The hair on my arms was black as a bear's; my hair was like a rush candle. . . . I walked through the camp and people ran away screaming—why are you looking at me so?"

"What does it mean?" I asked hoarsely. In the distance the gun "Christian" fired. The grassy cemetery split open in my head.

Rosalita folded the shirt carefully in her lap. "All my dreams are such bad omens anymore, I don't think about them much."

"Rosalita, I wish—"

"What?" She tilted her pale, undernourished face. "Can I help?"

"No, no." I got up hastily, looking at her bruised, swollen feet. I would not involve her in this; she was just out of prison. It would not be fair. Her experiences had been so terrible that she whimpered in her sleep; tears poured from her eyes when she dreamed. "I must go work on my . . . the papers. They're serving the stew over there." I pointed. "Don't forget to eat."

When I reached Lopez's stockade, I saw two soldiers trying to feed dead rats to the jaguar. They stood back a few steps from the length of the chain and twisted them through the air by the tails. As they fell, thudding on soft grey bellies, the jaguar leapt, snarling. The rats must have sickened him, though, for he backed off. Back of Lopez's villa, behind the huge earthwork, the air smelled pleasantly of oranges and limes.

Without stopping to catch my breath, I rapped hard on Elisa Lynch's door. The usual wrinkled brown woman in a black skirt embroidered with red crosses admitted me silently. Elisa Lynch sat on the piano stool, her fingers poised over the keys as if I had interrupted her, although I had heard no music. The room had been redecorated in pea-green chintz, patterned with palm leaves and tiny mandarins, which covered the walls, the chairs, the divan and even the picture frames. An ornate marble mantelpiece had been installed. A plaster of Paris head of Medusa, white snakes coiling wildly, had been placed on a lace doily in the exact center, reflected double in the mirror. The bird cages had been painted white, and the birds made a shifting kaleidoscope with their colored feathers.

Elisa Lynch's tense face softened when she saw me. "If this were Paris, there would be silver ice coolers all over the room, and we could have a long chat, Molly." She wiped her forehead delicately. "It's too much effort to fan oneself, isn't it?"

"It's very hot."

"You look so agitated." She brought her fingers down with a loud, clanging jolt on the keys. "Please sit down. What's wrong?"

I sat down on the divan. My throat ached. "Nothing. I just . . . the funeral, I guess."

"Of course." Her lashes fluttered down. "He was your friend." She played with the amethyst on a velvet ribbon at her neck. "Francisco actually cried, Jose was so close to him." She began to chatter aimlessly, her voice unnaturally high, and I had the impression that she was listening for something, for her head tilted at unexpected sounds; her eyes ran nervously around the room. "It was such a silly accident. It shouldn't have happened." She pulled out a batiste handkerchief. "But Jose was always so impetuous, wasn't he? He gave the Brazilians quite a scare, you know. They thought it was the resurrection, bodies rising from the dead. And the way he asked to be sent *agua abajo* to London—ah, it's so sad!" She paused. "You look peaked, Molly. Are you getting ill?"

"No, not that; I—" Once again the cemetery exploded; I was lying in my hammock, covering my head with a blanket. "I'm not ill."

She flushed. "All right, then. You've been crying, though. Your eyes are all red."

"Elisa, I'm afraid."

"No!" She jumped up, her hands over her ears. "Don't tell me any more about that; don't say anything!" She squeezed her eyes so tightly that they appeared as only a fold of wrinkles across her face. "Please understand my position. I'm the mother of four children, *his* children—!" She leaned close to me, opening her eyes. Her breath smelled of spearmint. "Don't you think I'm afraid, too?" she whispered. "Sometimes I think Napoleon there"—she pointed to the parrot's cage, covered with the same green chintz that covered everything else in the room—"sometimes I think he repeats everything I say."

A knock sounded. She whirled away from me, her hand to her mouth. The old woman flashed past in the hallway. By the time Lopez, in an embroidered black overcoat, had entered the room, Elisa Lynch sat casually at the piano, picking out a few preliminary notes, humming.

"Look what I've got for you, Elisa."

She turned, smiling. "What is it?"

"A diorama. The Admiral sent it over. It was captured off that little gunboat we sank last month." He handed it to her, sniffling as though he'd caught a cold. "There are only four views, though." He grinned at me. "Of your civil war, Mrs. Companion. You should be interested. Fort Sumter, Vicksburg, the ironclads. Let me put the pictures in, Elisa; you can't see anything like that." He grabbed it away from her and inserted one of the translucent frames from his pocket. "Now go to the window."

She held it to the light. "That's Fort Sumter, Elisa."

"How small compared to Humaitá!" Handing me the diorama, she smiled, bright and hard. I looked at the silvery scene for only a moment before agreeing.

# Eleven

A few minutes after the old woman had served maté in little silver cups, Wisner de Morgenstern arrived. He swept off his big-brimmed straw hat immediately, turning it around agitatedly in his hands. A straight, handsome Roman nose, pale and delicately colored in contrast to his reddened skin, had been expertly modeled to his face. Lopez, grinning, picked up the jeweled knife with which he had just peeled an orange and snipped playfully at Wisner's nose. Wisner smiled weakly, but his hands trembled and he stuttered, attempting to speak.

"I thought you weren't going to be back here for another week," Elisa Lynch interrupted, putting her hand on his arm. "What's wrong, Wisner?"

"Elisa, your excellency, I . . . I . . . it was so . . . never—no, once before—but this . . . !" He coughed, covering his mouth with his handkerchief, holding the wax nose in place with one careful finger. "I couldn't believe it."

"Sit down, idiot." Lopez waved at a chair. "Don't keep babbling such nonsense. What's wrong?"

"They arrived four days ago. I took the first boat, you see; it shook me so, I—"

"What arrived?" Lopez grabbed another orange from the bowl on the table, cut a small circle in the top, and squeezed a stream of juice into his mouth.

"*Capincho* heads, five of them."

"Water hogs!" Elisa Lynch shook herself. "What?"

Wisner nodded. "Five severed water hog heads, beginning to rot. Wrapped in shawls."

"But why—?" Elisa Lynch poured maté for Wisner. "It's a stupid joke, but why . . . you're so upset, Wisner."

"Because of this." He tapped his nose. "Someone's mocking me." He sagged back in his chair. "Once before, in Venice, it happened. I told you about it— some urchins threw pigeons in my open window. The beaks had been severed. I thought about killing myself then."

"Was there a note, anything?" Lopez hooded his eyes. He picked up the decanter of brandy on the table, poured a finger into the hole he had cut in the orange, swished it back and forth, then squirted the brandy into his mouth. He wiped his lips with the back of his hand.

Wisner cleared his throat. "Yes, but it's ridiculous. The note is a joke, too."

"Who was it from?" Lopez tensed, his fingers tearing into the orange so that juice and brandy bubbled over them. "Tell me, Wisner."

"Washburn. But of course he—"

"The beast!" Lopez flung the orange across the room. It smacked the bust of Medusa in the eyes before tumbling against the vase of flowers in the false fireplace. "Only he . . . of course."

"But I don't believe Mr. Washburn . . . " Wisner began in a small, wavering voice.

"It was Washburn. Tyrant, inhuman pig! Those were effigies of his own face, Wisner."

"But I played whist with Mr. Washburn only the night before!"

"He suspects you're a spy; that's it."

"He knows I'm a spy. We've discussed it." Wisner pulled out his handkerchief again. "He's careful to say nothing in my presence. But Mr. Washburn is a gentleman!"

"He's a beast."

Wisner looked at the floor. "I can't believe it."

"This is it!" Lopez banged on the table, rattling the cups and spoons. "I can't have the United States minister insulting my advisors; why, doesn't he think I might use it as an excuse to declare war?" His face turned slightly blue. The red veins in his eyes looked like sharp wires. Elisa Lynch, nervously twisting her hands in her lap, abruptly got up and went to the parrot's cage, where she flicked off the cover and began to stroke its tailfeathers. Lopez looked at me. "What do you think, Mrs. Companion? *Is* Washburn capable of such vulgarity?"

"He's capable of . . . " The shadow of the cemetery hill, the way it appeared at twilight when you looked up, the tall angels almost lost in gloom, materialized before my eyes. "I think he could even—"

"What?" Lopez leaned closer. I seemed to see a

gleam of fire in his eyes, the explosion reflected. "What could he even, Mrs. Companion?"

"Blow, I mean, throw—throw dirt at his own mother's grave."

Lopez looked at me queerly. "He's vulgar."

"Yes." I shut my eyes. "Yes, yes."

"He's responsible for Diaz's death, too. Did you hear about Diaz, Wisner?"

"General Diaz is dead?" Wisner put his cup down with a clatter. "How did it happen?"

"Washburn again." Lopez's fingers, I saw when I opened my eyes, trembled as he played with the knife. Imperceptibly, I moved back a little from the table. Out of the corner of my vision I saw Elisa Lynch take her parrot out of the cage on her wrist. She was frowning. "We intercepted some letters written by Washburn to Mitre and Caxias. 'Kill Diaz,' he told them; 'whatever you do, kill Diaz.' So they shot him with a poisoned shell. The doctor cut off his leg, but it was too late; the poison had spread."

"This is terrible!" Wisner bit his thick lips. "Diaz was a real soldier! All the men loved him."

"I'm giving him a hero's funeral tomorrow. . . . Pig!" Lopez slashed the tabletop with his knife. I jumped halfway off my chair with an uncontrollable whimper. Wisner put his hands behind his back, as if Lopez had threatened to cut them off. The gesture recalled Lopez's first threat to me. I slipped my own hands under the folds of my skirt. "Take that, Washburn, and that!" Lopez laughed, slashing again and again at the table.

"Francisco, what are you doing?" Elisa Lynch, the green parrot on her shoulder, the chintz cage cover in one hand, turned fiercely on him. "You're ruining my table!"

"That bird, Elisa—it's poisoned. Kill it!"

"What?" She reached to protect the bird. As she did, Lopez leapt over a footstool, knocked her back, grabbed the ruffling parrot around the neck, and plunged his penknife into the feathers. "Empress!" the parrot blurted once, then shrieked loudly.

"Francisco! Francisco!" Elisa Lynch's voice, trapped in her throat, was hardly audible. Lopez stabbed the bird again, then flung it on the carpet, where it writhed its wings, making sobbing, human sounds before it was still. Wisner covered his face with a handkerchief. Elisa Lynch flung herself over the bird, rubbing her cheek against its bloody feathers.

"It's poisoned, Elisa; don't touch it! All these birds—" Lopez ran past me, where I sat paralyzed on my chair, to the wall of wicker bird cages. He sliced the leather thongs tying the doors shut. The birds, small blue parakeets, grey doves, Penelope birds and little green pigeons, whistled and chirped wildly; the parrots squawked, beating their wings. As Lopez flung the cages open, the birds flapped dizzily into the room, fluttering against the mirror and the windowpanes. He grabbed hold of a blue parakeet with a silver throat and strangled it to death. An apricot bird perched on my hair, its tiny sharp claws stinging me out of my paralysis, but when I attempted to stand up, darkness welled behind my eyes. Elisa Lynch raised her face, her cheek stained with the parrot's blood. Lopez had a big white cockatoo by one wing, his knife ready; a Penelope bird shrieked past his arm, startling him so that the cockatoo escaped and fled to the man-

telpiece, shaking its hurt wing. All over the room
birds dipped and chattered. Lopez opened another
cage, more slowly, to get at a parrot. "Francisco!"
Elisa Lynch screamed. "Stop it! Stop it!"

"Washburn poisoned them, Elisa." The parrot dipped
at his hand with its sharp yellow beak. He slammed the
cage door; in the next cage he found a magenta parakeet
which he squeezed so tightly in his hand that I buried
my face in my lap until he had finished. Again I was
afraid to move.

"Oh, my God, Francisco! Stop it! He never poisoned
them!"

"He poisoned your birds, Elisa, and sent Wisner a sack
of capincho heads."

"You did it yourself, Francisco; you know you did."
She stood up, the dead parrot wrapped in her skirt.
"You sent those heads to Wisner. You did it! You in-
cluded a note from Washburn." She reached up to touch
the blood on her cheek. "I saw you write the note, Francisco; I heard you give the orders for your horrid little
joke."

"Liar!" Lopez flung the suffocated bird against her
breast. She didn't flinch. "He's poisoned you, too, Elisa.
Like Bruguez. Did you know Bruguez is sick?" He
glimpsed Wisner, who still had his handkerchief to his
eyes. "Get the doctor, Wisner. Madame is poisoned."

Wisner slowly lowered his handkerchief. He had
turned pale and breathed heavily through his open
mouth. "Yes, yes, your excellency, yes, yes."

"Mrs. Companion, get her to bed, do you hear?"
Lopez ran to the window as Wisner shuffled out, opening
the blinds, shooing the birds out; he had dropped the
knife. Elisa Lynch tumbled the dead parrot from her
skirt onto the scarred table.

"Napoleon," she whispered, "Napoleon." She looked at Lopez, beating his arms at the remaining birds like some plump featherless turkey. As if in a daze she walked over to the desk, rolled the top open, fumbled in one of the tiny drawers inside, and pulled out a snuffbox. "Look, Francisco. Look at me!"

Lopez turned, frowning. The rage had drained out of him, leaving his skin strangely sallow, as if he had recovered from a fever. "You're sick, Elisa."

"Look at me." She pulled out a big speckled spider by one leg. "These are dead, but sometimes I eat live ones, too." She put the spider in her mouth and swallowed. Lopez winced. She pulled another spider from the box. Three of the dried brown legs crumbled off and drifted along her silk skirt. "Will you ever kiss me again, Francisco?"

"You're sick, Elisa. You need to be bled." With his clenched fist he knocked the snuffbox from her hand. It smashed on the floor; the hinged ivory lid broke off. Several small black spiders floated across the Oriental carpet, where it was difficult to see them in the swirling purple pattern. "Get her to bed, Mrs. Companion. We've got to get the poison out of her before it's too late." He opened the bedroom door. "Hurry up, put your arm around her—there. I'll see what's keeping that idiot Skinner. I know he hasn't gone back to Humaitá yet." He slammed the door once I had helped her to the bed, leaving us alone in the dim, blue-papered bedroom.

She shook off my arm. "It's all right."

"He's going to bleed you, did you hear?"

"He bleeds me whenever he thinks I've been difficult. I don't mind. Doctor Skinner sticks a few leeches on my arms and neck, but he always brings a vial of calf's or goat's blood, and I stay in bed a few days." She lay down, propping her head against the round bolster. "This time, I don't care. I wouldn't care if he drained every ounce of blood out."

I heard a scratch at the door; then a little boy with straight dark hair poked his head through a crack. "Mama? The parrot's sick. All the birds are gone away. I didn't do it, Mama."

"Mama's sick, Teodoro. Go away now."

The boy looked at me, blinking his wide black eyes. "Who's the Señora, Mama?"

"Just a señora." Elisa Lynch sat up, pulling the pins out of her hair. "Go away, Teodoro. Go play with your brothers." The boy shut the door. She pulled more pins from her hair, then uncoiled several false braids from the top. Her scalp shone pink at the part; her hair was much thinner and greyer than it appeared when wound with all the curls and switches. "You look so pained, Molly. Don't. After I'm bled he'll probably kiss me and give me presents." Her lip twitched. "It's a simple system, really. Blood for gold. Give me that comb over there, please."

As I handed her the comb, her face crumpled. She threw herself flat on the bed, her hands clenching and unclenching, sobbing in loud, choking gasps. I stood awkwardly by the bed, playing with a tassel of the canopy. When she sat up again, her skin was embossed with the pattern of the coverlet. She had chewed on some strands of her hair in her grief, and they hung like limp worms across her cheek. "You don't understand my ambitions, do you?"

"Your ambitions?"

"I don't understand them myself anymore. But I thought—I still do, if this miserable war ever ends—

Francisco has a good chance of becoming an emperor."

"I've heard rumors."

"About the crown he ordered in Paris? It's in the treasury at Asunción. For a while he talked of marrying the Brazilian princess, but that was absurd—the only way is Bonaparte's way." She laughed bitterly. "When I was a girl in Ireland, I had a little penny-etching of Bonaparte. I kept it pinned to my mirror, so that whenever I looked into the glass, *he* was looking back at me. Is that Skinner?"

The rap on the door came again. When I opened it, Skinner stood outside with his case, biting the tip of his mustache with his sharp front teeth. "The Bishop is looking for you, Mrs. Companion; something about the funeral arrangements. I'll take over here."

In the outer room, Teodoro, who wore a blue suit with a lace collar, had arranged the three dead birds in a row on the table and was pouring maté from one of the cups over their mashed feathers. He looked up with his finger on his lips. "This is a funeral, too, Señora. Be very, very quiet."

When I reached the church, Bishop Palacious, an unhemmed satin surplice over his cassock, was supervising two soldiers on a ladder. They were hanging Diaz's dress uniform from the rafters over the altar, trying to position it above the tabernacle. A young girl sat stitching a piece of velvet on the altar steps, while a turtle-faced old woman made ineffectual little dips at the Bishop, trying to catch the surplice in her fingers. "Later, later!" The Bishop pushed her away. "We've got to do this first. A little to the left, idiots!" He pointed up.

Diaz's uniform, the gold cuffs gleaming, swung gently

back and forth. I felt the soft, sobbing mucus back of my nose again. "What are you doing?"

"Ah, Mrs. Companion. We're hanging the General's uniform over the altar. It'll hang there until it decays, rots off—years, years! A great honor." He leapt away from the old woman's clamping fingers. "Leave me alone. Not yet. You see, Mrs. Companion, it's an honor, reserved for . . . for Cardinals, I believe, and the Pope, but Lopez has ordered it for General Diaz. A great honor. Put that ladder away, you two."

"But that's his dress uniform! What will he be buried in?"

"Nothing, Lopez says. Like his last great raid."

The two soldiers carried the ladder down the aisle. The uniform spun slowly around on its rope and wire contraption; a pale, barely discernible shadow rotated over the altar. The Bishop pulled the unfinished surplice over his head, panting and grunting. I was glad he could not see my face for a minute.

"Witches!" he muttered. "I should have got them to make the shroud first."

"I've got the shroud."

He puffed his cheeks. "You've got the shroud?"

"A big piece of ñandutí lace. I've had it for a while."

"Lopez said satin."

"Lopez will never see the shroud; you know that."

He frowned. "I suppose the body's begun to stink, it's so hot." He looked up at the hanging uniform. "That won't last long, either. Did I say years?" He laughed, his chin shaking like a pudding. "It'll mildew in a month. Ashes come, ashes go, eh, Mrs. Companion?"

I turned away from him. "What did you want me for?"

"To write a paean."

"A paean!"

"Lopez wants the Golden Combs to sing. There'll be three bands. I thought if you wrote a paean to Diaz . . . "

"Let them *Te Deum* something you know."

His face twisted. "I'm a poor country priest, Mrs. Companion. I don't know any Latin except for the mass, and sometimes I think it doesn't sound quite right. But when I ask those sweet-assed Franciscans about it, they just bow their bald heads and grin."

"Ask them for a song, then. I can't write a song."

"Just something like—" He hummed. *"When he rode, the monkeys fled, knowing death was their sure bed . . .* you know what I mean?"

"No, I can't do it. You do it."

"This may be the grandest funeral in Paraguay, Mrs. Companion. After the mass, we carry the coffin up to the cemetery, three bands, an honor guard of women lancers, the Golden Combs in black dresses, singing *your* song, the staff officers—barefoot. Lopez wants everyone barefoot except himself, then every soldier who can be spared from the trenches; afterwards the cavalry will place their spurs on the coffin—that's my suggestion— then dancing, champagne to assuage the grief, *slow* dancing, Mrs. Companion." He pulled me back, as I had started to leave. "Very appropriate."

"I'm sorry. I can't do it."

He sighed. "Then I'll get that fellow Bliss. Revolting, to have a song composed by a traitor." He watched me hopefully. "What do you think Diaz would think?"

"He'd laugh. You'd better try on your surplice again; they've got it ready."

I hurried out of the church. He called after me once, but I didn't stop. The cemetery loomed like a dark cloud at the edge of my vision. I imagined standing by Diaz's grave, my head bowed, while the thin voices of the Golden Combs sang *"When he rode, blah blah blah. . . . "* The ground trembled. I flew through the air clutching Diaz's naked body, wrapped in the spider web lace. Deep in the jungle Calvin's sallow face peered through a screen of leaves, waiting for the debris and flames to settle. General Bruguez turned in his hammock, smiling at his gouty leg as he thought of all the gold in the treasury at Asunción—the jeweled, waiting crown. In a few days the thousands of torn, mutilated bodies would blacken; the Brazilians combing the camp for loot would keep damp cloths over their noses because of the stench. Some enterprising officer would discover a head—Lopez's head—the torn lips pulled back in an awful grin as if he were ready to speak, and carry it triumphantly about on a long pike. My terrible fantasy left my eyes sottish with tears. I stopped under a tree and pulled off some leaves to wipe them; it was Pancha Garmendia's tree. A girl with thick black bangs, her forehead pressed against the trunk when I came up, jumped back nervously, looking at me.

"What are you doing? Are you ill?" I asked, for her face had turned rather pale as she stared at the leaves in my hand.

She squeezed her toes nervously. "I'm praying for General Diaz."

"Under this tree? Why not in church?"

She touched the rough bark. "Because this is a holy tree. I'm praying that General Diaz will be resurrected, so he can go *agua abajo.*"

"How do you know he wanted to go *agua abajo?*"

"Everyone knows. He wanted to go down to the end of the river after the war, to London, to see the bears dance with the queen."

"Why this tree, though?"

"Because this is the tree where Pancha Garmendia was taken to heaven." She pointed up through the canopy of leaves. "When a live person is taken to heaven, there's always an exchange; a dead person comes back."

"Maybe it's already happened."

She shook her head. "No, not at this spot. The dead person comes back to the same spot the live person left." She folded her arms sadly. "But there's no time in heaven, you see. It might be centuries. But I'm praying it will be General Diaz."

"What would happen if Diaz came back?"

She smiled. "Well, he would ride his big grey horse again, shooting Brazilians, and take a boat to London. We'd win the war." She scooped up the leaves I had let flutter to the ground. "I'll put these under my pillow, and I'll dream of the person who'll be resurrected. I might not recognize him, of course." She held the leaves up to the light as if trying to read their veins. "You can't pick the leaves yourself, you see, or even ask anyone to do it. But you've come and done it for me! That's a good sign." She tucked the leaves into the neck of her blouse and bowed her head against the bark, moving her lips soundlessly. I walked on. I didn't think there was much chance of Diaz's resurrection, especially since Pancha had died of common drowning; her bones were probably caught in a snag somewhere, in some eddy of current, long since cleaned white by piranha.

I walked to the telegraph office; it was useless wandering around the camp. There was probably some news from Asunción—the citizens' wild demonstrations of grief for Diaz, no doubt—which I could write up into an article for the *Lambaré*. I wanted to go to a dark room, wrap my head in a blanket, soothe my aching palms, which had always been a barometer of my grief even at times when I couldn't cry somehow, and sleep for hours, maybe days. But it was impossible. Always the cemetery exploded in some chamber of my brain; the women in their fresh white dresses tumbled over each other in the sky; Lieutenant Saguier howled like a dog as his belly opened; Elisa Lynch's son Teodoro suffocated under a wall of stony earth from which even worms could not extricate themselves. I had to work to keep my mind off these paralyzing visions, for they prevented me from thinking of a solution. Solution. The word had a nice, settled sound to it. But the easiest solutions were both suicidal, and while I could contemplate them abstractly, carrying them out was another matter. I had already faltered in telling Lopez outright about the explosion; the other solution, to attend the funeral, knowing it was my own funeral, too, required a numbness of spirit that I had once had—there had been times in my life when it would have been easy—but now had no longer. I could risk my life actively or passively and still maintain virtue. Calvin's plan, the unvirtuous plan that I should play sick and save my life, was suicidal as well, for I could never survive with the burden of guilt it entailed. Let them blow up. Again I saw Calvin's face through the screen of leaves, but this time I crouched beside him, my skin whey-colored, my body so stiffened that a touch would topple me. My father, in his rusty black graveclothes, leaned to whisper in my ear, "Tell Lopez . . . if you've got a soul, that is."

When I reached the telegraph office, Lieutenant Cela was leaning against the door frame, his arms folded. "She's here. Maybe you can get rid of her for me."

"Who's here?"

"That old woman who used to be Pancha Garmendia's duenna. She thinks I'm her son now. She wants to know where the stew pot is." He rubbed his ear. "Damn nuisance. She ought to be in prison; that's where she belongs. She's batty." He looked at me closely. "I saw that Argentine girl outside your hut, the one who tried to escape with Pancha."

"They've released her from the prison camp."

"That's right, they released some prisoners a couple of days ago in honor of something or other. I forget."

"To make room for more."

His small, light brown eyes slipped away from my face to a point on my shoulder. "Lopez's brothers have publicly declared themselves traitors and asked for forgiveness from the nation. His sisters have been arrested, too. His mother is under house arrest."

"His mother?"

"She's been counterfeiting paper money."

"But paper money is useless! Why would she counterfeit it?"

"Who knows? You'll have to write the article, though."

"Am I to think up the reason, too?"

He moved his face closer to mine. "Let me tell you something, Mrs. Companion," he said softly. "Major Olabarrieta has the hut next to mine. Yesterday I went to see him. All his things were gone—his hammock, his

clothes, even the stuffed crocodile he was so proud of
. . . some other stuff was in there. I asked a soldier
outside if he'd seen Major Olabarrieta. 'No,' he said.
'Has he moved?' I asked. 'Yes.' 'Where to?' The soldier
didn't know. At that point I realized I'd asked too many
questions." He touched my arm. "And that's not all.
Major Olabarrieta used to take Madame Lynch's sons
out riding, you know? When I was at headquarters later,
the children were playing and one of the boys said,
'Where's Major Olabarrieta?' They all told him, smiling,
'He's gone.' This morning I heard he was bayoneted to
death."

I jerked my hand away from him. "Please—"

"Mrs. Companion, don't you see? Be more cautious."
He bit his lip. "I shouldn't have spoken." He turned,
yelling into the telegraph office. "Hey, Madonna?"

The old woman hobbled slowly out, leaning on a
twisted stick with a knob like a monkey's face, more
wasted than ever; as she smiled, her few black teeth
wiggled, ready to fall out. Her skirt and blouse were
torn and filthy, speckled with straw and grease. "Lopez
is drowned," she whispered, recognizing me.

"She ought to keep her mouth shut." Leopoldo
sighed. "Can you get her away from me? Take her to
the women's camp and give her a pot."

"I make good soup." The skin of the hand she placed
on Leopoldo's arm was buckled and ridged, like badly
cured leather. "Out of chicken feet, but there's no salt."

"Get her away from me." Leopoldo detached the old
woman's hand from his arm as if it were a slug and
ducked back into the office. The old woman stood blinking after him.

"Let's go make soup." I took the crook of her elbow.

She hobbled willingly with me, her staff making little puck, puck sounds in the dust. We circled by headquarters where, outside the stockade, several soldiers wandered around with big nets, looking at the sky. A couple of others tossed bread crumbs about. One soldier noticed me watching him as he swung his net energetically through the air above his head.

"All Madame Lynch's birds have escaped! It's a miracle! At the moment of Diaz's death, the cages flew open."

I looked up at the flat, dull blue sky. "There aren't any in sight."

He made a running leap with his net. "They might be invisible, Lopez says." He wiped his forehead. "I don't think we'll catch them, though. They're too quick. They probably flew *agua abajo* with Diaz's soul."

# Twelve

By the time the brief grey twilight had descended and lights flickered on across the camp, a line of triumphal arches had been built from the church to the cemetery. The soldiers constructed them quickly of light wood, while the women decked them with boughs of flowering orange, brilliant parasitic creepers which they had hacked down in the jungle, orchids, jasmine and wild roses. I had spent two nervous hours in my hut, trying to decide what to do, and now I could stand it no longer. I had to get air. The bands practiced by torchlight in front of headquarters, and sometimes, between their silences, I thought I heard the thin voices of the Golden Combs, although it may have been only the wind or the shivery hum of insects. A group of drummers, their red, blue and white drums marked "Vencir o Morir" or "Republica del Paraguay" piled beside them, sat smoking under a clump of trees. A tall armless man, his empty sleeves pinned up on his shoulders like little wings, stood up with a rapid, snakelike movement when he saw me pass.

"Señora, please! Is it true?"

"Is what true?"

Torchlight flickered over the man's drawn face, casting red shadows over his skin. "That when General Diaz died, his severed leg grew back? You were there, Señora. Is it true?"

"No, it isn't."

The man's mouth opened wide, as if he were going to shout something horrible. Then it closed. "Ah!" he said in a small voice, walking away until he disappeared out of the red circle of the torches.

"We told him it wasn't true," one of the drummers said, butting out his cigar in the dirt.

"He was our best drummer," a boy with a square dark face added. "His arms were shot off in battle. He's only just out of the hospital."

"He likes to listen to us, poor fellow. We can't send him back to Asunción, not yet," the first drummer said. "He sleeps with his head on his drum."

The square-faced boy stood up, strapping his drum around his neck. "He's afraid that even in heaven he won't have his arms, because they weren't found. But that's nonsense. All the ashes fly together at the last judgment; everyone knows that. Then he'll play his drum forever."

"Still, Faustino, you're too young to understand," an old man growled, holding up his gnarled hands. "I used to drum to monkeys in the jungle, during those years when El Defuncto forbade music." He put his finger to his lips as if he had said too much, or might even have been overheard by El Defuncto himself. He coughed, continuing, "Poor Estevan, there, if he could only have believed that Diaz had regrown his leg like that—" He looked at me sadly. I felt that I had disappointed him immensely. "Well, who knows what good it might have done him?"

"And Diaz's leg will be buried with him, too. He's lucky it's not lost. If Estevan could only have *seen* his arms again." The first drummer sighed.

"Diaz has bad luck, too," Faustino said sullenly. "He wants to go *agua abajo*. He doesn't want to be buried in clay."

"Poor Diaz; if I were Lopez I'd . . . " Shaking his head, the old man put his arms behind his neck and leaned back against the tree. The drummers all looked at me uneasily.

"Diaz should be sent *agua abajo*," I said slowly. The words startled me as I said them. I felt as if I had spit out blocks of wood. The drummers looked at me, nodding.

"It's bad luck not to give the dead their wish." Faustino rapped his drum. "It's bad luck for the war."

"Float him down to London, that's what I say." A man with a bald head scarred delicately like a cracked eggshell hulked to his feet, pointing in the direction of the river.

"It's up to Lopez."

"Someone should talk to Lopez."

"*Agua abajo!*"

"Good night," I said under my breath, hurrying away in the midst of their sudden spirited conversation. I felt like a balloon filled with hydrogen; any moment I would rise to the treetops. I knew what to do now. I would float Diaz downriver. Without a body no funeral was possible.

I ran past two sad-faced harpists whose thin, separate notes fell like ice through the night air, out of the torchlit area into moonlight. *Agua abajo.* The words echoed through my head. I had to get the shroud from my hut first, and I was surprised to see yellow light filtering through the reed walls. Inside, the old woman crouched on the floor, tightly clutching the edge of the hammock while Rosalita tugged at her sleeve.

"Oh, Señora, she won't go! There's a hut for her, but she won't go."

Rosalita dropped her hands. The old woman looked suspiciously around, then, brightening when she saw me, revealed her black teeth. She rocked back and forth, singing "bim bim bim" under her breath.

"She made a soup out of cracked bones and these thick, salty leaves. She wants you to come eat it, she says."

"I don't have time."

I unstacked a couple of crates, scaring brown roaches in all directions, and found the yellowed paper in which I kept the lace. It appeared to be intact. I held the delicate spider web up to the candle that burned on the table.

"What's that? A wedding veil?"

"A shroud."

Rosalita took a corner of the lace suspiciously between her fingers, looked at it for a second, then dropped it as if it were poisoned. Through the open-worked lace I saw the old woman grab her staff and flutter to her feet like a pile of rags roused by the wind.

"That's for Lopez," she muttered, picking up the candle from the table. Before I realized what she was doing, she glided the flame against the lace that I held

stretched out in both hands before my face. It caught
fire immediately. Gasping, I fell on the ground on top of
it.

"Señora! Señora!" Rosalita screamed.

The fire must have been snuffed out at once. When I
stood up, Rosalita held the candle in one hand and
waved her fist at the old woman, who huddled in the
corner, whimpering. My dress was scorched in front. I
held out the lace. A big hole with blackened edges had
been eaten in the center, ruining the beauty of the pattern. Tendrils of straw from the floor were caught in the
weave. I pressed it against my face, crying openly.

"Ah, Señora, don't! Don't!" Rosalita wailed. "It's only
a little hole!"

I shook myself, then rolled the lace into a bundle.

"You're so pale, Señora. What's wrong. Can I help?"

"No, it's nothing." I turned around, rather dizzy. The
exaltation that had coursed through me when I talked to
the drummers had drained away. "I must go out for a
while, Rosalita." I swept past her, not looking at either
her face or the old woman's. I knew that Lieutenant
Urdapilleta would be sitting with Diaz's body; he would
have to help me. I glanced up at the moon, which was
shadowed at the edges as if it were a hole you could
climb through. The air was bright in spite of the darkness. The faces of the few men I passed on the way
shone white as masks. Already the spiders had been at
work, and the clumps of scrub grass along the way were
hung with spider web wheels. The preparations for the
funeral had ceased, for it was quite late, and Diaz sector
was deserted. A triumphal arch, heavy with mock
orange and mimosa, had been erected outside his door,
and some feathery leaves dripped over my forehead as I

entered. I was surprised—and disappointed—to hear voices, for I wanted to involve only Lieutenant Urdapilleta in this matter. Inside, Wisner de Morgenstern stood staring down at the open coffin; and Monkey-Snout, blending in with the shifting brown shadows the way he did in my dreams, sat with his arms wrapped around his legs in a corner. Lieutenant Urdapilleta, crumpled in the same chair in which I had left him this morning, turned his pale, grief-sunken face slowly toward me.

"The Bishop said you had a shroud."

"Here it is." I held it so that he could not see the hole. I walked over beside Wisner, who coughed and cleared his throat, trying to wave me away. In a minute I saw why. Diaz was completely naked except for a silver bowl that covered the end of his severed leg. His long thin body had turned a glossy yellow color as if he had been dipped in wax. Two silver coins pressed over his eyes gave him a stare as blank and meaningless as a statue's.

"Oh, Mrs. Companion, you're ripping it; you're ripping it!" Wisner grabbed the shroud out of my hands, which I had begun unconsciously to tear apart. He flung it over Diaz. The lace floated, settling, and clung like a real spider web, blurring the lines of Diaz's face. "Let's just move that burned part off his heart, tuck it under his shoulder, there . . . a handsome man, Mrs. Companion." Wisner pulled the lace momentarily off Diaz's face. "A fine nose, too. That's rare. A mark of character."

I turned away while he shut the coffin. Monkey-Snout's eyes were fastened on me, but he had not moved or said anything.

"I guess you'd better nail it up, eh, Urdapilleta?" Wisner clapped his hand on the young man's shoulder. "Like a father to you; I know how it is."

Urdapilleta shook off Wisner's hand. "I can't stand the thought of him buried, nailed up."

"Diaz wanted to go downriver." I looked at Urdapilleta hard.

He nodded. *"Agua abajo."*

"Then we must send him *agua abajo*, Urdapilleta."

Urdapilleta, who was bent over staring at his knees, lifted his head. "Send him?"

"Float him downriver."

A little silence isolated everyone in the room for a minute, so that the candles' sputtering sounded overly loud. Monkey-Snout shifted his haunches. Wisner touched his finger to his nose; in the side of one nostril there was a little depression from the habit. Finally Urdapilleta stood up, a spot of color in both cheeks. "We will, Señora! We'll float him downriver. Tonight!"

"You're crazy!" Wisner's voice cracked.

"That's what he wanted, Wisner." I pointed at the coffin.

"But Lopez! The funeral—!" Wisner covered his mouth, coughing.

"Lopez wants this, too," I said carefully. "He just doesn't want to be *publicly* responsible."

Wisner shook his head. "You're crazy." He glanced at Monkey-Snout. "Tell her she's crazy!"

Monkey-Snout shook his head. "It's bad luck to deny a dead man a wish. To deny *any* man a wish from the heart is bad luck." He looked at me.

Again Wisner sputtered. "But Lopez . . . !"

"Lopez secretly wants this," I lied. "He'll be

223

pleased." I looked at the coffin, which appeared much heavier than I remembered. "Will you help, Wisner?"

Confused, Wisner turned around in a complete circle to look at Urdapilleta. He pulled out a lace-edged handkerchief, patting his forehead. Urdapilleta pointed to the coffin. "You take that end, Wisner, you and Monkey-Snout. Señora, you carry that small coffin with his leg. There, behind you. We can't forget his leg."

The three men heaved the coffin onto their shoulders. It tilted precariously for a moment, as Urdapilleta was taller than Wisner and Monkey-Snout. He stooped to adjust to their height. At first Monkey-Snout had trouble getting a good grip with his missing fingers. "We'll go near the Laguna Concha," he said in his raspy old voice. "The current comes in close to shore there. Then Diaz will float down to Curupayty, under the chain, and past the fleet to London."

"Will it float?" Wisner puffed. "And what about the fleet?"

"It will float. The fleet will think it's only a log."

Outside, the moonlight had been partially eaten by clouds, so that the darkness washed deeper and there was less distinction between night and shadow. The small coffin, although cumbersome, was not heavy. Instinctively we circled wide of Lopez's stockade, which was the only place we were likely to run into sentries until we reached the river, the edge of the wide enceinte. Patrols in the swamp or the carrizal were possible, but I preferred not to think of them yet.

"I think Wisner and I can handle this," Urdapilleta said when we reached the swamp. "Monkey-Snout had better walk ahead. I don't know the way."

From then on we went single file. No moonlight

penetrated the thick moist growth of palms and parasitic creepers. In the distance, but sometimes closer at hand, the large *cururu chini* toads barked like a pack of hounds. Once the small coffin almost slipped out of my hands. I imagined the toads' ugly muzzles popping up and down in the pools of mud sucking between the trees on both sides of the loma on which we walked. Sometimes, too, I could hear the parrots chewing bark, then screaming as we passed.

Monkey-Snout stopped. I ran into him, knocking his shoulder with the coffin. "Quicksand!" he said. "Urdapilleta? Be careful; try to step where I step."

We circled deeper into the undergrowth, treading anxiously on a series of rotten logs sunk along the edge of a small black pool. Once we were over, the ground seemed drier and higher. Urdapilleta and Wisner set the coffin down.

"So that's quicksand." Wisner picked up a stick and threw it into the pool, where it sank slowly out of sight under the viscous black surface. By now we had adjusted to the dark enough to see one another's faces. Wisner crouched down beside the pool, dipping his fingers into the mud.

"Be careful," Monkey-Snout said. "A giant lives underneath there. That's his mouth."

"A giant!" Wisner laughed.

"One of the giants who stand on a rock in the center of the earth. Once the heads and shoulders of these giants stuck out all over the world, but they've all sunk below the surface now." Monkey-Snout sat down on Diaz's coffin. "I don't know why."

"Someone's coming," said Urdapilleta, tensing beside me. "Listen!"

"I don't hear anything."

"Twigs breaking."

"I hear it." Monkey-Snout stood up. "Following on the loma." In a minute he added, "Women."

"Women!" Wisner looked at him, startled. "How can you tell?"

In a minute two figures came into view, one shadowy and indistinct, the other ghostly in a long white dress. "Quicksand!" Monkey-Snout shouted. "Be careful."

"Señora Companion? Are you there?"

"Rosalita?"

"It's the old woman," she called. "She's been following you all night; I couldn't get her back!"

"What old woman?" Wisner asked under his breath.

"A crazy one," I told him. "Rosalita? Come along here on those logs. Watch out for the quicksand."

Carefully guiding the old woman, who still appeared insubstantial because of the dark rags she wore, Rosalita circled the quicksand pool. In her white dress she looked as if she could have floated across, but I held my breath, for I did not trust the old woman; like a figure in a dream, she was capable of dragging Rosalita into the pool with a wild yell. I was glad when they reached us. Immediately the old woman knelt down and tried to open the coffin, but Urdapilleta put his foot on top of it. "No, no you don't, you old hag."

The old woman began to beat on the coffin with her fists.

"Oh, Señora, I'm sorry. I couldn't stop her. I was afraid of what she might do if I let her go alone."

"It's all right."

"What are you doing?"

"Floating Diaz downriver."

"What?" Startled, Rosalita stumbled backward over the small coffin, her legs kicking up into the air. Wisner got his arms under her shoulders and pulled her to her feet. Unexpectedly she started sobbing, rubbing her hurt shoulder as though she had finally reached the limit of all the pain that had previously been inflicted on her. The old woman watched her for a minute, then began banging on the coffin again, crying "bim bim bim" in unison with Rosalita's sobs. Finally Urdapilleta, who kept running his fingers through his hair, could stand it no longer. He shoved the old woman away from the coffin. She rolled over once; then, huffing, crawled to her feet. Immediately she stepped off the loma into the quicksand pool, which sucked her up to the knees. Rosalita screamed. Wisner ran forward, his arms flailing, grabbing at the old woman's head. Her shawl came off in his hands. I clamped hold of Wisner's legs, for he had almost tumbled in on top of the old woman. This time he clutched her tangled grey hair and pulled, while beside him Urdapilleta and Monkey-Snout reached out their hands. The old woman, sinking deeper, did not seem to realize what was happening, although her mouth gaped in a wide O, for she stuck both hands into the mud, avoiding Urdapilleta and Monkey-Snout. Wisner held on to her hair. Urdapilleta, balancing precariously, finally got his arms around her neck, but she began choking and sputtering, her tongue forced out.

"You're strangling her, you fool!" Wisner cried. "Lower, lower, under the shoulders."

"Let her go." Monkey-Snout stood up, folding his arms. "She's already dead; let her go."

"She's not!" Urdapilleta had her by one arm now, and Wisner, still holding her hair in one hand, managed to get a firm grip on the other. "She's not dead, you idiot!" They both set their feet and pulled. I got out of Wisner's way. The old woman was up to her waist now, but slowly, like some ugly black toad, she emerged from the sucking, bubbling mud as they tugged at her. Overhead, parrots, disturbed by the noise, chattered and scolded; I kept listening beyond the present noise for the noise of an alerted patrol on its way down the loma, but could make out nothing. Finally, with a fierce yank, they freed the old woman. Urdapilleta and Wisner stumbled backward, leaving her beached on the dry ground like some loathsome root. Urdapilleta caught himself, but the force of momentum sent Wisner head over heels in a somersault. Unhurt, he got up, immediately clamping his hands over his face. "My nose! It's . . . it's gone! My nose!"

He scrunched down on his knees, patting the ground. "My nose—I've got to find . . . "

"You've saved a demon." Monkey-Snout, his arms folded imperturbably, glanced down at the old woman, who lay slowly writhing beside the pool. Indeed, in the darkness, her rags coated with black slime to the waist, her hands black as if scaled, she did not look human. Rosalita, who had knelt down to help the old woman, paused, looking up at him.

"It's true," he said. "Look at her! Years ago she must have committed some great crime and gone straight to hell. Since then, a demon has lived inside her, sucking water from her eyeballs and every drop of yellow milk from her dugs, bit by bit gnawing her brain like a white cheese, slurping around her heart. . . . "

Rosalita, who had been about to touch the old woman, withdrew her hand and stood up.

"Let's throw her back!" Monkey-Snout shouted.

At that moment a horn sounded nearby. I heard a rush of feet in the underbrush. My heart pounded. "It's a patrol!" Urdapilleta grabbed my arm, trembling. "They'll take him back and bury him!"

"Open the coffin," Monkey-Snout whispered fiercely into our ears. "Hurry up; open it!"

Dazed, Urdapilleta pushed off the lid. Monkey-Snout jumped on top of the old woman and dragged her over to the coffin. In the distance I could hear the voices of the soldiers. Wisner was still on his knees searching for his nose, moaning under his breath. Picking up the little coffin, Rosalita stepped back into a screen of leaves and was hardly visible. "Drop her in!" Monkey-Snout held the old woman's arms. "Get her legs, Urdapilleta."

"What?"

"Hurry!"

Shaking his head in bewilderment, Urdapilleta grabbed the old woman's legs. Together they heaved her into the coffin on top of Diaz and put the lid back on. "Now sit on it, Señora." Monkey-Snout pushed me to the coffin. I sat down, feeling sick, imagining the muddy old woman inside crawling over Diaz's naked body; over the white lace she had already burned. She tapped and thumped on the lid and sides, her voice muffled to a croak. In a minute the lanterns of the patrol flashed over our faces. I recognized Lieutenant Quinteros by the fuzzy beard spread over his face.

"What's going on here?"

"It's a crocodile," Monkey-Snout said.

"What?"

"We've caught a crocodile in this box."

Several of the soldiers peered at me over Quinteros's

shoulder, raising their lanterns for a better view. Inside the coffin the old woman banged against the lid. "Listen to it," one of the soldiers said. "It must be huge!"

"It's already eaten Señor Wisner's nose completely off," Monkey-Snout added, pointing at Wisner, who sat on the ground with his back to the soldiers. At the mention of his nose, he groaned and buried his face in his sleeve.

Quinteros, frowning, took a lantern from one of his soldiers and approached Wisner. "Is this true?"

Wisner looked up suddenly, revealing his deformed face in the full glare of the lantern. Quinteros sucked in his breath. "My God, how . . . !" He moved the lantern rapidly away from Wisner's face, his own face twisted in revulsion. "What are you doing with it in the box?"

"We're taking it to the river," Monkey-Snout said calmly. "There Señor Wisner will blow off its snout with his pistol and let it go . . . to bleed or starve to death in the river."

"Why don't you just shoot it?" Quinteros shook his rifle. "I'll shoot it."

"Don't you see, he wants revenge," Urdapilleta added slowly, sitting down casually on the coffin, for the old woman was beginning to bounce the lid up and down as I sat there. "Killing it would be too easy, but blasting off its snout, then letting it live . . . eh, Quinteros? You understand?"

Quinteros smiled. Then he laughed loudly, his whole body shaking. "This is fine; this is fine! Wait until we tell the others. I only wish I could go with you, Urdapilleta, but we've got to get back to Paso Pucu. The fleet's acting strangely tonight. Something's up." He muttered

under his breath, looking at Wisner still sitting deso-
lately on the ground, "Poor fellow."

"This'll cheer him up," Urdapilleta said.

Inside the coffin the old woman screamed.

"Awful noises they make, don't they?" Quinteros
shook his head.

After the patrol had disappeared down the loma into
the darkness, we let the old woman out of the coffin and
started again for the Laguna Concha; it was a strange
procession from a dream, led by Monkey-Snout, who
fluttered one of Wisner's lace-edged handkerchiefs over
his head so we could see him, and brought up in the rear
by the old woman leaning on a stick, slimy with mud to
the waist, muttering "bim bim bim" at irregular intervals. In the darkness her voice echoed hollowly, like a
bird's warning. Rosalita, carrying the small coffin now,
followed Monkey-Snout; ever since he had called the
old woman a demon, she had refused to go near her. I
helped Urdapilleta and Wisner carry Diaz's coffin, for
Wisner seemed to have lost all his strength with his
nose, and kept almost dropping his end, causing Diaz to
bump ominously against the sides. The tight wall of
vegetation thinned abruptly, and the loma swept around
the edge of the Laguna Concha, which stretched like a
long sheet of ice in the moonlight, almost blinding me
after the tunnel closeness of the jungle. We crossed a
bridge made of brushwood covered with sod, which
shifted under our feet like a boat. On the other side of
the laguna, Monkey-Snout stopped to gather some
leaves from a thin stand of thornless pindó palms, a good
emetic, he said, and we passed through a bamboo forest
to the river. The bank here was thick with foxtail grass,

and Monkey-Snout sliced an opening with his knife.
Then we saw the water, although we had heard its rushing sound a long way off. The bank, half a foot above the
level of the water, was spongy; carefully we lowered the
coffin. Urdapilleta lifted the lid and flung it away, almost
striking the old woman, who shrieked and jumped back.

"What are you doing?" I asked, turning away, unable
to look at Diaz again. "Please don't—"

"He's got to *see!* Let me get these coins off."
Urdapilleta sighed. "He feels like soap."

"Put the lid on!"

"He'll suffocate."

Out of the corner of my eye I saw Urdapilleta take off
his own shirt. "What are you doing now?"

"Get that stick from the old hag," he said. "I'm making a sail." He did not wait for me to act, but shoved past
me, pulling the stick easily from the old woman's hand.
She scurried away from him, hiding herself in the bushy
foxtail grass. Monkey-Snout gave him Wisner's handkerchief, and he stood the stick upright at one end of
the coffin, tied it to the rope handle, then fastened on his
shirt. Monkey-Snout adjusted the shroud; when he saw
the burned hole, he looked at it closely, then turned to
me. "That was the good-luck charm."

Together he and Urdapilleta lowered the coffin into
the water, for Wisner would not take his hands from his
face because of the bright reflected moonlight. Rosalita
knelt on the bank, peering at the water, ignoring everyone. Urdapilleta pulled the lace shroud away from
Diaz's face and forced his eyes open, but only the whites
seemed to show. His mouth had a curve to it, as if he
smiled. "You ought to be crazy by now," Diaz had said,
and I could almost hear him whispering now, "You are!
You are!" Spitting on the hem of my dress, I wiped a bit

of mud off his cheek. The coffin floated gently out from
the bank. Away from the shadows of the foxtail grass,
the moonlight streamed over him like silver.

The coffin washed back against the bank, little waves
gently lapping its side. "I'll have to swim out."
Urdapilleta unfastened his belt and pistol, but Monkey-
Snout stopped him by jumping into the water with a
startling splash. He grasped one end of the coffin and
nudged it farther out. When the water reached his neck,
he gave it a shove. It shot forward, sucked into the current. The shirt ballooned. Swiftly the coffin flew past.
Urdapilleta saluted as it disappeared, a black shadow
among the many other moving shadows on the river.

"Now the little coffin." Monkey-Snout lifted his wet
arms. Urdapilleta lowered the other coffin down beside
him into the water. Once again Monkey-Snout nudged it
into deeper water.

"It's sinking!" Urdapilleta called. The little coffin had
almost disappeared under the surface. Monkey-Snout,
his head floating in the water, disembodied, his black
hair spread around him like eels, attempted to dive
under and force it up. Suddenly he surfaced, screaming.
Beside him a long shape emerged; I glimpsed a crested
tail, then a churning that may have been foam or teeth
or both. Urdapilleta grabbed his pistol and fired three
times into the water, but Monkey-Snout had disappeared below the surface and did not rise again.

"It's the old woman!" Rosalita grabbed hold of me,
sobbing again, while I stared, dazed, at the spot where
Monkey-Snout had disappeared. Slowly Urdapilleta
lowered his pistol. For a moment I thought I perceived a
long shape just under the surface of the water. "It's the
old woman!" Rosalita pressed her face against me.

"What's she saying?"

"I don't know."

"The old woman!" Rosalita raised her head. "She turned into a crocodile!"

I looked at Urdapilleta, who shrugged his shoulders. Wisner had parted the foxtail grass with one hand, still covering his face with the other. "She's gone, that's all," he said.

"She's run off again, Rosalita, that's all."

Rosalita jerked away from me. "She turned into a crocodile and ate that old man. I was there, looking into the river. . . . I can't see my reflection in the river; the water carries it away too quickly. . . . " She knelt down in the same spot. "I was *here*. I heard this sound. The old woman jumped suddenly into the water and turned into a crocodile. I *saw* her, Señora!"

"The old woman's gone," Wisner repeated in a dull voice.

"She's run off," Urdapilleta said. "She's crazy." He looked out at the water. "Poor old man."

I clutched my arms, shivering. Although I felt horror at Monkey-Snout's death, I had no sense of loss. Instead, I kept seeing Diaz out on the dark river, floating *agua abajo*, not to London but to a feast for crows and vultures who would quickly spot him and dip to feed. Or, if the coffin sank like the other, I saw a school of caribe fish darting in to strip his bones. Or one of the ironclads of the fleet might hook it up; I saw the sailors marveling at yet another atrocity of Lopez, while the story circulated about the hundreds of tortured dead men sent downriver in coffins. "Let's go," I said. "It's almost dawn."

Urdapilleta called the old woman a few more times, while Rosalita smiled bitterly and Wisner watched the growing light with alarm.

The rising red sun revealed the whole camp in disarray as we crossed the marsh and circled around Lopez's stockade to the long barracks; poor, dull-coated horses with prominent ribs had been brought from the paddock and were hitched at various places around the officers' huts, some covered with red wool, others with large doubled-over pieces of leather. Only a few had saddles lined with sheepskin, and leather stirrups with buttons at the end for bare feet. Some of the guns on the stockade itself which were never used had been dismounted. Officers and men scurried everywhere with guns and bundles and official-looking papers. Some of the soldiers were tying up their belongings; one group was systematically tearing down a barracks. Dogs yelped, running anxiously under our feet. I turned around to say something to Wisner, but he had disappeared, probably to locate another of his wax noses. Urdapilleta cornered one of the officers hurrying past. "What the hell's going on?"

"It's the fleet," the officer panted. "Listen!" Over the noise and tumult of the camp I could hear the boom of guns in an unexpected direction. "They're bombarding Humaitá. They've sunk the chain."

Urdapilleta paled. "The way's open to Asunción, then."

"They could be in Asunción in three days, the bastards. But they're too stupid. They want to take Humaitá first. So Lopez is going to leave a skeleton garrison and a lot of Quaker guns. Ha!" The officer wiped his brow. "This position's useless now."

"Where are we going?"

The officer shook his head. "No one knows. Across to the Chaco for now, at Timbó, then probably to the Tebicuary. If the fleet concentrates on Humaitá for a few weeks, there's time to establish a new position upriver. Anyway, Lopez has ordered the capital and the treasury moved to Luque." The officer waved his papers. "I've got to get these to Major Resquin." He ran off through the growing crowd.

Urdapilleta looked around him, dazed. "I'd better report. Have they forgotten Diaz?"

"It seems so."

I walked through the camp with Rosalita, whose face grew greyer and more sunken, the brighter the sun shone. She kept stumbling and knocking against my shoulder. "They're taking me farther away, aren't they?"

"What?"

"I'll never get back to Corrientes."

"When the war's over, Rosalita."

"It'll never be over."

When we passed near the tree where Pancha Garmendia had been chained, she ran over and embraced the trunk, startling a red parrot from the upper branches. Then she began to climb the tree, swinging herself up by the lower branches until she disappeared into the foliage. "Rosalita! Come down from there— you'll fall!" I cried. She didn't answer. For a while I heard branches crackling, then only the natural sound of the wind in the leaves. Sometimes I thought I glimpsed a bit of white, but it may have been only the silver undersides of the leaves. I was about to call her again, but stopped myself as a file of soldiers marched past. If she could wedge herself up there for a few days while the army pulled out, perhaps she had a chance of escaping and making her way to the Argentine army. I doubted it. I looked up the dark hood of the tree. A lit-

tle light filtered through like coins. I had the strange impression that Rosalita was no longer there. Shivering, I
hurried to the telegraph office. The carpet over the
door of the next hut was rolled up. Bliss sat on the floor,
leaning against a crate, his manacled legs stretched out
before him. "Molly!" he called.

I walked over.

"The guard's gone. Blast it, what's happening?"

"A retreat."

His pale eyes bulged a little. "What about the
funeral?"

"The funeral?" I looked at him sideways. Calvin had
somehow relayed word to him about the explosion. "I
don't know. I guess it's off."

"Off?" His voice shook with real anguish. "It can't be
off!"

"I don't know." I looked up over the steaming corrugated rooftops of the camp to the cemetery hill, which
had raw red clay sides from this angle and a blur of
blue-black foliage across the top. "Why do you care?"

"Molly!" His face twisted. "Look at me. Look at these
things on my legs." He reached down to roll up his
trouser leg so that I could see his puffy, hair-matted leg
better. "You think you'll fare any better?"

"I don't think so." I closed my eyes. "I haven't had
much sleep tonight; I haven't . . . Shall I bring you
some food?"

He buried his face in his arms. "I don't care. I don't
care."

I left him, plunging into the confusion of the camp
which seemed to increase by the minute. A carriage
body mounted on an oxcart rumbled through the center
street, dressed chickens and turkeys hanging all around

it. An officer pricked his diseased horse with a sword, trying to get its legs moving, but the horse merely moved its milk-colored eyes and trembled on its spindly legs.

Outside the stockade, where much of the activity was centered, three men with guitars balanced on their protruding bellies strummed furiously, but the music was barely audible above the tumult. I picked my way through the confusion, trying to get back to the women's camp; as I cleared the worst crowd, I saw many women out in the fields with long bags, gleaning what grain there was left.

On the road across the marsh, Elisa Lynch passed me swiftly on horseback. For the first time she wore the uniform jacket of a colonel with her riding skirt and was followed by two young lieutenants who waved their whips over their heads. No doubt she was going to muster the women lancers. The road was choked with soldiers moving in from abandoned positions in the swamp and jungle, and she did not notice me.

Suddenly the ground swayed under my feet. The cemetery hill on the left spewed open, almost the way I had been imagining it over and over in my dreams, like a volcano; the explosion roared in my ears—a hundred trains. Calvin, I thought. . . .

A huge black cloud obscured my vision. I was sprawled on the ground. All around me soldiers crouched with their arms over their heads. Then I realized that my dress had caught fire, and I staggered up, flames flowering around my ankles, and began to run, tripping over men who yelled up at me. I was unable to stop. Earth fell like rain—clods and rock and shattered trees and fine dust that stung my eyes even though I protected them with my fingers; a long, yellowish thighbone thumped across my back and tumbled beside me. The rain of earth pelted down until it seemed that it would fall forever; then smoke and dirt swirled around me, creating a foul mockery of twilight into which I ran, a growing wheel of fire, in erratic circles. A strange pain ascended my legs, and once I fell, my hand smashing an ancient skull that powdered away between my fingers.

Around me the soldiers shook themselves, amazed that they weren't hurt, amazed that the cemetery hill had disappeared. In the brown air their laughter sounded ghoulish. When they caught sight of me, their faces stiffened in horror. "Lopez! Lopez!" A group cheered in the distance, waving mud-covered arms. "They didn't unhorse him, not Lopez! It's a miracle!"

I turned around. Lopez must have been following Elisa Lynch when the cemetery exploded. The silver trappings of his horse, which an officer was trying to quiet, shone like a coat of mail. The wind from the explosion swept his scarlet poncho out behind him like wings. As three men leapt at me, shoving me to the ground and beating my flames with their shirts, I glimpsed him riding by, his angry yellowish face streaked red and black from the ruptured earth.